"You are mighty quick to dismiss me, Miss Raleigh. What if I, too, had an offer to make you?"

Rebecca's heart raced. She turned away, retreating behind her desk. "I am not interested in the type of offer a gentleman might make to me," she said. "They usually involve the sort of work that is…not my forte…"

Lucas was following her, his footsteps slow, soft and inevitable. He was smiling. "And what sort of offers might those be, Miss Raleigh?"

"You know full well," Rebecca said, her mouth dry.

"Yes, I think that I do. Have you ever accepted such a commission, Miss Raleigh?"

The angry sparks lit Rebecca's blue eyes. "You should mind your own damned business, my lord."

Lucas's smile deepened. "You could become my business."

* * *

The Rake's Mistress
Harlequin Historical #767—September 2005

Winner of the Lories Best Published Award 2005

Dear Reader,

It is 1803, and along the coast of Suffolk the threat of French invasion is at its highest. Smugglers, pirates, treasure seekers and spies are all drawn to the quiet Midwinter villages, where the comfortable surface of village life conceals treason and danger as well as romance and excitement....

This is the world that I have inhabited for the past year whilst I wrote the BLUESTOCKING BRIDES trilogy. It has been a wonderful experience. I have always loved the county of Suffolk for its remoteness, the peace of the woods, the wind in the reeds at the water's edge and the sunset over the sea. It is one of the most atmospheric and inspiring places for a storyteller.

About a year ago I was reading a book about "The Great Terror," the years between 1801 and 1805, when Britain was permanently on the alert against the threat of Napoleonic invasion. It made me wonder what life would have been like in the coastal villages of Britain, where there was always the chance that the business of everyday living would conceal something more dangerous. I thought about a group of gentlemen dedicated to hunting down a spy—gentlemen for whom romance was no part of the plan, but who found that the ladies of Midwinter were more than a match for them! And so the idea of the BLUESTOCKING BRIDES trilogy was born....

I hope that you enjoy these stories of love and romance in the Midwinter villages! It has been a real pleasure to write this trilogy.

Nicola Cornick

The RAKE'S MISTRESS

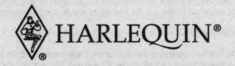

HARLEQUIN®

TORONTO • NEW YORK • LONDON
AMSTERDAM • PARIS • SYDNEY • HAMBURG
STOCKHOLM • ATHENS • TOKYO • MILAN • MADRID
PRAGUE • WARSAW • BUDAPEST • AUCKLAND

ISBN 0-373-29367-4

THE RAKE'S MISTRESS.

www.eHarlequin.com

Printed in U.S.A.

Look for

"The Fortune Hunter"
in
A Regency Invitation
to the House Party of the Season

Coming November 2005

Please address questions and book requests to:
Harlequin Reader Service
U.S.: 3010 Walden Ave., P.O. Box 1325, Buffalo, NY 14269
Canadian: P.O. Box 609, Fort Erie, Ont. L2A 5X3

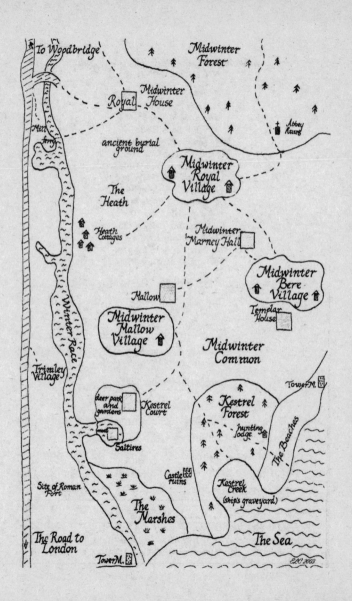

To Woodbridge

Midwinter Forest

Royal   Midwinter
          House

Abbey Ruins

ancient burial
ground

Midwinter
Royal
Village

The
Heath

Midwinter
Marney Hall

Heath
Cottages

Midwinter
Bere
Village

Mallow

Templar
House

Midwinter
Mallow
Village

Winter Race

Midwinter
Common

Trimley
Village

Tower M.

deer park
and
gardens

Kestrel
Court

Kestrel
Forest

hunting
lodge

Saltires

Tipe Beaches

Site of Roman
Fort

Castle
ruins

Kestrel
Creek
(ship's graveyard)

The
Marshes

The Road to
London

Tower M.

The Sea

E.P.C. 2003

Chapter One

October 1803

The young man who climbed into Miss Rebecca Raleigh's carriage that night looked as though he had escaped from a bawdy house.

It was not an encounter that Rebecca had been expecting. The carriage had paused briefly to avoid two drunken gentlemen who were weaving their way across Bond Street in the thin autumn rain. Rebecca, twitching the curtain back into place with a sigh, wished that she had not left it quite so late to return home from the Archangel Club. This was the time of night when the young bucks were out on the streets in search of an evening's entertainment, and the fact that she was travelling in a coach with the crest of the Archangel on the door would be protection from some, and provocation to others, for it was known to be the most exclusive gentleman's club in the whole of London.

The carriage was just picking up speed again when

the door slammed open without warning and a young man tumbled inside in a welter of tangled limbs. On closer inspection—and Rebecca was able to make a very close inspection indeed—he looked to be about nineteen years of age. He had the sort of boyish good looks that would melt the heart of the sternest dowager: dark hair, hazel eyes and a sweetness of expression that was well nigh irresistible. He was also missing quite a quantity of clothing, he smelled pungently of a mixture of stale wine, cheap perfume and strong tobacco, and his face was covered in red carmine patches as though he had received a quantity of over-ardent kisses. Rebecca was hard-pressed not to laugh.

As soon as he saw that there was a lady in the carriage, the youth made a sound like a strangled cat and flapped his hands about in a vain attempt to cover those parts of his anatomy he evidently thought would cause her offence. He was still wearing his shirt, if little else, and had he kept still it would have successfully covered the one thing he most wished to hide. Unfortunately in his confusion he gave Rebecca a very clear view of precisely that which he was trying to conceal.

In her professional work, if not her private life, Rebecca had seen far worse sights than a semi-naked youth and, as he collapsed on to the seat, his hands in his lap, she calmly removed her cloak and passed it to him with a kindly smile.

'Take this,' she advised. 'It will preserve your modesty and keep you warm. Indeed you look chilled to the bone. It is a cold night to be out without the proper attire.'

The young man grasped the cloak to him gratefully, though his gaze was still wary, as though he were waiting for her to swoon—or call out the Constable.

Rebecca pushed the hot brick across the floor towards his bare feet and nodded encouragingly at him. After a moment's frozen surprise, the youth had wrapped the cloak about his person and now rested his feet on the brick with a little sigh of relief.

'Thank you, ma'am,' he said. 'I must apologise for this intrusion. Indeed, you must think it quite odd in me.' He was well spoken, with the ingrained charm and confidence of the aristocrat. Rebecca placed him unerringly as a young sprig of fashion who had been caught out in a prank.

'I do think it odd,' she agreed, 'but I am sure that there is a perfectly sensible explanation.'

The young man did not look so certain. He gave her a timid look from beneath his ridiculously long black eyelashes.

'Well, of course…' He was trying to sound like a man of the world, but his tone was a little too lame to convince and the chattering of his teeth did nothing to add to an impression of sophistication.

'May I introduce myself, ma'am?' he said. 'Lord Stephen Kestrel, at your service.' He leaned forward and held out a hand to shake hers. The cloak slipped a little and he withdrew hastily, curling up as though he had been scalded.

'Pray do not stand on formality with me, Lord Stephen,' Rebecca said, smiling. 'I am pleased to make your acquaintance. I am Miss Rebecca Raleigh.'

There was a short silence in the carriage. Rebecca

knew that Lord Stephen was trying to work out, on
the basis of this meager information, just who Miss
Rebecca Raleigh might be. She could read his
thoughts, for his expression was transparently puzzled.
Here was an unmarried woman travelling alone at
night. She was soberly and inexpensively dressed, if
the dim light thrown by the carriage lanterns was any
guide. She was past the first flush of youth, but not
old by a long chalk. She spoke like a lady but could
hardly be one of the gentry…

Rebecca smiled inwardly and decided not to enlighten him. If he had seen the Archangel crest on the
door of the coach as he had leapt in, then he would
also be leaping to some rather more interesting conclusions about her identity. The Archangel Club ca-
tered to gentlemen of the *ton* who had exotic tastes
and the financial means to indulge them. Rebecca had
known all about the Archangel's reputation for de-
bauchery, but she had accepted the commission anyway. Business was business, and she had to earn a
living.

But evidently Lord Stephen had not noticed the
Archangel crest; when he spoke again, he had clearly
decided to give her the benefit of the doubt and to
treat her as the lady she appeared to be.

'Once again, I must apologise, Miss Raleigh,' he
said. 'I had been at my club—' there was a hint of
pride here, as though membership of White's or Boo-
dle's was still a novelty to him '—and some of the
other fellows decided to pull a hoax on me.' A frown
furrowed his forehead. 'I suppose we had all had
rather too much brandy, but it seemed amusing at the

time. They placed a bet that if they gave me two minutes' start I could evade the pack and find my way home before the hunt caught up with me. Fifty guineas said that I could do it.'

Rebecca looked at him, her lips twitching slightly at the forlorn figure he cut. 'I take it that you lost?' she said sympathetically.

'I *got* lost,' Lord Stephen said gloomily. 'Thought I knew my way about London, but it's dashed difficult to find one's way in the dark on foot, without a servant to give directions. Before I knew it I was up Norton Street and the other chaps were closing in on me, so I headed into the nearest building and it was a...' He paused, looking awkward.

'A bordello?' Rebecca guessed.

Lord Stephen blushed. In the dark it was almost possible to feel the heat of his embarrassment radiating from his face.

'Well, yes, I suppose one would call it so.' He shifted uncomfortably on the seat. 'I dashed inside and they fell on me with a great degree of enthusiasm and I only just managed to escape with my life.'

Rebecca doubted that it was his life that the light-skirts had been after, but she managed not to smile.

'That is very unfortunate,' she agreed.

'I'll say!' Lord Stephen's eyes rounded at the memory. Rebecca realised that, for all his semi-sophistication, he had been quite out of his depth.

'I was stripped practically naked within a second and then they started to tie my wrists to a bedpost and—' Lord Stephen broke off. 'But perhaps you do not wish to hear about that, Miss Raleigh.'

'Perhaps not,' Rebecca agreed.

'No.' Lord Stephen looked crestfallen. 'It is no tale for a lady's ears. Fortunately I managed to break free, but then the Watch came, so I ran away—'

'And jumped into the first carriage you saw,' Rebecca finished.

Lord Stephen shifted with embarrassment. 'Well, yes. I do apologise, Miss Raleigh, but you were my only chance. Lucas will be absolutely furious with me,' he added, with gloomy relish.

'Lucas?' Rebecca said.

'My brother, Lucas Kestrel.' Stephen's face had lit with a hero-worshipping smile. 'He is an all round out-and-out bang-up fellow, Miss Raleigh, quite the Corinthian. When he hears what has happened he will give me a roasting. A well-deserved one,' he added, with a sigh.

'Perhaps you need not tell him,' Rebecca suggested. 'If you are able to creep into the house unseen, why should your brother know?'

Stephen looked at her with a spark of hope gleaming in his eyes. 'You mean you will not give me away? I say, Miss Raleigh...' his voice warmed '...you are a capital girl!'

Rebecca laughed. There was something about Lord Stephen Kestrel that made her feel quite maternal, for all that she could only be five years or so his senior. He had an endearing air of innocence about him.

'I do not see why I should carry tales to your brother,' she said. 'I am not your nursemaid.'

The carriage had been proceeding towards Rebecca's home in Clerkenwell, but she doubted that this was the correct direction for Lord Stephen, who would surely be more likely to be found in Grosvenor or Berkeley Square.

'I do not suppose,' she said 'that my coachman will have the same difficulty in finding your home that you did, Lord Stephen. If you will give me your direction I will ask him to take us there.'

This was soon accomplished. Lord Stephen did indeed live in Mayfair, as Rebecca had suspected, and the coach was turned around and headed back towards the West End. On the way Lord Stephen confided a great deal more about himself and his family; that he was down from Cambridge at present, that he was the youngest brother of the Duke of Kestrel and had no less than two other brothers and two sisters, and that his favourite brother was Lucas, who was an Army man and a great gun. By the time they turned into Grosvenor Street, Rebecca's ears were heartily tired with the repetition of Lord Lucas Kestrel's name. He sounded to be precisely the sort of gentleman of fashion that she instinctively disliked and she could only be grateful that she would have no requirement to meet him.

The coach drew up outside an elegant townhouse and Lord Stephen peered out of the window, drawing back with a curse.

'Devil take it!' He recollected himself. 'I beg your pardon, Miss Raleigh, but I do believe Lucas is at home. What cursed luck! I was hoping he would still be at his club for several hours and I could hurry inside undetected.'

'Could you not go around the back and go in at the

servants' entrance?' Rebecca suggested. It was the route that was most familiar to her, but the idea had evidently not occurred to Lord Stephen before, for his face lit up.

'What a splendid idea! I say, you are up to all the rigs, Miss Raleigh! I am most indebted to you—' He broke off.

There was an ominous click as the door of the coach unlatched from the outside. An icy gust of air blew in, bringing with it a spattering of rain. In the aperture stood a man with a lantern in one hand. He looked like an avenging angel with the light illuminating his dark auburn hair and casting shadows across the hard planes of his face. A cool hazel gaze swept over Rebecca in challenging appraisal.

This man was older than Stephen Kestrel—ten years older at a guess—but he had enough of Stephen's spectacular good looks to make him instantly recognisable. Here there was a harder edge, something altogether more intimidating than Stephen's boyish charm. This, Rebecca thought, must be the infamous Lucas Kestrel himself.

It was clear that Lord Lucas had returned home for the night, for he was dressed with an informality that only befitted his drawing room. His jacket was unbuttoned and his neck cloth loosened. The casualness of his attire did little to soften the impression of uncompromising maleness. Rebecca shivered. This was the sort of man about whom the chaperons would issue dire warnings. Every instinct that she possessed told her to tread very carefully. She had no difficulty at all in identifying him as an out-and-out rake.

Rebecca drew back into her corner as the icy wind whipped inside the carriage. Lord Stephen made a vain grasp at the cloak, but it blew aside to leave him once more half-naked and caught in the lantern light in all his glory.

'Stephen?' Lucas Kestrel said incredulously. The dark frown on his brow deepened. His gaze shifted back to Rebecca and seemed to pin her to her seat. She felt a strange, swirling sensation in her stomach, a wariness with an edge of excitement. It set her heart racing. She turned hot despite the icy draught.

'Stephen,' Lucas Kestrel said again, without taking his eyes from Rebecca, 'what the devil is going on?'

'Hello, Lucas.' Stephen Kestrel was stuttering. 'I…I do apologise. This must look quite bad…I… This is Miss Raleigh…'

'How do you do, Miss Raleigh,' Lucas Kestrel said. His voice was lazy and smooth and it sent a ripple of awareness down Rebecca's spine. A smile that was not in the least friendly lifted the corner of his mouth as he looked at her. 'I do not believe we have met before.'

'How do you do, Lord Lucas,' Rebecca said. She inclined her head politely. 'I am sure that we have not met. I would most certainly have remembered. Your family do seem to make quite an impression.'

That earned her another look, hard and unsmiling. 'Pray excuse me a moment,' Lord Lucas said, with exemplary courtesy. He took his eyes from her at last and Rebecca managed to breathe again. She made a small business of smoothing her skirt and adjusting her gloves. It was unnecessary, but it helped to settle her nerves. She had been unprepared for the impact of Lucas Kestrel's presence and it had disturbed her far more deeply than any man had done before.

'Out of the coach, please, Stephen,' Lord Lucas said. 'I shall see you in the library in half an hour. Fully dressed, if you would.'

Rebecca watched as Stephen drew the cloak about him with the forlorn dignity of a dethroned emperor and descended the carriage as decently as he could. Once he was standing on the pavement he turned back to her and sketched a rather comical bow, hampered as he was by keeping the cloak tightly wound about him.

'I am indebted to you, Miss Raleigh,' he said. 'If you would give me your direction I shall call to convey my sense of obligation. And to return your cloak, of course—'

'Enough, Stephen,' Lucas interrupted. 'I will deal with Miss Raleigh.'

Rebecca did not like the sound of that. She arched her brows haughtily. Ignoring Lucas, she turned to his brother, who was now shivering in the chill autumn breeze.

'It was a pleasure to meet you, Lord Stephen,' she said. 'I am glad that I was able to be of service.'

That brought Lucas's eyebrows snapping down in an intimidating stare. Stephen gave her a tentative nod and sped away up the steps into the house, where a blank-faced butler held the door open for him. Stephen disappeared. Lucas did not. Despite the fact that her insides were quaking, Rebecca turned a disdainful gaze upon him.

'I assure you that I do not require dealing with, Lord Lucas,' she said. 'If you would be so good as to close the carriage door, I will make my way home at once. I have already been delayed far too long.'

In response, Lucas held the door open a little wider. 'If *you* would be so good as to come inside, Miss Raleigh,' he said, with unimpeachable politeness, 'then we might continue this conversation in the warmth.'

'No, thank you,' Rebecca said.

Lucas's lips almost twitched into a smile. Rebecca felt herself warm to him slightly. She did not seem able to resist. The man evidently had a sense of humour, deep though it might be buried.

'It was not an invitation,' Lucas said gently.

Rebecca smiled. 'It was not an acceptance,' she said.

Lucas's eyes narrowed on her face. 'Step down, Miss Raleigh,' he repeated, his tone harder this time.

'No, thank you,' Rebecca said again. 'A lady would need to be quite mad to agree to enter the home of gentlemen she had only just met.'

Lucas's lips set in a thin line. He said a few words to the coachman and then swung himself up into the coach and slammed the door behind him. Immediately the space in the carriage seemed to shrink and become nerve-rackingly small. Rebecca had not found Stephen Kestrel daunting even when he was half-naked. Lucas was another matter. He was just plain intimidating, fully dressed or not. Rebecca tried to calm the erratic tripping of her heartbeat.

The coach set off with a small jerk, the horses'

hooves striking loud on the cobbles. Rebecca felt panic rise in her throat and once again tried to quieten her nervousness. She could not pretend that the situation looked promising. The servants of the Archangel Club were accustomed—and well paid—to take orders from gentlemen without any argument. For all she knew, Lucas Kestrel could be a member of the Club himself. So if she were to call out, or demand that the carriage be turned around, the coachman would very likely ignore her. She could be dead in the Thames before anyone lifted a hand to help her.

Despite her attempts to keep such thoughts from showing on her face, something of how she was feeling must have penetrated the mask, for Lucas Kestrel put a hand out to her and said silkily,

'Have no fear, ma'am. Since you would not join me I thought it easier to join you. I have merely instructed the coachman to drive around for a while to prevent the horses from becoming chilled. This will all be over quickly if you choose to oblige me.'

His tone was even, but Rebecca could not miss the threat implicit beneath the words. She raised her chin, an angry spark in her blue eyes, her own voice cutting.

'And in what way may I assist your lordship?'

Lucas's gaze slid over her lazily, from the thick chestnut hair beneath her plain round bonnet to her feet encased in nankin half-boots. He considered her with insulting thoroughness and Rebecca felt her temper catch beneath the scrutiny. She was not accustomed to tolerating the impertinent inspection of a rake.

'I can think of many ways you might assist me,' he

murmured, 'but for the moment I am concerned only for my brother. For the moment.'

The angry colour had come into Rebecca's face at his words and now she subjected him to a scrutiny of her own. It proved a mistake, for once she had started looking, she found it difficult to tear her gaze away.

Lord Lucas Kestrel had a striking face, thin and sunburnt, with high cheekbones, dark auburn hair that was almost brown and very dark hazel eyes beneath strongly marked brows. He was not conventionally handsome, but the sum of all the elements was so unusual that it had a potent impact. Rebecca found that she wanted to go on looking at him and not just because he was shockingly attractive. She made her living as an engraver, and as such she had an eye for a striking image. Lucas Kestrel had a face an engraver could lose herself in, all hard lines and angles. As for his body, he had a compact elegance that would translate well into a sculpture or picture. That powerful body would be quite magnificent without its clothes... Rebecca felt herself blush all over, as though someone had locked her in a hothouse. This sort of instant reaction to a man never happened to her normally. An artist of any discipline, be they painter, sculptor or engraver, was accustomed to viewing the human body as an art form. They were accustomed to being completely detached. Alas, detached was not the word to describe her response to Lucas Kestrel.

He was watching her with one of those dark brows raised quizzically and a smile lingering on his lips, as though he knew what she was thinking. It turned Rebecca hot with annoyance, rather than awareness, to have been caught staring.

'So you should be concerned for your brother,' she snapped, to cover her embarrassment. 'A youth who gets drunk at his club and indulges in foolish pranks with other young men running riot in the streets—'

'And ends up in the arms of a Cyprian from the Archangel Club, having sexual congress in a carriage,' Lucas finished softly for her. 'Yes, Miss Raleigh—if that is indeed your name—I do so agree with you. Stephen's exploits are a matter for alarm. Boys will be boys, but I wish Stephen had chosen another place to indulge himself than in the dangerous hands of the Angels. They will ruin him.'

Rebecca felt a violent flash of outrage that almost got the better of her. She calmed herself with a deep breath and when she was able to speak she was pleased that her voice was almost steady.

'I fear that you are labouring under a series of mis-apprehensions, my lord,' she said. 'I first made your brother's acquaintance when he climbed into the carriage in Bond Street only a half-hour ago. On learning of his plight at the hands of his friends, who had abandoned him in a bordello, I agreed to convey him home. That is the sum total of our acquaintance.' She looked at him defiantly. 'On the basis of that short meeting, however, I can assure you that his company is far preferable to yours!'

Lucas laughed. 'I imagine so,' he agreed. 'I expect that Stephen was most charming to you, whereas I, having knocked about the world a good deal more than he has, am not as gullible as a youth in his salad days.'

Once again, his gaze assessed her, studying the curve of her breast beneath the thick, unfashionable worsted of her dress and returning to linger with disturbing concentration on her mouth.

'How much did you take him for, Miss Raleigh?' he asked softly. 'One hundred guineas? More? What is your price?'

Rebecca shrugged, feeling inordinately angry. 'Your judgement is not as sound as you pretend, my lord,' she forced out. It was an effort to speak politely, but years of dealing with her uncle's customers had schooled her temper. 'A gentleman who cannot tell the difference between a Cyprian and an artisan has little discernment indeed.'

Lucas looked incredulous. He lay back on the seat, crossing his long legs at the ankle. Rebecca moved her skirts aside to avoid touching him. He watched her manoeuvre with amusement.

'My dear Miss Raleigh,' he said, 'surely the facts speak for themselves?' He gestured about them. 'This is a carriage owned by the Archangel Club for the exclusive use of their customers. I find you inside it, with my brother. He is half-naked, smelling of drink and perfume, and covered in painted kisses. You are—'

'I am what?' Rebecca retorted. 'Fully dressed? Your imagination runs away with you, Lord Lucas. Matters fell out precisely as I told you, as you will find when you interrogate your brother. In fact, I suggest that you go and do so now. I find your company grates on me!'

Lucas was laughing. 'What a charming manner you have, Miss Raleigh. Do you practise it on your clients—in whatever trade it is that you profess to perform?'

Rebecca bit her lip. Hard. She found that she wanted to do him some sort of injury, preferably a painful and nasty one.

'My customers deserve civility, my lord,' she said. 'You forfeited that right by your own discourtesy.'

Lucas gave her an ironic half-bow. 'I beg your pardon, Miss Raleigh. Would you care to explain the manner in which I have insulted you?'

Rebecca glared at him. 'Surely that is quite obvious, my lord? You are a gentleman who has a positive talent for offending a lady. I deeply regret the act of kindness that led me to offer my help to your brother. If I had known that it would require me to spend any amount of time with you, then I would have thought not once but twice!'

She saw the gleam of Lucas's teeth as he smiled. 'A neat insult of your own, Miss Raleigh. You defend yourself with spirit. Alas, you are doing it too brown.' His tone changed, became cynical. 'No one associated with the Angels ever acts out of kindness. Why not come clean and tell me the truth? You may be sure that Stephen will not hold out for long when I speak to him.'

Rebecca closed her eyes, counted to ten and opened them again. Her voice was measured.

'I assure you, my lord, that my meeting with your brother fell out exactly as I have related it. As for myself, I would say that that is none of your business. I am not a Cyprian, I am not out to fleece your brother or drag him down into the moral depravity you evidently fear. In fact, I am not in the employ of the Archangel Club at all…' She hesitated for a fraction of a second, for that was not entirely correct, and Lucas pounced.

'Why the hesitation, Miss Raleigh? You had almost convinced me there…'

Rebecca shrugged angrily. 'Very well. The reason that I am in this carriage is that I have undertaken a piece of engraving work for the Archangel Club. I have a commission from them—' She broke off as she saw Lucas's expression of sardonic amusement.

'A commission,' he murmured. 'I suppose one might call it that.'

'I do not see why I have to protest my virtue to you, my lord!' Rebecca said hotly. 'It is none of your business.'

'Indeed, you have no need to protest at all, Miss Raleigh,' Lucas agreed smoothly. 'Not when there are easier ways to prove your innocence.'

Before she could guess his intentions, he took her hand in his and with studied deliberation stripped off her glove. His gesture was so sudden and so sensually provocative that Rebecca gasped. She tried to withdraw her hand, but Lucas held it firmly between both of his, running his fingers over her skin with the lightest of strokes. His touch was cool and she felt the effect of it jolt right through her body. The colour flooded her face; her nerves prickled. She was unable to repress a shiver.

'You will see that they are not the hands of a lady,' she said, 'but an artisan.'

Her voice came out a little huskily and she hoped

that Lucas had not noticed. He was insufferably arrogant as it was, without giving him the advantage.

He looked up and met her gaze, and Rebecca realised that it was a vain hope. Lord Lucas Kestrel was quite experienced enough with women to know when he had an effect upon them. She could see it in his eyes.

His thumb was stroking her palm gently now, sending flickers of feeling along her skin. 'I agree that they are the hands of someone who works for a living,' he agreed softly. 'That does not make you any less of a lady, Miss Raleigh.'

'I do not wish to discuss semantics with you, my lord,' Rebecca said. 'In fact, I do not wish to discuss anything at all. However, I will accept an apology.'

Lucas gave her a very straight look. There was the very faintest hint of a smile in the depths of his eyes and Rebecca's insides trembled. She was aware of an insidious feeling of attraction growing between them and fought against it wholeheartedly. Lord Lucas Kestrel was clearly a dangerous man.

'You have it, Miss Raleigh,' he said softly. 'My most humble apologies.'

Rebecca drew her hand from his grasp and cleared her throat.

'I think that it is time for you to go now, my lord.' She rapped on the roof of the carriage. 'Stop, please! Lord Lucas will be leaving us here.'

She half-expected the Archangel's coachman to ignore her command, but the carriage slowed obediently to a halt. Lord Lucas was not so biddable. He sat watching her, a challenge in his gaze as though he were defying her to throw him out bodily.

'What, are you to abandon me here?'

'I am certain that you will be able to navigate the streets of London better than your brother,' Rebecca said sweetly, 'and since I have no desire to remove your clothes you will not be in need of begging a cloak from a kindly traveller.'

Lucas grinned. 'You put ideas into my head, Miss Raleigh.'

Rebecca blushed. The ideas were in her head as well, erotic and disturbing, no matter that she tried to ignore them.

'Disabuse yourself of them, my lord. I will bid you good night.'

Lucas held her gaze for a long moment. There was something lazy but watchful about his scrutiny. 'I am not entirely sure that I wish to go, Miss Raleigh,' he murmured.

Rebecca slipped her free hand into her reticule. Her fingers closed around the cold, reassuring shape of her engraving scribe. She whipped it out and levelled it at his throat. 'Allow me to encourage your departure, my lord.'

'The devil!' Lucas's eyes lit with unholy amusement. He kept his gaze on the wickedly sharp diamond point. 'What is that?'

'A diamond-pin scribe for cutting glass. I use it for the very profession you derided a short while ago.' Rebecca touched the point of the pin with one gloved finger. 'Diamonds are the hardest substance known to man, my lord.'

Lucas rubbed his chin ruefully. 'Then it seems that you have something in common with them, Miss Raleigh.'

'I do not think that you should be in any doubt of my profession now, nor of my sincerity in wishing you gone,' Rebecca said.

'No, indeed.' Lucas's gaze came up to her face and he smiled again, a real smile, wholly disarming, seriously dangerous. Rebecca felt her pulse skip. He inclined his head in a gesture of acknowledgement. 'Very well, Miss Raleigh, I shall leave you, but I shall see that your property is returned to you, all the same.'

'Please do not trouble yourself,' Rebecca said.

'It is no trouble. Cloaks are expensive commodities, particularly for a lady obliged to earn her own living. I shall return it in person.'

Rebecca felt her temper flicker again. 'Pray save yourself a tiresome task, my lord, and send a servant with it. That would surely be more appropriate.'

She saw Lucas's amusement that he had got under her skin. 'That would be too shabby. Will you furnish me with your direction, Miss Raleigh?'

'Certainly not,' Rebecca said.

Lucas sighed. 'I shall find it out anyway.'

'But not from me.'

Lucas sighed again. 'Then I shall leave you, Miss Raleigh, with the promise to see you again soon.'

He opened the door of the carriage and sprang down without bothering to lower the steps. Rebecca's last view of him was a tall figure standing beneath the street lamp, a dusting of raindrops already on his hair. She sat back as the carriage moved off again and

gave a huge sigh. She did not regret helping Stephen
Kestrel for he seemed a pleasant enough young man.
His elder brother was another matter. Forceful, confident, with a face like a fallen angel and a touch that
threatened to overset all good sense… Rebecca shook
her head. She had a rule about staying away from gentlemen like Lucas Kestrel, men who were rakish and
dangerous and who could spell disaster for a woman
who had her own way to make in the world.

She hoped that he would not seek her out again.
She knew he would.

Lucas Kestrel stood on the wet pavement and
looked about himself in some perplexity. He realised
that he had no notion where he was. He had spent the
entire journey with his attention focussed on Miss Rebecca Raleigh to the exclusion of all else. They could
have been halfway down the London to Brighton road
for all he knew. He could not remember the last time
that had happened to him when he had been in conversation with a woman.

He started walking. He knew that he would soon
see a familiar landmark. Having navigated his regi-
ment across half of Egypt, he had no concern that he
would get lost in the outskirts of London. The only
thing that he regretted was failing to put a coat on.
That showed lack of foresight. He had not thought that
Miss Raleigh would occupy him for long and certainly
had not foreseen that she would throw him out of her
coach and leave him to walk home.

A rueful smile tugged at his mouth. He found Miss
Rebecca Raleigh a fascinating combination of confi-

dence and vulnerability, strength and innocence. When he had first set eyes on her he had felt her gaze like a physical blow to the heart. He had never known anything quite like it.

He had had ample proof that night that Miss Raleigh was no Cyprian. Despite the misleading circumstance of finding her in the Archangel's carriage, her appearance and demeanour were as far removed from that of a courtesan as was possible to find. The Angels would not be seen dead in the shabby gentility that had characterised Miss Raleigh's clothing. Not that she was in any way an antidote. Lucas suspected that, if suitably attired, Miss Raleigh might outshine some of the accredited beauties of the season. Her hair had been a lustrous dark russet beneath that ugly bonnet, her figure was extremely neat and her blue eyes were magnificent. He had noticed. Of course he had. He would defy any red-blooded male to look at Miss Rebecca Raleigh and not feel a flicker of interest, to study her mouth and *not* want to kiss her...

Lucas shifted his shoulders beneath the damp material of his jacket. If Miss Raleigh defended herself so effectively against all comers, then such thoughts were quite pointless. Lucas had been on the wrong end of plenty of weapons in his time in the army, but this had been the first on which he had been menaced by an engraver's scribe. He accepted wryly that it was no more than he deserved for trying his luck. It had been a deliberate challenge he had thrown down to her— and she had responded with a coolness and a courage that had won his admiration. Lucas smiled to himself. Miss Raleigh had not liked him, but all the same, she had not been indifferent to him as a man. She had been unable to hide that from him. He had seen it in her eyes when he had touched her. There had been a vulnerability about her then that she could not conceal.

He finally turned into Grosvenor Square and ran up the steps into the house. Byrne, the butler, noted his rain-soaked jacket but made no comment beyond the very faintest of raised eyebrows. The servants were accustomed to Stephen arriving back in all manner of disarray. To see Lucas in a like state was very unusual.

Stephen was awaiting him in the library, faultlessly attired in buckskins and a jacket of blue superfine. Lucas shrugged off his own jacket and handed it to the footman before making his way across to the table and pouring himself a brandy. He waved the glass at Stephen.

'One for you, little brother?'

Stephen nodded. There was a wary look in his eyes as he watched Lucas pour for him. He took the proffered drink with a word of thanks and waited until Lucas had taken his seat by the roaring fire before he did the same.

Lucas sat back with a sigh, removed his neckcloth and stretched his legs out towards the blaze. His eyes were fixed on the flames. By now he was fairly convinced that Miss Raleigh had been telling the truth and he certainly did not believe Stephen capable of carrying off a deception. Without turning his head, he said, 'So tell me, Stephen, how comes it that I find you conveyed home in a carriage belonging to the Archangel Club?'

Out of the corner of his eye he saw Stephen jump

and spill his brandy on his jacket sleeve. Stephen cursed under his breath. He had paled and now fixed Lucas with a pleading look.

'The Archangel? But I had no notion... I mean... Oh, Lord!'

'Oh, Lord, indeed,' Lucas said, very drily. He smiled. 'Are you telling me, Stephen, that you have had no dealings with the Angels before tonight?'

'I haven't had any dealings with them at all!' His brother protested. 'I only jumped in the curst coach because it was passing and I did not know what to do!'

Lucas looked at him. His younger brother had never been the brightest apple in the barrel, and when Lucas had discovered that he would be nursemaiding Stephen around London for a few weeks he had roundly cursed his elder brothers who had assigned him the task. It could not be helped—Justin, the Duke of Kestrel and head of the family, was at his estate in Suffolk and Richard was on his honeymoon, and not even Lucas could blame him for prioritising his married bliss above keeping an eye on a wayward youth. Besides, Lucas had business to attend to in London, and had therefore been the obvious choice to rein in Stephen's wilder excesses. It seemed, however, that this particular incident was not as serious as it had originally appeared. Both Stephen and Miss Rebecca Raleigh were telling the same tale and Lucas was inclined to believe that it was a true one.

'You did not know that you had appropriated a carriage belonging to one of the most notorious clubs in town?' he repeated, just to be sure.

'No!' Stephen was looking most unhappy. 'Lucas, I swear I had no idea—'

'Very well,' Lucas said. He eyed Stephen closely, aware that his brother was trying to utilise seldom-used mental machinery. A deep frown marred Stephen's brow. Lucas waited patiently.

'But if Miss Raleigh was in the carriage,' Stephen said slowly, 'and the carriage belongs to the Archangel Club, then that would make Miss Raleigh—' He broke off, a look of horror crossing his face. 'Oh, no! That must make Miss Raleigh a Cyprian! I say, Lucas, that cannot be right!'

Lucas laughed. He was interested to see the loyalty that Miss Raleigh had inspired in Stephen, even on so short an acquaintance. Stephen's face had set in a stubbornly disbelieving expression.

'That cannot be so,' he said again.

Lucas raised his brows. 'Why not?' he asked, curious to know Stephen's reasoning.

'Because it was clear to see that she is a lady,' Stephen said. His face lightened. 'In fact, she is a capital girl! Do you know, Lucas, she did not scream or have the vapours when she saw me? She offered me her cloak in case I caught a chill. I thought that most practical of her.'

'It was indeed,' Lucas murmured. For a moment he wondered. Miss Raleigh might not be a courtesan, but such coolness when confronted by masculine nakedness did argue some prior experience.

'And,' Stephen added, warming to his theme, 'she even suggested I might creep inside the house by way of the servants' door to prevent you from seeing me.

I thought that very clever of her. So you see, there is not the least possible likelihood of her being a courtesan. She is far too—'

'Too?'

'Too special,' Stephen muttered, turning scarlet.

Lucas viewed his young brother with some pity. It was clear to him that Stephen was suffering the first, unavoidable pangs of calf love. It had been bound to happen sooner or later, and rather Miss Raleigh than some *genuine* Cyprian who would take all Stephen's allowance, turn his untried emotions inside out and probably sue him for breach of promise into the bargain. Remembering an episode from his own youth that had involved an older woman, an unguarded marriage proposal and a large sum of money from his father to buy the harpy off, Lucas repressed a shudder. It was fortunate that Stephen's admiration for Miss Raleigh seemed of so innocent a nature. In point of fact, *he* was the one who had entertained decidedly less than innocent notions of Miss Raleigh, *and* attempted to act on them. He was the one who had thought of Rebecca's thick, russet hair released from its confining pins and spread across his bare chest, had imagined her mouth crushed ruthlessly beneath his own, had dreamed of freeing those voluptuous curves from the restraint of that disfiguring worsted dress. Miss Rebecca Raleigh had been very tightly buttoned up and he had wanted to unbutton her. He would have given a great deal for the privilege. He shifted in his chair as his thoughts had their inevitable physical reaction.

'I say, Lucas,' Stephen said, looking at him closely, 'are you feeling quite the thing?'

Lucas shook his head slightly to banish the images of Rebecca, naked and wanton in his arms. Damnation! The more he tried to dismiss the thoughts, the more they crowded in on him. And he was no callow boy. He had suffered his own youthful infatuation years ago and these days preferred to keep such matters on a far more businesslike footing. Not for him the pitfalls of love, nor the placidity of marriage either. He would leave that to his elder brother, Richard.

'I was thinking of Miss Raleigh,' he said truthfully. 'Pray do not concern yourself, Stephen. As you so perceptively noted, she is no courtesan. In point of fact, she is a glass engraver. She tells me that she is undertaking a commission for the Archangel Club. That is all.'

Stephen looked slightly puzzled, as though he had not previously realised that the profession of glass engraving existed.

'Oh well, then…' he said, his brow clearing. 'As I said, she is a capital girl.'

'She is indeed,' Lucas agreed, 'and I shall be calling on her to convey our gratitude for the service she rendered you. I do not think that we need say any more on the subject.'

Stephen looked slightly shocked, as though he could not quite believe that he was getting away with matters so lightly. He got to his feet, his gaze going to the ormolu clock on the mantelpiece.

'I say, Lucas, do you think that I might be able to go back to White's—'

'No,' Lucas said.

Stephen deflated. 'Oh, very well then. Good night.'

'Good night,' Lucas said, with a smile. 'I wonder in which part of London Miss Raleigh has her engraving workshop?' he added, half to himself.

'I have not the slightest idea,' Stephen said, sounding startled that his brother had even asked him. 'I have not given the matter any thought.'

'Of course not,' Lucas said. 'I am surprised that I even thought you would.' He raised his glass in a toast. 'Sleep well, little brother. I thought that we might go to Tattersall's tomorrow afternoon if you would like.'

Stephen flushed with pleasure. The hero-worshipping look was back in his eyes again. 'Oh, may we? I should like that above all things!'

He went out and left Lucas shaking his head ruefully. Outside in the hall, he could hear Stephen regaling Byrne, the butler, with a highly coloured version of his adventures.

'How very exciting for you, my lord,' he heard the butler say expressionlessly.

Stephen's voice faded away and there was no sound but the crackle of the fire and the click as Lucas replaced his brandy glass on the table. His thoughts had returned to Miss Rebecca Raleigh, but there was a more professional interest in them now.

It was a curious twist of fate that had delivered to him Miss Raleigh, engraver, when he had spent the past three weeks checking every single glass engraver's workshop in London, from the showrooms of the great practitioners to the garrets of the artisans.

Lucas went over to the desk, took a small key from his pocket and unlocked the top drawer. There was a list within, marked with small ticks, crosses and additional notations. Lucas scanned it quickly. Miss Rebecca Raleigh's name was not on the list, but perhaps she worked for someone else. She had not made that clear. Or perhaps, as he had originally thought, there was more to her story than she had disclosed to him.

Lucas took out the most recent letter from his brother Justin in Midwinter. For the past six months, the Kestrels and their friend Cory Newlyn had been involved in the delicate task of finding and catching a French spy, a criminal so cunning that he—or rather, she—had so far evaded all their attempts at a trap. Gradually they had drawn nearer to their target. They had eliminated all those who must be innocent and had identified a core of people who must be guilty. As yet they had not caught them red-handed and the spy and her allies grew ever more brazen, operating under their noses.

In the course of the investigation both Cory Newlyn and Richard Kestrel had found themselves brides from amongst the ladies of the Midwinter villages. It was a fate that Lucas was determined would not befall him.

In his most recent letter, Justin wrote that the hunt for the Midwinter spy was entering its final phase. They had identified that the culprit was still passing treasonable information to the French on such crucial matters as harbour defences and troop movements. They knew that the spy ring communicated by a pictorial code rather than a written one. And they now knew that the original cipher, the key to the entire code, was engraved on glass. They had some examples of the code in their possession, and Cory, who was a specialist in code breaking, was working on it even now.

All they had to do was catch the spies in the act—and find the engraver. The latter task had been allocated to Lucas and was the reason why he was currently in London.

Lucas put the letter down slowly. Finding the engraver had been like looking for a needle in a haystack. It was not that there were hundreds of glass engravers in the city, for it was a highly specialised trade. The difficulty lay in the fact that he was trying to identify a certain style of engraving. He had questioned each man, examined their work and inspected their premises in minute detail on the pretext that he was about to place a very large order with them. During the course of his enquiries he had found nothing to match the patterns he was looking for. The mystery engraver had proved tiresomely elusive. But now perhaps she had found him rather than the other way round…

Life was hard, Lucas thought. It must be a damnable business for a young and unprotected woman to be obliged to survive by making her own living. If Miss Raleigh was tempted by work that was not quite legal, who could blame her? If she accepted a commission from the Archangel Club, one could not be surprised. There might even be a connection between the Midwinter spy and the Club. The Archangel Club was a shadowy organisation with some downright dubious members. One heard rumours…

Lucas pulled the inkpot towards him, selected a sheet of paper from the drawer, and started to pen a letter to Justin. If there *was* a link between the Midwinter spy and the Archangel Club, then only Justin had the necessary authority to penetrate the club's mysteries. He would have to concentrate on Miss Raleigh herself and see what he could persuade her to divulge.

Lucas paused. Under the circumstances it was imperative that he should rid himself of any designs on Miss Rebecca Raleigh. There was nothing that confused rational thought so much as unbridled passion. He liked to keep the two matters entirely separate and had determined after the disastrous *affaire* in his youth that he would never make the mistake of letting his feelings cloud his judgement ever again. It was a vow that had been surprisingly easy to keep. Until now.

Lucas's quill scratched as he outlined the situation to his brother. Of course, he could be getting ahead of himself and the girl might prove to be quite innocent. He paused. Innocent was, in fact, a word that would fit Miss Rebecca Raleigh. For all that she was not a schoolroom miss, for all that there was a certain robustness about her as a result, no doubt, of earning her own living, regardless of all those factors there was also a vulnerability and an inexperience to her. It was a curious mix and an intriguing one. A woman who was not overset at the sight of a naked man, yet retained a certain demureness...

Lucas twitched the pen between his fingers. He did not delude himself that he was going to find the situation easy to manage. In some ways it would be his pleasure to pursue the acquaintance with Miss Raleigh and in other ways it would be the very devil to keep his mind on his work. But first, he needed to find her.

He reached out and pulled the bell. When Byrne trod softly into the room he looked up from his letter.

'Byrne, would you be so good as to send for Tom Bradshaw first thing in the morning?' he said. 'There is someone I need him to find.'

'Very good, my lord,' Byrne said impassively. Bradshaw, who had originally been employed by Cory Newlyn on some of his more dubious adventures, was a frequent caller in Grosvenor Square. All of the servants knew not to question why.

The butler went out. Lucas sat back in his chair and picked up his list again. He could be jumping to conclusions, of course. Miss Rebecca Raleigh might be precisely what she said she was and his quarry was somewhere else on the list. A prickling instinct, a certain excitement, told him otherwise. Lucas had always had a finely developed sense of danger. It had kept him safe and gained him a legendary reputation amongst his men for having more lives than a cat. Now it was telling him that the end game had begun. His quarry was within his grasp.

Chapter Two

It was the sound of carriage wheels on the cobbles outside, followed by a peremptory rapping at the door, that roused Rebecca from sleep the following morning. She turned her head and squinted at the clock on the chest of drawers opposite her bed. It was ten o'clock. The light from behind the thin curtains was bright and the street was alive with noise.

Rebecca went across to the window and threw the casement wide. Down in the street was the familiar green and gold coach with the angel crest on the door, and hanging from the coach window was a buxom beauty with tumbling golden curls and a plunging red silk dress. When she saw Rebecca peering out she let out a shriek.

'Becca! Come down and let me in!'

Dragging a shawl about her shoulders, Rebecca ran down the wooden stairs and threw back the bolts on the workshop door, then went to unfasten the shutters. The light flooded in. It showed the room to be narrow, neat and plain, with a workbench beneath the window and shelves displaying engraved glassware on the op-

posite wall. Despite its austere emptiness, the studio
had touches of elegance. There was a polished rosewood desk where Rebecca took orders and a brocaded
chaise-longue on which the customers might sit whilst
they discussed their requirements or waited for their
commissions to be packed. Rebecca's uncle, who had
run the business until his death some four months previously, had impressed upon her the need to present
an efficient and prosperous face to the world, no matter the underlying truth. Prosperity begat further business, George Provost had told her, so the workshop
was always swept clean and tidy, a fire always burned
in winter and the shelves displaying the glass engraving were illuminated by candlelight to show the work
to advantage.

This morning, however, there was no fire since Rebecca had overslept and she had had no maid to help
her since the death of her aunt and uncle. She lived
and worked alone, doggedly enduring with a business
that was failing as surely as the icy rain fell on the
London streets. First it was the apprentices and the
journeymen who had left, shuffling their feet and
avoiding her eye as they made excuses of better paid
work elsewhere. She had known that they did not wish
to work for a woman; had known that the vintner
whose premises abutted hers on the left and the gold-
smith who penned her in on the right were making a
wager over who would get her workshop when she
was forced out. The commissions had fallen off with
the news of her uncle's death and she had had to let
the maid go after only a month, unable to pay her
wages any longer. She felt nervous living on her own,

for although Clerkenwell was a far more salubrious neighbourhood than many, it was no place for a woman alone. Nan had told her this before and here she was to tell her again.

Nan Astley swept into the workshop in the manner of a duchess visiting a hovel. She held her red silk skirts up in one dainty hand for all that she knew the floor was clean enough to eat her dinner off. Once upon a time little Nan Lowell had grown up with Rebecca on these streets, and these days, widowed and embarked on a very different life, she never lost an opportunity to make a fuss over her newfound position as the mistress of a wealthy lord. To those who looked askance and told her she was no better than she ought to be, Nan turned up her nose and swept past in a cloud of jasmine perfume. It was Nan who had gained Rebecca the precious commission from the Archangel Club, for she had once been one of the famous Angels herself before Lord Bosham had taken her under his sole protection. Now she viewed Rebecca as something of a protégée and was determined to help her gain a rich protector and escape her penury. In vain did Rebecca argue that she would rather die then sell her body. Nan ignored her protests, being something akin to a force of nature.

'Darling!' Nan approximated a kiss an inch from Rebecca's cheek. 'You look so peaky. And here was I thinking I would find you already hard at work on the vase and rose bowl for the Archangel. Whatever can have happened to you that you are still in bed at this time?' Her big blue eyes darted around the room as though expecting to find a gentleman effacing himself against the panelling. 'My darling Boshie positively forced me out of the house to call on you, Becca darling. Boshie, I said, nobody but nobody calls at ten, or at least only if they are most ill bred. But Boshie was very insistent.' Nan arched a plucked eyebrow. 'It is very cold in here, my dear. I shall get Sam to light a fire whilst you dress. Ten minutes, mind you! Do not keep me waiting!'

Rebecca trailed meekly back upstairs to dress. There was no point in resisting Nan on the small things when it took all her strength to oppose her on the large ones. It took her a mere five minutes to dress in the plain brown gown she wore when working, and to bundle up her thick, dark hair under the old-fashioned lace cap. Pausing to inspect her reflection in the speckled mirror, she thought that she did indeed look pallid compared to Nan's glowing and painted beauty. But such beauty came at a price and it was a cost that Rebecca had never been prepared to pay. Even now, as she faced ruin head on, she shuddered to think of it.

When she descended she found the workshop candles lit, a fire burning in the hearth and Sam the coachman fetching a tray of tea in from the scullery. Nan was reclining on the *chaise-longue,* her feet up on Rebecca's workbench, her head tilted as she admired the red shoes that peeped from below her petticoats. She looked abandoned and beautiful, all tumbled fair curls and creamy flesh. She looked up as Rebecca came in and gave a little shudder.

'Brown, darling? So disfiguring!'

'I do not dress to impress in my profession,' Rebecca said, without rancour.

Her friend's blue eyes mocked her. 'And how it shows!'

In reply, Rebecca pushed Nan's feet gently off the workbench and sat down opposite her. Sam the coachman put the tea tray down on the rosewood desk and gave Rebecca a huge wink. She found herself smiling back. Sam had the bearing of an old soldier and a granite-hewn face to match, and he might work for the Archangel, but then so did she after a fashion. He also made an excellent strong cup of tea, and that went a long way towards gaining Rebecca's appreciation.

'Call back for me in a half-hour if you please, Samuel,' Nan said sweetly, kicking off the red shoes and tucking her feet up under her on the *chaise-longue*. 'I have matters of business to discuss with Miss Raleigh.'

The coachman bowed, gave Rebecca another smile, and went out into the street.

'Your business must be urgent indeed if it brings you out so early,' Rebecca said. She remembered Nan once saying that one of the benefits of being a kept woman was that one worked all night and could sleep all day. Rebecca privately thought that it was not worth it, even to be the mistress of an amiable buffoon like Lord Bosham. For better or worse, she had inherited a large amount of pride and a streak of independence from her family, and that pride revolted at the thought of being any man's mistress.

Nan did not answer immediately. She allowed her gaze to travel around the workshop, pausing as her eye fell on a slender vase on the windowsill. It was engraved with a picture of a sailing ship, a privateer with elegant lines and furled sails. She smiled slightly.

'How is your brother these days, Rebecca? Have you heard from him lately?'

'Not in a long time,' Rebecca said. Her chest tightened and she took a deep breath to steady herself. No matter how much time went past, it always hurt to be cut off from Daniel; now that her aunt and uncle were dead, the isolation was much more acute.

'A pity,' Nan said, her blue eyes sharp. 'Now there is a man who could persuade me into marriage...'

'I do not believe that Daniel is a marrying man,' Rebecca said with a small smile. 'He is wedded to his ship.'

'Show me a man who is the marrying kind, darling,' Nan said, a little bitterly. 'They are all out for what they can get, which is why we have to fleece them first.'

Rebecca pulled a face. She had heard Nan speak like this before and seen her friend's pretty face crease with cynicism and bitterness. Rebecca herself had never had a great deal of time for love. As a child, she had been a voracious reader and had devoured everything that came within her grasp, be it romances or treatises on engraving. Once she had started to work, the time for reading and any other pursuit had become very limited indeed and Rebecca had come to the conclusion that romance belonged only between the pages of a book. As far as she could see, marriage was a matter of comfort, convenience and sometimes of financial benefit, and yet she had never seen fit to enter the married state for any of those reasons. Not even when her aunt and uncle had died and, lonely and almost destitute, she had received three offers of marriage and had been tempted to take them simply for security… She had held out because a stubborn instinct had told her that, despite her cynicism, there had to be something better. She hoped it was true, yet in her heart she did not really believe it.

Rebecca drew a piece of paper towards her and extracted a pencil from the drawer of her desk. She started to sketch idly—little cherubs, larger angels with grave faces, wings folded, hands held piously in prayer. The angel motif was the perfect engraving for her commission. But perhaps a saintly face was not the correct image for the Archangel Club. Angels with wicked faces would be more appropriate, angels that looked like Lord Lucas Kestrel…

Rebecca bit the end of her pencil and tried to concentrate.

'Lord Fremantle was asking for you,' Nan said. 'He was most impressed when he met you last night.'

The pencil broke between Rebecca's fingers but she did not look up. 'By my engraving, I hope,' she said colourlessly.

Nan drummed her fingers on the brocaded edge of the sofa. 'You understand precisely what I mean, Becca.'

Rebecca sighed. 'I hope that you told him that I was not interested,' she said.

There was a pause. 'Rebecca,' Nan said, 'will you not at least consider it? Fremantle is rich and generous—'

And depraved and revolting, Rebecca added, though she did not voice her thoughts aloud.

Nan waved a hand to encompass the workshop. 'What are you trying to prove here? You know that you cannot continue. This week, next week, it will all be the same in the end.'

Rebecca looked up and met the steely blue of her friend's eyes. She felt angry and upset. So this was why Nan had called so early. Lord Fremantle, Bosham's crony and one of the gentlemen of the Archangel Club, had made no secret of his admiration for her when they had met the previous night. Rebecca had ignored his veiled hints and had concentrated on business, but now the inevitable had happened. Fremantle wanted her to be his mistress and he had sent Nan as a go-between, to negotiate the arrangement. Perhaps there was even a financial reward in it for Nan herself, when Rebecca complied. The thought made her skin crawl.

Nan was still looking disparagingly around the empty workshop. Rebecca knew there was no point in pretending. Her friend had seen the desperate state to which she had descended. Nan had even checked that Daniel, Rebecca's brother, was not inconveniently on hand to defend his sister's honour, and then she had passed on Lord Fremantle's proposition. And the worst of it was that Nan was right. Sooner or later Rebecca would lose the roof over her head and would need to find alternative employment, although she was utterly determined that it would not be in a house of ill repute, even one so exclusive as the Archangel Club.

Rebecca thought about Lord Fremantle and felt her skin shudder. He had been everything that was courteous the previous night, but his dead fish eyes and his waxy hands had repelled her. Even had she been starving she could never have accepted his offer. The thought of those hands on her body was so repellent that she felt sick.

'His lordship is very kind,' she said, trying to swallow the lump of nausea in her throat, 'but I fear I must decline his proposal. Even if I cannot continue with my own workshop I am certain I shall find employment elsewhere.'

'As a drudge in someone else's workshop?' Nan asked, the derision clear in her voice. 'You are too good for that, Becca.'

Rebecca almost said, 'Better a drudge than a whore', but managed to hold back, both out of friendship and also because she was not at all certain that it was true. Was her own parlous situation so much more enviable than her friend's pampered life? Most people would think not.

'I cannot do as you suggest,' she said.

She knew that her voice was nowhere near as steady as she would have wished, but she also knew that Nan was canny and would not push too far. She had planted an idea and she would watch it grow as Rebecca's plight became more acute. Sure enough, Nan shrugged lightly now.

'No matter. It was merely a thought. Your decision will not affect your commission, of course. Lord Fremantle was most impressed by your work.'

'Thank you,' Rebecca said. She looked at her friend,

her shoulders slumping. 'You know how grateful I am that you got me the work, Nan, but I cannot do as Lord Fremantle wishes.'

Nan's hard little face softened slightly. She put a hand out to Rebecca. 'I know you think that you could not do it, Becca, but it is not so difficult in the end…'

'I understand that,' Rebecca said, shuddering. 'That is what frightens me.'

She picked up her pencil again and sketched a few more angels. Lord Fremantle had been entranced by her suggestion that she should take the Archangel image and transfer it to the medium of glass. He had placed an immediate commission for a large shallow rose bowl and a matching vase to grace the dining table of the Club, and he had offered her a huge amount of money as payment for her work. Rebecca felt cold inside. She had an unpleasant feeling that she might be obliged to offer Lord Fremantle various other services before she ever saw her money, whatever Nan said.

The difficulty was that she was trapped. If she undertook the work and the Archangel Club refused to pay then she was ruined, with no recourse. If she refused the commission because she suspected Lord Fremantle's motives, then she would starve all the sooner, for she had only one other customer at present and no prospect of that situation changing. She had no choice.

'I hear,' Nan said, holding her teacup delicately between painted fingernails, 'that you had a most exciting encounter with Lord Lucas Kestrel last night, Rebecca.'

Rebecca pushed her sketches away with an impatient hand. 'I suppose that Samuel told you?'

'Of course. He was most concerned for your safety, my love. He would have stepped in at any moment, you know, had his assistance been required.'

'Handsome of him,' Rebecca murmured, remembering the alacrity with which the coachman had taken orders from Lucas Kestrel. 'Fortunately I was in no real danger.'

'Tell me all about it,' Nan invited, leaning forward. 'You are flying high there, Becca. The Kestrels are monstrously high in the instep.'

'I am scarcely pursuing their acquaintance,' Rebecca said drily. 'Indeed, I should be happy if I never set eyes on a member of that family again. One meeting was quite enough for me.'

'It sounds as though you set eyes on quite a lot of Stephen Kestrel,' Nan said, arching her plucked eyebrows knowingly. 'Almost all of him, in fact. Sam was concerned that he might catch his death of cold when he hopped into the carriage half-naked.'

Rebecca stifled a laugh. 'Happily for Lord Stephen, I lent him my cloak. And I averted my gaze as best I could.'

Nan opened her reticule and popped a sugared almond into her mouth, crunching with fervour. 'I hear that he is a sweet boy.'

'Very,' Rebecca said wryly. 'I felt very sisterly toward him.'

'I wonder if he has a penchant for bawdy houses and low company?' Nan mused. 'Perhaps I could make his acquaintance?'

Rebecca gave her a very sharp look. 'He has no money of his own,' she said. 'I think he is beneath your notice, Nan.'

'Oh, well…' Nan put her reticule aside with a pettish gesture. 'I doubt the game would be worth the candle. Young boys…' She shrugged. 'They are usually grateful and eager, but it is seldom worth it in the end.'

'Besides which, you would incur the wrath of Lord Lucas Kestrel,' Rebecca said feelingly, 'which is not a fate I would wish on anyone.'

Nan's blue eyes lit with laughter. 'What did you think of him, Becca? I doubt that *he* aroused any sisterly feelings in you. That is not the sentiment he generally produces in the ladies.'

'No,' Rebecca said. 'I imagine that it is not.' She thought of all the feelings that Lucas Kestrel had aroused in her: the anger and the edgy excitement and the longing. She fidgeted with her teacup, impatient with herself, wishing that it was possible to dismiss Lucas from her thoughts.

'Have you met him?' she asked.

'Only in passing,' Nan said with every evidence of regret. 'He is not one of Bosham's set.'

'Nor a member of the Archangel Club?'

Nan put her head back and gave a peal of laughter. 'I should think not! Lord Lucas Kestrel is far too straight for the Angels!'

Rebecca raised her brows. She did not like the sense of relief the news brought her. 'I thought him a rake.'

'Oh, he is, but…' Nan wrinkled up her nose '…his

tastes do not run to the exotic.' She shot Rebecca a curious look. 'Did you like him, Becca?'

Rebecca reached for her pieces of paper and idly sketched a few kestrels. She was good at drawing hawks. Their grace and fearless pride had always attracted her. She felt tired. It had been Lucas Kestrel who was responsible for the fact that she had overslept that morning, for even after the carriage had finally delivered her home the night before she had found that she could not sleep immediately. Lord Lucas's face was before her when she closed her eyes. She imagined that she could still feel his touch against her skin. She could hear his voice and see the way his eyes had darkened with disturbing intentness when he had focussed on her. No man had ever stirred her in such a way before.

After two hours of tossing and turning in her cold bed, she had risen to warm some milk and make herself a soothing drink with nutmeg and honey. And finally she had slept, only to be troubled by a tumble of broken and erotic dreams that left her wide awake, flushed and aroused, and distressed to find herself so.

'Lord Lucas is like many of his type,' she said now. 'He is arrogant, overbearing and damnably sure of himself. I always avoid men of that stamp.'

There was a great deal more feeling in her voice than she had intended and Nan opened her eyes very wide.

'So there *is* a man who can wring a passionate response from you, Rebecca! How very interesting.'

Rebecca made an exasperated noise and folded her

arms tightly. 'Nan, the only feeling I have for Lord Lucas Kestrel is one of extreme dislike!'

'What better welcome could a man have?' an amused masculine voice said from the doorway. 'Good morning, Miss Raleigh. It is such a pleasure to see you again!'

Lord Lucas Kestrel was standing with his hand on the latch and now he swung the door closed behind him and stepped into the workshop. He was immaculately dressed in a dark-green morning coat and buff pantaloons, and his black hussar boots gleamed almost blue in the patches of sunshine that speckled the floor. Under his arm was a brown paper package tied up with string, which he brought across to the table and presented to Rebecca with a small, ironic bow. Rebecca, conscious that her face was bright pink and that she was extremely flustered, muttered an incoherent word of thanks and wished that she might be anywhere other than right there under Lucas's laughing hazel gaze. She felt at an extreme disadvantage.

Nan was not so reticent. She slid from the *chaise-longue* with a certain feline grace and held out a hand to the newcomer.

'I fear that my friend's powers of speech have deserted her, my lord, so that I am obliged to introduce myself. Anne Ast-ley, delighted to make your acquaintance.'

Lucas took her hand and bowed over it with an old-fashioned style that clearly charmed her.

'Miss Astley. Lord Lucas Kestrel, at your service.'

'We were speaking of you only a moment ago,' Nan

said artlessly, making Rebecca glare at her. 'Rebecca was telling me of her experience last night.'

Lucas's mouth quirked into a grin. He shot Rebecca a wicked sideways look.

'I hope that Miss Raleigh found it as bracing an incident as I did myself,' he said.

'I am happy to say that I do not require my life to be braced by such events,' Rebecca said. She gestured to the parcel. 'I thank you for your kindness in returning the cloak, my lord, but as I said last night, it was quite unnecessary for you to call in person.'

Lucas smiled into her eyes and she felt his gaze like a physical touch. 'Wild horses would not have kept me away from you, Miss Raleigh,' he said gently.

'Well,' Rebecca said, feeling her temper start to simmer at the mocking light in his hazel eyes, 'I wish that I could offer you some refreshment as reward for your persistence, Lord Lucas, but I fear that Miss Astley and I have just taken tea. Besides, I am persuaded that you must be quite extraordinarily busy, so I shall not delay you a moment longer.'

Lucas laughed. 'You quite mistake the case, Miss Raleigh, for I have set aside the entire morning in order to come and see you.'

'Then I am desolated to disappoint you, my lord,' Rebecca said, 'but I must continue with my work.' She turned away, intending it as a dismissal, but was very conscious that Lucas had not left.

In fact, he was politely holding the door for Nan with the words, 'Miss Astley, I do believe that your carriage is waiting. It was a pleasure to meet you…'

Rebecca hurried across the workshop. To be left

alone with Lucas Kestrel was not in the least what she wanted. She felt quite breathless at the thought. She caught Nan's sleeve between urgent fingers. 'Nan, wait! There is no need for you to hurry away.'

'I fear that I must be at the Club within the hour,' Nan said, smiling at Lucas with a complicity that Rebecca found both frustrating and irritating. 'I shall be back soon to see how you fare, Becca. In the meanwhile, think about Lord Fremantle's offer. It is a good one.' She glanced at Lucas again. 'You will receive none better.'

Rebecca could feel Lucas's quizzical gaze on her face and coloured up again. Nan leaned over and kissed the air by Rebecca's cheek, then gave Lucas a flirtatious look over her shoulder. 'I shall hope to see you again soon, my lord.'

'The pleasure will be all mine,' Lucas said, with an expressive lift of his brows.

Rebecca watched him give Nan his hand up into the carriage. She was sorely tempted to bolt the door against him whilst he was outside, except that he struck her as the sort of man who would probably climb in at the window. So she waited, her jaw set, a stormy look in her eyes.

'You look quite put out, Miss Raleigh,' Lucas said, as the coach rolled away down the street. He closed the workshop door quietly and came across to her. 'Whatever can have happened to put you in so poor a temper?'

Rebecca pressed her lips together hard. 'I apologise if I appear unwelcoming, my lord. The fact of the matter is that I have an important commission to fulfill and have already lost time today through Miss Astley's visit. You must excuse me—'

'Must I?' Lucas murmured. He took a step closer, his eyes on her face. 'But I have gone to an inordinate amount of trouble just to find you, Miss Raleigh.'

'Then you would have done better to save yourself the effort, my lord,' Rebecca said, above the swift beating of her heart, 'for I have no time to spare.'

Lucas's gaze searched her face. 'You are mighty quick to dismiss me, Miss Raleigh. What if I too had an offer to make you?'

Rebecca's heart raced. She turned away, retreating behind her desk. 'I am not interested in the type of offer a gentleman might make to me,' she said. 'They usually involve the sort of work that is…not my forte…'

Lucas was following her, his footsteps slow, soft and inevitable. He was smiling. 'And what sort of offers might those be, Miss Raleigh?'

'You know full well,' Rebecca said, her mouth dry.

'Yes, I think that I do.' Lucas came to stand in front of her. His voice hardened. 'They are the kind of propositions made by the likes of Lord Fremantle, are they not?' His gaze drifted over her thoughtfully. 'Have you ever accepted such a commission, Miss Raleigh?'

The angry sparks lit Rebecca's blue eyes. 'You should mind your own damned business, my lord.'

Lucas's smile deepened. 'You could become my business, Miss Raleigh.'

'You mistake, my lord. That could not happen.'

'No?' Lucas tilted his head thoughtfully. There was

a challenge in his eyes. Rebecca saw it and her heart stuttered.

'No.' She did not sound even a quarter as certain as she would have liked.

Lucas watched her for a few seconds, his expression very still, then he drove his hands into his pockets. 'We shall see. As it happens, you quite mistake me, Miss Raleigh. The offer I intended to make was a commission for a piece of work.'

Rebecca was startled. 'A commission?'

'Of course.' Lucas's dark hazel gaze mocked her. 'I am quite offended that you think me callow enough to offer you *carte blanche* when what I really wanted was a set of engraved glasses as a wedding present for my brother.'

Rebecca was neatly trapped and she knew it. She had not the slightest belief that Lord Lucas had even thought of commissioning a piece of engraved glass before the previous night. Very likely the matter of glass engraving had not been one on which he had had any opinions at all. Yet she could scarcely accuse him of lying…

The words broke from her. 'I cannot believe, my lord, that you have had a long-cherished intention of ordering a piece of engraved glass for your brother's wedding!'

Lucas laughed. 'Of course I have not, Miss Raleigh, but there is a perfectly simple explanation. I have been cudgelling my brains this fortnight past to think of what I might give Richard and Deborah as a wedding present. When I met you—' he gestured airily '—the problem was solved.'

Rebecca sighed heavily. It was a plausible enough explanation and, goodness knew, she should be grateful for the commission. A piece of work done for an eminent family like the Kestrels might lead to other orders and before long her business would be flourishing again. And beggars could not be choosers, no matter how much she wished to avoid Lord Lucas Kestrel.

'I take it,' Lucas said lightly, 'that you will not be declining my offer?'

'No,' Rebecca said guardedly. The words seemed to stick in her throat. 'I should be happy to accept.'

'Capital!' Lucas smiled at her. 'You must tell me how we proceed, Miss Raleigh.'

Rebecca waved at the display shelves. 'If you would care to take a look at the work I have on display, my lord, you may choose the type of glass you want and the design that you would like me to engrave on it.'

Lucas nodded. He moved across to look at the shelves. 'I may take a little while, Miss Raleigh, so pray do not let me distract you from your work. I shall come over when I have decided.'

Rebecca felt a little put out. It was true that time was precious and she should be starting to sketch out the angel patterns on the glass bowl, but she was not at all sure that she could concentrate on her work whilst Lucas was there. She went into the storeroom that led off her studio. The room was cold and dark, and the ranks of glasses, bowls and vases that were normally stacked there to await engraving had dwindled until there were only a few items left. This was the last of her uncle's stock and Rebecca knew that she would have to order more glass in soon, but she did not have the means to pay for it yet. When the commission for the Archangel Club was completed, perhaps... But that was assuming that she would gain more orders. It would be dangerous to buy more glass when her business was so precarious. With a sigh, Rebecca reached for the large glass rose bowl at the back of the shelf and took it back out into the workshop.

Lucas was studying one of the engraved glass panels that Rebecca had hung from the ceiling. His head was tilted and Rebecca watched the fall of dark auburn hair across his forehead and the hard, shadowed line of his cheek in the candlelight, and something strange happened to her insides. Her heart gave an erratic thump.

She went over to her workbench and placed the bowl carefully on the top. She had a small pot of paint in a drawer, which she always used to make a delicate outline on the glass before she started the engraving. She took out her brush and edged the top off the pot, sketching with delicate strokes. An angel with a wicked face... She could see it in her mind's eye, head bent in prayer, the line of its cheek and jaw a straight slash in the glass, giving the impression of strength and grace. Rebecca stuck her tongue out slightly and concentrated hard, trying to block out Lucas's presence.

She did not succeed. She was too aware of him. He took his time, examining all the pieces on the display shelves with close attention. She could see his shadow crossing the deeper barred shade on the floor, coming closer. Despite the fact that her back was turned to him, his presence disturbed her, stirring the air, creating currents.

'Is this all your own work?' Lucas questioned.

Rebecca pushed a stray strand of hair away from her flushed face. 'The majority of the display pieces are my uncle's work. This was his studio up until his death four months ago. I engraved the glass panels and some of the other items plus the vase.' She gestured to the windowsill.

'Your work is very good.' Lucas's voice was quiet. 'There is so much passion in the pieces…'

Rebecca dropped her brush and bent down to retrieve it. Passion—and Lucas Kestrel. It was a combination that made her stomach drop. Her mind filled with images that were nothing to do with engraving at all, images of his hands on her body, his mouth against her skin…

'Thank you.' Her voice was muffled.

Lucas was standing by the window, looking at the slender vase with the ship engraved on it. He traced the curve of the engraving with one finger. Rebecca repressed a shiver and bent back over her work. She had never experienced such a strong physical reaction to anybody in her life and it frightened her. She wanted him gone.

He came back to the workbench and Rebecca put the paintbrush down, eyeing him warily.

'Have you made your choice, my lord?'

Lucas nodded. 'I think so. I would like a set of the slender glasses like the one that you have on the shelf engraved with an anchor. A set of six would be perfect. They are quite beautiful. I believe you must be extremely talented, Miss Raleigh.'

There was no mistaking the sincerity in his tone, and after a moment Rebecca gave him a shy smile. 'Thank you,' she said again. She did a quick mental inventory of the contents of her storeroom. She thought that she had just enough stock to cover the order.

'You have made a good choice,' she said. 'And the design?'

Lucas frowned slightly. 'I am not certain…'

'I usually advise clients to choose a design that has a significance to the recipient,' Rebecca said hesitantly. 'Flowers for a gardener, or a ship for a sailor, for example.' She looked at him. 'A kestrel for the Kestrels, perhaps?'

The lines about Lucas's eyes deepened as he smiled. 'What a splendid idea, Miss Raleigh. A kestrel it is, then.'

Rebecca put her head on one side and did a rough drawing of a bird of prey in flight, proud and predatory.

'How appropriate,' she said softly. She looked up to find Lucas's eyes upon her, bright and hard. For a moment their gazes locked and held.

Then Lucas said, 'So, how much are you going to charge me, Miss Raleigh?'

Rebecca tore her gaze away from his. For a brief moment, trapped in the compelling power of his eyes, she had forgotten everything else. She plucked a figure at random.

'I…erm…twenty guineas, my lord.'

Lucas looked astounded. He straightened up. 'Twenty guineas? That is ridiculous, Miss Raleigh.'

Rebecca was shocked. She had not anticipated that he would argue over cost. Plenty of people did, but she had not imagined Lucas Kestrel to be a miser. She supposed that twenty guineas was a little expensive, but she was not backing down now. She raised her chin in a determined fashion.

'Twenty guineas it is, my lord.'

'I will not give you a penny less than sixty.'

Rebecca recoiled. 'Sixty guineas for six glasses? Do not be so foolish, my lord!'

'It is sixty guineas or nothing, Miss Raleigh. Not a penny more and not a penny less. If you do not wish the commission…'

Rebecca had also got to her feet by now. She faced him across the desk. 'This is idiotic, my lord! Most people negotiate downwards, not upwards!'

Lucas looked down his nose. 'I am not most people, Miss Raleigh.'

Rebecca glared at him. 'You do not understand. I have given you a fair price for the work.'

'Must you sell yourself short? You will never make enough money to survive if you do not value your own work.'

Rebecca shook her head with frustration. 'It is the market price, my lord. Allow me to know more about that than you do. Only Adams or Woolf could command such prices!'

Lucas shrugged. 'Do you accept the commission, Miss Raleigh?'

'Of course, but—'

'Then you must accept the sum I offer.'

Lucas came around the desk and stood in front of her. His dark gaze scanned her face, softening slightly as it lingered on the indignant colour in her cheeks. He shook his head slightly. 'Pride, Miss Raleigh, is one of the seven deadly sins. But then—' he took a step closer and his fingers brushed her cheeks with a featherlight touch '—so is lust…'

Rebecca went hot all over, then cold. Lucas's gaze dropped to her lips and she knew with a certainty and a tingling anticipation that he was about to kiss her. She backed away until she came up the hard edge of the desk and put out a hand to ward him off. 'My lord—'

'I am still not sure about you, Miss Raleigh,' Lucas said slowly, 'despite your claim last night that your association with the Archangel is entirely innocent.' His fingers drifted down the line of her throat and rested momentarily where the pulse beat hectically in the hollow at its base.

'I am not at all sure whether you are as virtuous as you claim to be…' His hand was sliding to the nape of her neck now, tangling in the curls there, stroking softly. His tone was hypnotic and so was the intent look in his eyes. Rebecca felt her knees tremble. The desk creaked as she unconsciously leaned against it for support.

She put up a hand and tried to push his aside. It seemed to take an inordinate amount of effort and so did her words. 'Whereas I am in absolutely no doubt about you, my lord.' It came out as a whisper.

Laughter lightened Lucas's eyes. Somehow he had

captured her hand in his, diverting it from its purpose. His touch was warm and intimate against her skin. 'Are you not?' he said. 'And what do you think of me?'

'That you are a rake, my lord,' Rebecca said.

'And I suppose that you do not have any time for rakes, Miss Raleigh?'

His thumb was rubbing the back of her hand now, sending tiny quivers of feeling along her nerves. Rebecca frowned, trying to concentrate.

'You suppose correctly, my lord.'

He was drawing her closer. There was something inevitable, something inescapable about the way his arms went about her. She did not struggle. She found that she wanted to know what it would be like.

His lips were cool and light and for a second hers clung to his before he released her. The way that she trembled in his arms was out of all proportion to the kiss and yet she felt shaken to her very soul.

'Why not?' he said, very softly.

'Why not what?' Rebecca was so confused she could barely stand.

'Why not give rakes—or at least this one—some of your time?'

For a moment, Rebecca could not think of any reason why not. Then she shook her head sharply to dispel the seductive spell he was weaving. 'Because I have my own way to make, my lord, and I doubt that you are likely to make that any easier for me.'

'You mistake,' Lucas said. 'I could make life much smoother for you.'

Rebecca closed her eyes for a moment against the

temptation. She barely knew this man and yet she knew with an instinct as old as time itself that he was dangerous to her. There was a predatory intensity about him that forced a reaction from deep within her.

'I am sure that you could make my life smoother, my lord,' she said, taking a deep breath to steady herself, 'if your patronage gains me more work.'

Lucas laughed and released her. 'Very well, Miss Raleigh.' His tone sobered. 'How long will it take you to complete the work on the glasses?'

'About a week, I imagine.'

Lucas bowed. 'Then I shall return in a week's time. Good day, Miss Raleigh.'

Rebecca sank down on to the *chaise-longue* as he went out, closing the door quietly behind him. She felt physically exhausted, as though she had been working ceaselessly for hours. She was not at all sure what had happened between the two of them. It was not something that had ever happened to her before. But Lucas had had a word for it.

Lust.

Nothing could have spelled out more clearly the role Lord Lucas Kestrel foresaw for her in his life. He might have held back from an offer of *carte blanche* now, but it was only a matter of time. And in truth, there was something a great deal more appealing about accepting an offer from such a man than from the likes of Lord Fremantle.

Rebecca felt herself tremble at the thought. What had Nan said? *It is not so difficult in the end…*

Rebecca could see just how easy it could be.

She picked up the rose bowl and peered at her reflection in the polished glass. Her face was flushed and her eyes bright. She felt wide awake, stirred up. Once again, she remembered the blissful feeling of Lucas's arms around her. It had felt absolutely right to be there, exciting, pleasurable and at the same time deeply comforting, like coming home.

Rebecca put her face in her hands for a brief moment, then bent to scoop up the pencils and the sheets of paper that were still lying scattered on the floor. She reminded herself that bliss was a very short-lived and deceptive feeling, for when it had gone, as it surely would, one was left counting the cost.

She must be practical. She had a living to earn and she wanted matters neat, tidy and simple. There was no room in her private life for passion when it all went into her work. Nothing must induce her to accept *carte blanche*. Not Lucas's persuasions, nor her own desires. She owed it to herself to keep that pledge.

All the same, she was tempted.

Chapter Three

Lord Lucas Kestrel was feeling guilty. It was not a sensation that was familiar to him and he did not care for it. It was a guilt that had crept over him during the previous few days and had finally driven him out of the house at nearly midnight to take refuge at White's, where his friends had greeted him with great pleasure and had promptly set out to relieve him of a large part of his army pay. Since Lucas could not concentrate he lost very quickly, and had just thrown his cards in for a final time when someone touched his shoulder and Cory Newlyn's voice said in his ear, 'Would you care to join me for a drink, Lucas, before you lose your shirt?'

Lucas looked up, his dark scowl lightening into a reluctant smile. Cory had been a friend of the Kestrels for many years and the two of them had met only the previous week when he had called on Lord Newlyn at the British Museum to discuss the pictorial code being used by the Midwinter spies.

Lucas stretched. 'I'll gladly join you,' he said, moving to sit with Cory at a quiet corner table where a bottle of port already resided on the table between them. Cory sat down, crossed his long legs at the ankle and viewed Lucas with a meditative air.

'The only time I have seen a man lose like that was when your brother Richard was suffering the pangs of ' unrequited love for Deborah Stratton,' he said cheerfully. 'There must be something weighing heavy on your mind. What is going on, Luc?'

Lucas scowled. 'Damn it, Cory,' he said feelingly, 'must you be so shrewd?'

Cory laughed. 'Forgive me. If you do not wish to talk…'

Lucas shrugged, trying to shake off his irritation. 'I feel guilty because I am behaving like a cad,' he said bluntly. Briefly he told Cory the tale of his dealings with Rebecca Raleigh. 'Tom Bradshaw discovered that she worked out of a studio in Clerkenwell,' he finished. 'Until four months ago it belonged to her uncle, George Provost. He was a well-respected engraver, if not a particularly eminent one, and he would have been the perfect choice to make the Midwinter engravings, for he would welcome the business but not be famous enough for anyone to recognise his work.'

Cory grimaced. 'You are sure?'

'Certain.' Lucas toyed with his glass of port, watching the deep red liquid glow in the light. 'I have been to the studio. There were some pieces there that matched the patterns on the Midwinter glass precisely, and Miss Raleigh confirmed that they were her uncle's work.' Lucas sighed and sat back. 'There can be no doubt.'

'So we have found our engraver.'

'It would appear so. But as he has so inconveniently died, his niece is our only contact to the Midwinter spy ring and I need more information from her.'

Cory pulled a face. 'I see your dilemma.'

Lucas nodded. 'I am taking advantage of Miss Raleigh's vulnerability because I want her to confide in me,' he said. He pulled a disgusted face. 'Good God, it sounds even worse when I express it like that! I can scarce believe what I am doing.'

Cory did not reply immediately. He lifted the bottle and poured another glass of port slowly, watching Lucas's face as he did so.

'It sounds to me,' he said perceptively, 'that you are suffering an excess of remorse over this, Luc. We all know that espionage can be an unpleasant business, requiring the sort of actions one might not normally contemplate.' He looked closely at his friend. 'Are you sure that your feelings are not involved?'

Lucas drew rings on the highly polished surface of the side table with his wine glass. He tried to block out the memory of kissing Rebecca and the promise of passion with which she had responded to him. That had not been part of his original plan. He had intended to draw her out and gain her confidence, nothing more, but the mutual attraction between them had made a mockery of his good intentions. And then it had taken little to change good intentions to bad ones...

He had been reading the poetry of Ben Jonson the previous night. God only knew why—he was a man of action, not a scholar. He suspected that it was a book his brother Richard had left lying around and he had picked it up because he was bored and restless and thinking too much on Miss Rebecca Raleigh. He should have known better. Poetry never helped a man to think straight, and when he had stumbled across a line from the 'Queen of Love' he had paused and thought of her even more, for he seemed powerless to resist.

'You will turn all hearts to tinder…'

He told himself that he had kissed Rebecca because he had been testing her, suspicious of the innocence that cloaked her like a shield. He had wondered if that purity could possibly be genuine. Yet there had been nothing calculated about their embrace. Lucas himself was experienced enough to know the difference between real and counterfeit emotion, the type that men could buy from courtesans. There was nothing counterfeit about Rebecca Raleigh. He had acted on impulse and her response had shaken him. And when he had seen the confusion of desire in her face as he released her, he had been overtaken by such a wave of tenderness… He shook his head. That was no way for a rake to think. More to the point, it was no way for him to be thinking when he was conducting an investigation.

Cory cleared his throat gently and Lucas glanced up.

'I confess that I find it difficult to be detached about this,' he said morosely, answering the question in his friend's eyes. 'I cannot conceive how it happened.'

Cory's lips twitched. 'How many times have you met Miss Raleigh?' he asked.

'Twice.'

'And what do you know of her?'

'Very little, as yet.'

Lucas realised that in terms of fact this was probably true, but that in terms of instinct, on a deeper level, he felt that he already knew Rebecca intimately. It was a disquieting feeling. The little that he did know prompted him to trust her, to take her into his confidence. He was sure that she could not be guilty of involvement in the Midwinter spy ring. Perhaps even her uncle had not known the nature of the business he was involved in. When Lucas had studied the pieces on display in Rebecca's studio, his heart had sunk like a stone at the likenesses between the engraving on the glasses there and the ones in his possession. It was the first time he had visited an engraver's studio *not* wanting to find the patterns he sought. But the style was unmistakable.

'Ask her to tell you the truth.' Cory was watching him, his face grave. 'Either that, or disengage until Justin returns from Midwinter and can question her himself.' He grimaced. 'When do you expect him back?'

'In a week or so.' Lucas rubbed his brow. 'I cannot disengage, Cory. We cannot take the risk that Miss Raleigh is involved with the Midwinter spies. If she were to suspect anything and disappear, we would have lost the lead. Worse, she would warn the others what had happened and then all our work would be destroyed.'

'And if she is innocent?' Cory questioned. 'How will she feel to discover that you have approached her under false pretences?'

Lucas's lips thinned. It was the one question that he

had not permitted himself to consider. 'I cannot allow that to influence me.'

There was a silence between them. 'I appreciate your difficulty, Lucas,' Cory said slowly. 'Sometimes, however, a man must follow his instinct.'

'Following one's instinct can get one killed,' Lucas said bleakly.

'And ignoring it can lose a man the one thing he most desires,' Cory pointed out gently.

Lucas shifted irritably. 'Marriage is making you soft, Cory Newlyn. Why tie yourself to one woman when there is an entire legion of them out there?'

'Perhaps,' Cory said, 'because one particular woman is all you need?'

Lucas gave him a cynical smile. 'Definitely soft, Cory.'

'All rakes reform in the end,' Cory said, 'unless they want to end as sad old roués leaning on their canes and leering at the débutantes.'

Lucas shuddered. 'You paint such an attractive picture.'

'Think about it,' Cory said, smiling. 'Look at Richard.'

Lucas shook his head. 'Richard was ready to reform,' he said slowly. 'He was in love. I…' he hesitated, '…I am not.'

Cory sighed. 'Nor ever shall be? I thought that you had recovered well enough from your youthful disappointment to realise that not all women are designing harpies.'

Lucas laughed. 'Oh, I have. My antipathy does not stem from that.' His face stilled. 'It is more that I have never met a woman to whom I wished to be faithful. Ever after is a long time.'

'You are thinking of your father,' Cory said acutely.

Lucas shrugged. 'I am thinking of my mother,' he said. 'She detested Papa's philandering, but she never said a word against him.' He shifted uncomfortably in his chair for, even now, the memories were hard to recall. 'She never said a word, but she lost the happiness that once lit her eyes. I could not ask for such stoicism from my wife.' He fixed Cory with a sardonic look. 'If you start to tell me, in that exasperating manner of happily married people, that I shall feel differently when I meet the right woman, then—'

Cory held up a hand peaceably. 'I should not dream of it, Luc.' He got to his feet and slapped Lucas good-naturedly on the shoulder. 'I wish you good fortune. I am away, home to my wife.'

Lucas watched Cory's tall figure thread its way through the milling crowd about the card tables. He saw Cory pause to greet an acquaintance here and there, but there was a barely repressed impatience about him that soon had him on the move again. Lucas noticed that he turned down at least two offers of a round of piquet and several invitations to join some cronies for a drink. He shook his head thoughtfully. He had the greatest admiration for Rachel Newlyn, but he could not see why Cory should be in such a hurry to return to her side. Petticoat government… He had done very well without it these twenty-eight years past and he was not about to succumb to its lure now. This business with Rebecca Raleigh was a different matter entirely. The only reason he felt badly about deceiving her was because she was young and alone. She had struck him as gallant. Yes, that was the word to describe Miss Raleigh. She was gallant in the face of all the odds and he admired her courage whilst being in danger of trampling that very gallantry underfoot.

'Devil take it!' Lucas said bad-temperedly, slapping his glass down so hard that the table shook. He had come out to drown his sorrows and yet it seemed there was nowhere to hide. He felt the greatest scoundrel in the whole world.

With two commissions to complete, Rebecca rose each day when the bleary London dawn spread across the sky and worked late into the night. During daylight she would throw the shutters wide to draw as much natural light into the workshop as possible. When night came she would light the candles and continue until her head ached and her eyes itched. There was no sound in the studio but for the diamond scribe scratching the glass as she meticulously picked out the pattern of the wicked angel. Beneath its point the figure came to life, wings folded neatly, the line of cheek and jaw giving the impression of strength and grace, head bent, as if in devout contemplation of sin. On the evening of the fourth day she laid her scribe aside and considered the engraving. She knew at once that there was something wrong with it. The problem was not in the execution, but in the finished picture. She had given the wicked angel Lucas Kestrel's face.

It was undeniable. The detail was perfect: the high cheekbones, the hard line of the jaw, the watchful eyes, the mouth... Rebecca put her head in her hands in despair. All this time she had been shutting Lucas out of her thoughts by concentrating on her work. She had refused to think of him, refused to dream of him. Yet he had come to haunt her nevertheless, taking life beneath the point of the scribe and showing her just how foolish she was to think that she could dismiss him.

Rebecca pushed the bowl away dispiritedly. She knew she should have spent longer practising on old glass before she started work on the crystal, but she had been desperate to finish the commission, desperate for the money, if she were truthful. And there was no real need to despair, for Lord Fremantle was likely to be very pleased with the work. She would deliver it to the Club in the morning. It was undoubtedly amongst her best work. Technically it was beautiful and perfectly executed. It was what it told her that was worrying.

Rebecca stood up, wiped the palms of her hands on her apron and walked restlessly across to the window. Night had fallen long since and the lights of the Jerusalem Tavern twinkled faintly in the dusk. A distant murmur of voices drifted on the night air.

Rebecca turned away. She knew that she should put in some time on her accounts, which consistently refused to add up. The mere thought of it made her head ache.

She wished with fierce longing that her uncle, George Provost, was here with her now. She had never felt so alone as she did these days, not even when she had been a child and her parents had died and she and Daniel were obliged to go their separate ways. George and his kindly wife, Ruth, had taken her in and over the years she had become much attached to them, but now she had no one. She knew that she had tried to bury her grief in her work, but every so often it would bubble up as it did now, making her eyes sting and her heart ache.

Rebecca had never minded working on her own before. Engraving was a solitary profession, but she was beginning to realise that there was a difference between working on her own commissions with the buzz of the workshop going on around her, and working in silence because she had lost all her colleagues.

With a little sigh, she went into the storeroom and took out an old wineglass that she used for practice. Now that the angel was completed, she needed to start practising birds of prey. She went back to her desk, sat down and picked up her diamond-point scribe and the little hammer. Stipple work engraving was slow and expensive, for each dot was placed individually on the glass with utter precision. For Lord Lucas Kestrel's commission, however, nothing but the best would do. Her professional pride demanded it.

She picked up her engraving scribe and the little hammer that she used for stipple work. She placed the scribe against the glass and tapped it gently.

An agonising pain shot through her left wrist, so sharp that it felt as though she were hammering into her own bones. Rebecca cried out, dropping the hammer so that it spun away across the bench. The glass fractured all the way around the top and broke off cleanly in a band half an inch wide. Rebecca felt sickness rise in her throat. She grabbed the edge of the desk to steady herself, then sat down and clutched her wrist with her other hand. The pain was receding a little now, a whisper of agony along her nerves. Eventually the faintness caused by the pain receded sufficiently for her to stumble across to the sofa and sit down.

She sat there for a very long time.

It had happened before, and she had dismissed it as an unlucky vibration from the hammer. Now, however, she knew she could not deceive herself any longer. She had seen it happen to other engravers, seen them work until the pain shadowed their every movement and they were obliged to give up their livelihood. The doctors shook their heads and said that nothing could be done and charged a guinea for the privilege of breaking the bad news.

Rebecca had worked at her craft since she was fourteen years old, and now, a decade on, the pain had come to take her too.

She looked around the dim workshop, at the light glancing off the crystal on the shelves and the tools of her trade lying discarded on the bench. She loved her work so much that she could never bear to let it go. The loneliness welled up more powerfully than before. She went across to the shelf and lightly touched the glass with the engraved anchor, as though it was a talisman. Beneath the elegant chase work was a motto. *Celer et Audax*—Swift and bold.

Rebecca wrapped both arms about her, as though to keep out the cold. If only Daniel was here. But Daniel had his own way to make. They had a made a pact when they were children and found they were to be apart. If ever the one needed the other, they had only to send a token…

For a moment, Rebecca was tempted. Then she sighed and moved back to the workbench. She would need to be in a great deal worse situation than this before she contacted her brother and drew him into danger.

She blew out the candles and made her way up to bed.

Early the next morning, on the basis that the longer she put it off the worse it would be, Rebecca picked up her engraving scribe and set to work. She was tentative at first, but when no pain troubled her, she soon fell into a rhythm again as she chipped delicately at the fragile glass. The work was absorbing and when a shadow fell across her workbench she realised that she had not even heard the knock at the workshop door. She looked up to see Lucas Kestrel there and her heart skipped a tiny beat. The strong morning sunlight from the window made his hair gleam conker brown rather than auburn.

'Miss Raleigh. How are you?' He smiled at her and Rebecca's heart did another quick flip.

'I am very well, thank you, my lord. How are you?'

'I am tired, I thank you,' Lucas said. He looked straight at her. 'I do not appreciate sleepless nights.'

Rebecca blushed. 'I suppose that you have something preying on your mind?'

'You suppose correctly, Miss Raleigh.'

Rebecca bent her head over the glass and polished

the surface with unnecessary vigour. Her hand was not quite steady. She tried to calm her singing nerves.

'I did not expect you to call again so soon, my lord,' she said. 'I fear that your commission is barely begun. We did agree a week and it is only five days.'

'I know it.' Lucas drove his hands into the pockets of his great coat. 'I did not wish to wait that long to see you again, Miss Raleigh, and as I may not meet you socially, this seemed the only way.'

Rebecca picked up the scribe and the hammer again. 'You are, of course, quite welcome to look around my studio, my lord. If you choose to spend more money here, then I shall not attempt to stop you, but not all the items are for sale.'

Lucas laughed. 'My dear Miss Raleigh, I believe we have established that already.'

Rebecca relaxed slightly. 'Very well, then…'

Lucas glanced towards the fireplace. 'You do not have a fire today?'

'I had not got around to building one,' Rebecca said evasively. She did not wish to tell him that she had run out of firewood and that her accounts had shown her it was something she could not afford to buy.

'If you show me where the wood is stored then I am happy to build one for you,' Lucas said. 'It is too cold today to be without a fire.'

Rebecca stared at him in the liveliest astonishment. '*You* will make a fire? You cannot!'

Lucas looked amused. 'I assure you that I am quite capable of it, Miss Raleigh. I have been in the army for years and have taken on far more challenging tasks than the building of a fire.'

Rebecca frowned. 'That was hardly what I meant, my lord. You would spoil the set of your jacket for a start and might even get soot on your pantaloons.'

Lucas's face lightened into a smile. 'Oh I see! You feel that I *should* not make the fire rather than that I *could* not. You relieve me, Miss Raleigh. I thought for a moment that you considered me the sort of frippery fellow who could not remove his boots without the aid of a valet.'

'You cannot make the fire because I have no wood!' Rebecca snapped. She put the wineglass down on the desk with a slap. 'Are you happy now that I have confessed it? I have no wood and I cannot afford to buy any more at present and whilst you distract me from my work I have no prospect of making any money that will enable me to buy firewood. Now will you go away?'

'I shall certainly go and purchase you some logs to build a fire,' Lucas said, 'and then when I return we may talk.'

Rebecca spread her arms wide with frustration. 'About what, my lord? There are plenty of penniless craftsmen working in London who cannot afford a fire. Why do you have to interest yourself in my case?'

Lucas shrugged. 'It is your misfortune that I am more interested in you than in the others, Miss Raleigh. I shall see you shortly.'

'Pray do not trouble to return!' Rebecca called, as he reached the door. 'And do not spend any money on me for I cannot repay you—'

'Please save your breath,' Lucas said, with scrupulous politeness. 'There is an entire crowd of people out here hanging on your every word.'

Rebecca ran to the window. She was distraught to see that it was true. Housewives with marketing baskets had gathered outside the door, their faces sharp and eager for entertainment. A group of shabby urchins was trailing Lucas along the pavement and apparently begging for money. The vintner was standing outside his shop in the sunshine, wiping his hands on a rag as he exchanged information with the silversmith. Rebecca gave a cry of aggravation and threw herself down on the *chaise-longue,* her face in her hands. Over the last six months her life had been growing progressively more difficult, but this new situation was both unexpected and utterly confusing. She did not wish to feel beholden to Lucas Kestrel and she was very afraid of where his charity might take her.

When Lucas returned a surprisingly short time later, Rebecca was still sitting on the sofa. She got up quickly when he came in and wiped her eyes with the back of her hand, hoping that he had not seen her tears. The wood merchant's assistant followed him into the workshop, hefting a very heavy sack of logs. The man took the sack through to the store, as he had done in Rebecca's uncle's time, and received a coin for his trouble from Lucas before he went out. It was then that Rebecca also spotted the parcel that Lucas had laid on the table containing a fresh loaf of bread, a pat of rich yellow butter, some cheese, a ham and half a spit-roasted chicken. Her stomach, treacherously, gave a loud rumble at the sight of food.

She seized a few logs and threw them higgledy-piggledly into the fireplace, venting her frustration on the inanimate blocks of wood until Lucas put out a hand to stop her.

'Wait! It will never light if you build it like that.'

'I know!' To her horror, Rebecca could feel the tears closing her throat. 'I know how to make a fire! I am also quite capable of feeding myself. I have managed perfectly well on my own for the past six months and I do *not* require some high-handed, arrogant lord—'

'That is tautology,' Lucas said.

Rebecca stared, jolted out of her train of thought. 'I beg your pardon?'

'Tautology. Gilding the lily. If I am high-handed, then the arrogance goes without saying…'

Rebecca gave an exasperated squeak. 'Arrogant, high-handed, conceited, self-important—'

Lucas raised a hand. 'Please, Miss Raleigh. I have taken your point. I am going to make some tea. Oh…' he paused '…and the food is for me to take home for supper…'

'I do not believe you!' Rebecca said sulkily.

Lucas shrugged. He disappeared into the scullery and Rebecca did not even trouble to try to stop him. Instead she took the logs out of the fire again, swept it clear and built it painstakingly from scratch. By the time the flames were taking hold, Lucas had returned with the tea and some Bath Oliver biscuits that Rebecca suspected might be stale.

He placed the tea on Rebecca's desk much as Sam had done the previous day, and came to sit beside her.

The tea, Rebecca was surprised to discover, was almost as good as Sam's brew had been.

'Now,' Lucas said, 'I would like you to tell me something about yourself, Miss Raleigh, and how you have ended in this situation. You said that you had managed very well on your own for the last six months. What happened before that?'

Rebecca looked at him. She was tempted to tell him everything, not just about the hardship following her uncle's death, but about her family and how her brother Daniel was the only one left, and he was a hunted man in as much trouble as she. She teetered on the brink of disclosure and then drew back a little. Lucas did not prompt her. He watched her steadily, but with so much gentleness in his eyes that she caught her breath to see it. It was grief and tiredness, she warned herself, that had weakened her. She needed to tell someone. She took a deep, refreshing gulp of the tea, set down her cup, and started to talk.

Lucas had not been entirely sure that Rebecca would answer his question. He recognised that she was living within her work at the moment; that it was the thing she used to blot out the grief. There were no signs of her personality at all in her studio, although it was the place where she lived as well as worked. He concluded that she had withdrawn into herself so much that nothing else could reach her. He wanted to be the one to break through that shell and touch her. He wanted it so much that it frightened him.

For his own sake he had to draw back. He had never felt like this before and it was the very devil. Even as he was questioning her and trying to gain her confidence, he felt the veriest traitor, the greatest betrayer in the whole world.

He had never met a woman like Rebecca Raleigh before. Affairs of the heart—he did not like to think in terms of love—had never been difficult for him in the past. Yet his current feelings prompted him to take Rebecca away from this hovel of a place where she tried so desperately to scrape a living. He wanted to cherish her, care for her and protect her. He pushed aside all the complex and unfamiliar emotions that pressed in on him and tried to concentrate.

He watched her face as she took a scalding mouthful of tea, watched the pure line of her throat as she swallowed and set down her mug. There was a slump to her shoulders, but she would never admit defeat. His heart swelled with an emotion he tried to dismiss as pity.

He sat quietly drinking his tea—a beverage that had never been his favourite drawing-room tipple—and listened whilst Rebecca talked. Her face was drawn and her blue eyes were full of pain, and it took every ounce of Lucas's self-control not to touch her.

'My uncle and aunt died of the sweating sickness four months ago,' Rebecca said, fiddling with the handle of her mug. Lucas noted that it had been broken and affixed again, slightly off centre. Presumably she could not afford to throw things away.

'I am sorry,' he said. 'So recent a grief must be very painful for you.'

Rebecca nodded. 'They had brought me up from the time I was a child. It was my uncle who taught me my profession.' She glanced quickly across at the workbench. 'He was a master engraver, one of the most talented men in the profession, though he never truly gained the recognition he deserved. I think...' for a moment she smiled '...I think that he taught me well.'

'I am sure that he did,' Lucas said, 'judging by the work on display here.'

Rebecca shot him a glance that had a tiny sparkle in it. Lucas noticed with a jolt how she came alive when she spoke of her work. 'And you are suddenly an expert, my lord?' she teased. 'You, who did not even know that the profession existed a week ago?'

Lucas gave a self-deprecating shrug. He felt guilty. 'I am a quick learner.'

The sparkle died from Rebecca's eyes. 'Whether or not I am good at my work is irrelevant now. When my uncle died, the business died with him. It was naïve of me to think that I could keep it running single-handed. One of the journeymen and the two apprentices took work elsewhere, for they did not wish to be employed by a woman. The other journeyman...' she hesitated '...he thought to persuade me into marriage as a way for me to continue the business.'

Lucas clamped down on his instinctive violence at the thought of some buffoon forcing himself on Rebecca and kept his voice level. 'You did not care for the idea?'

'No, I did not,' Rebecca said. 'I cared even less for the way that he tried to persuade me, and *he* disliked the means I took to dissuade him from his amorous advances.'

Lucas bit his lip on a laugh. He remembered her threatening him with the diamond scribe. 'What did you do?'

'I used the fire irons,' Rebecca said. 'They have a slight dent in them now.'

Lucas shook his head. 'So you used the fire irons on him and your engraving scribe to defend yourself against me... You are a dangerous woman, Miss Raleigh.'

Rebecca did not look at him. 'You were different,' she said softly.

Lucas felt his body tighten. He did not feel different. He wanted exactly what her journeyman and no doubt many another man had wanted from Rebecca Raleigh, and it was the devil's own job not to demand it from her.

'Not so different,' he said, wryly truthful. 'I wanted the same thing.'

Their eyes met and the tension seemed to spin out between them for an eternity. Rebecca broke the contact with an effort.

'You were quicker to understand,' she said drily, 'for with you I did not have to resort to physical violence.' She shifted a little. 'So once Malet had left, muttering of retribution, I was on my own but for Emma, the servant girl. I soon realised that when the men went they took all the work with them. So then I had to let Emma go too, since I could not pay her.'

Lucas's gaze narrowed with incredulity. 'You have been living here *alone* for four months?'

'Three months.' Rebecca's gaze flicked to his face and then away. 'Emma was with me for a few weeks after my uncle's death. I have managed well enough on my own. I have some work in hand…' She smiled. 'Quite a lot, thanks to you, my lord. And to the Archangel Club.'

She had given Lucas the opening he needed. He was astounded to feel himself hesitating to take it. At each step he became more deeply mired in deception. He was trying to obtain information from her under false pretences and his honour revolted at the thought. He ignored the squirming of his conscience and forced himself to press on.

'Do you have any other clients currently?' he questioned, allowing his gaze to range about the workshop as though the answer did not really matter to him.

Rebecca's gaze flickered. She rubbed a hand across her forehead. 'No, I have none,' she said.

'And no business outstanding from your uncle's time?'

Rebecca rubbed her eyes. It made her look like a child and it smote Lucas's heart. 'There are a few pieces still to be collected,' she said. 'My uncle completed some work for a gentleman who is a prodigious collector, but he has yet to send for it. I have it in the storeroom.'

Lucas's nerves prickled. If this mysterious collector was part of the Midwinter spy circle and he had yet to collect his order, then they might be about to catch him red-handed.

'What sort of engraving interests your collector?' he asked, as casually as he could.

Rebecca raised her brows. 'Why, all sorts of designs, my lord. Ships and birds and anchors… My uncle did an entire set for him with an astronomical motif—the phases of the moon, and the sun and stars. He has a wide interest.'

Lucas's attention was riveted. He had one of the Midwinter glasses in the pocket of his coat at that very moment and it was a match for a design he could see on the display shelves. He could feel the hard edge of the glass pressing against his thigh, reminding of the exact reason why he was in this studio, questioning Miss Rebecca Raleigh, glass engraver.

'What manner of man is he, this collector?' he asked, hoping he was not pressing too hard and raising her suspicions. It was difficult to tell what she was thinking. She gave him a direct look from her very blue eyes, but he could not read her expression.

'I have no notion, my lord. I never meet him. He sends his servant to place the orders and collect the finished engraving.'

Lucas shrugged, as though the matter was of no further interest to him. He would instruct Tom Bradshaw to keep the shop under observation until such time as the servant came to collect his order, and then he would have the man followed and see where that led them. He did not want to ask Rebecca any more questions on the topic now, both because he knew that she would become suspicious and also because he felt a traitor to be asking at all. He changed the subject to something more personal.

'Your friend, Miss Astley,' he said. 'Was she responsible for your commission from the Archangel?'

'No.' Rebecca smiled again, turning her empty beaker between her hands. 'My uncle did some work for the Club in the past, but Nan reminded Lord Fremantle of it when he was looking for an engraver to produce the rose bowl. She and I have been friends since we were children, for all that our way of life is quite divergent these days.'

'And does she seek to persuade you that her way is preferable to yours?'

'Of course,' Rebecca said. She looked around the studio, a rueful smile on her lips. 'Who is to say that she is not correct, my lord? There are easier ways than this to earn a living.'

'Yet you do not believe it?'

Rebecca looked him straight in the eye. 'Maybe it is a fault in me that the one commodity I am not prepared to sell is myself.' A little frown creased her brow. 'And that reminds me, my lord, that I must ask you not to give me any further charity. I cannot afford to pay you back.'

'I am not asking you to do so,' Lucas pointed out. He gestured to the fire. 'I could dismantle that, I suppose, and take it with me, but I am loath to deprive you of its warmth.' He stood up, smiling at her. 'I fear, my dear Miss Raleigh, that you will just have to bear with my quixotic gifts—and bear with me.'

Rebecca got up too. 'It would be better if you were not to call here again,' she said.

Lucas could see the reluctance in her face. 'Better for whom?' he queried gently.

'Better for me.' Rebecca fidgeted with the pencils on her work desk. 'Already people are starting to comment.'

Lucas raised his brows with arrogant disregard. He

had never cared for the opinions of others. To him the most important thing was that Rebecca should not starve. 'People are talking? Then tell them to go hang.'

Rebecca frowned slightly. He sensed that she was genuinely distressed. 'Then you will not promise to leave me alone?'

'I will not.' Lucas sighed. 'I cannot, Miss Raleigh.'

He waited, watching her try to work this out. There was a fugitive shyness in her blue eyes. These were the times when he sensed her vulnerability most acutely and it made him feel an utter scoundrel. He was torn in half. He genuinely wished to protect Rebecca and yet he knew he was taking advantage. This was caddish behaviour, abusing her growing trust in him in the hope that she might inadvertently pass on some useful information. Justin's return could not happen any too soon, so that he might hand over the entire investigation to him and withdraw before he hurt Rebecca Raleigh—and before his own feelings made a fool of him as well. Already he was in far too deep. And yet he had no real wish to withdraw.

He saw Rebecca's brow creased into a deeper frown. 'Why will you not promise to leave me be?' she whispered.

'Because I cannot keep my word.' It was the absolute truth. Lucas took her hand and kissed her fingers. He felt her try to draw away but did not let her go. He looked directly into her eyes. 'You see, Miss Raleigh, I have no *desire* to leave you alone. On the contrary, I wish to spend as much time as possible with you. So you see it would be quite foolish for me to make a promise that I have no intention of keeping.'

He watched the emotions flicker across Rebecca's face. 'You cannot spend time with me,' she protested. 'You distract me from my work too much. Besides…' she gave a little shrug '…it is quite pointless.'

Lucas smiled. 'Perhaps you will become accustomed to my presence?'

Rebecca shook her head. 'I doubt that I shall become indifferent to it.'

Lucas drew her a little closer. 'I am grateful for that. The last thing that I should wish for is that you be indifferent to me.'

Rebecca held him off with a hand against his chest. 'And what would be the *first* thing that you would wish for, my lord? For whatever it is, I cannot give it to you. I cannot see *any purpose* to your visits at all.'

Lucas turned her hand over and kissed the palm, feeling the shiver that went through her body as an echo deep within his own.

'All I desire is to see you,' he said. But already he was making a liar of himself, drawing her into his arms.

'My lord,' she said quietly, 'I thought that I explained—'

'It is only a kiss,' Lucas said lightly, 'and you can always decline.' He smiled into her eyes. 'You have already argued with me over countless other matters, Miss Raleigh. It should not be difficult for you to refuse me this…'

And as he spoke he drew her closer, allowing himself to forget the real reason that he was there, the purpose of his enquiries, the dual nature of his interest. Her softness and strength fascinated him. In that mo-

ment he wanted only her and everything else faded
into complete insignificance as he bent his head to kiss
her.

Rebecca was not sure why she had told Lucas so
much, nor why she felt relieved to have done so. She
had not confided in anyone since her uncle and aunt
had died, but had kept her feelings locked tightly in
her chest, repressed beneath the work that had kept
her mind and body occupied from dawn to dusk. Now,
though, she felt lighter in spirit than she had done in
a long while. It was this she blamed later for her poor
judgement in allowing Lucas to kiss her.

'It should not be difficult for you to refuse me
this…' he said.

Somehow his broad shoulders seemed to have
blocked out the rest of the studio, the rest of the world.
Rebecca could see only him.

'May I?' Lucas said softly.

Now that he was so close to her Rebecca found she
seemed incapable of doing anything other than look at
him. She knew the answer to his question was most
definitely 'No', but she was having some difficulty
with the word. Eventually what came out was 'Yes'.

She would probably have added a 'please', for good
measure, but Lucas was already kissing her by then, a
slow, lazy, languorous kiss that should have been light
and easy to dismiss, but somehow was not. His mouth
was warm and firm on hers, promising the sorts of
things that Rebecca was not even aware that she
wanted. As his arms went around her she felt her
whole body soften against his, pliant and suffused with

heat. Her legs trembled and the ground seemed to tumble away beneath her, which did not matter since Lucas was holding her hard now. She leaned against him and felt the world start to spin. *Now* she knew why she had never allowed a gentleman to kiss her properly before. *Now* she knew for sure that it was perilous and exciting and enough to make one forget everything—modesty and sense and propriety. Or, to be exact, that was what kissing Lucas did to her. She doubted that it would be the same with anyone else.

She was not sure how much time had passed before Lucas let her go, very gently, keeping a protective arm about her. Rebecca could not focus for a moment; all she was aware of was an intolerably strong ache to be in his arms again. She looked up into his face, saw the blaze of heat in his eyes, saw that he was about to pull her to him again, and stepped back in sudden panic.

'No! I... Oh, no!'

Lucas moved away at once. His face was a little pale and he was breathing hard. He ran a hand over his hair. 'Miss Raleigh—Rebecca—'

'Do not,' Rebecca said. There was a wrench in her voice. She could not believe that she had just invited Lucas Kestrel to kiss her. It seemed absurd, extraordinary. Yet she had ached to be in his arms and, once there, she had wanted him to hold her forever. And now that he had let her go she felt dreadfully lonely. She was evidently far more vulnerable than she had realised, to be drawn to the strength and assurance of a man she hardly knew.

She pressed a hand to her lips, moving to put some

distance between them. 'I do not know why I said yes,' she murmured. 'I never do such things—' She cut the words off before she gave herself away further and moved behind the rosewood desk. It made her feel better to put something solid between them. She hoped that Lucas was going to leave soon. Her legs still felt shaky and her head felt light, and she was not at all sure what was wrong with her.

Lucas was watching her. It made her feel hot and nervous.

'I think I have made a mistake,' she said.

'I am sorry that you should view my kiss in such a light,' Lucas said. He started to move around the desk towards her. A quick, heated excitement gripped Rebecca and held her still.

'Allowing for the fact that it was a mistake, how did you view the experience?' Lucas continued.

Rebecca drew a short breath. 'It was tolerable, my lord,' she lied.

Lucas raised his dark brows. A spark of devilment came into his eyes. 'Only tolerable? That is not how I would wish you to remember it, Miss Raleigh. You had better give me another chance.'

Rebecca backed away swiftly from her second error. 'There is no need whatsoever. It was passable, my lord—perfectly acceptable...'

Lucas was laughing now. 'I shall have to do better,' he murmured, reaching to pull her closer again. His voice roughened. 'Acceptable is simply not... acceptable.'

Rebecca wriggled, but Lucas had an arm about her and held her ruthlessly still. She felt his breath feather across her skin. She could see the shadow of his eye-lashes, spiky against the hard line of his cheek. His lips brushed her jaw, then his mouth was suddenly on hers, his hand tangled in her hair, tilting her face up to his. Sensation flared within her. The rosewood desk was smooth, the back of it hard against her thighs. She felt herself tremble. Lucas's hand brushed the cotton of her gown, his palm against her breast. He was kissing her with such urgency that her head reeled. His slightest touch could ignite her fiercest longings. She felt heavy, languid and tingly all over. Rebecca had never, ever imagined it could be like that.

The world shook. She felt herself lean back against the desk, scattering the pencil sketches all over the floor. The sound disturbed her and she tried instinctively to pull away, but Lucas did not break the kiss, prolonging it mercilessly until Rebecca had almost forgotten where she was and was held helpless and bewitched. This time when his lips left hers she gave a small gasp of disappointment that she could not repress, and she saw the masculine satisfaction in his expression as he scanned her face. Useless to try to deny his effect on her, for it was evident in her shaking hands and her flushed, aroused face.

'Acceptable?' he drawled.

Rebecca moved away, surreptitiously holding on to the desk for support. 'There is nothing acceptable about this behaviour, my lord. I desire no more from my clients than that they pay promptly, and you are no different from the rest.'

'No different?' Lucas's insistent tone made her blush. She knew that she was not telling the truth.

'I cannot allow you to be any different from the rest, my lord.' Rebecca knew she was weakening. If he touched her again…

But he did not. She saw the shadow of something come into his eyes, almost as though he had recalled some barrier that stood between them. He touched her cheek lightly in a gentle caress that she felt shiver through her body.

'Be careful, Rebecca Raleigh,' he said.

And it was odd, but later she wondered why his words had sounded like a farewell.

Chapter Four

'Rebecca, it is decided. You are coming with me to a ball this evening.' Nan Astley marched triumphantly into Rebecca's studio the following evening and surveyed her friend with amused disapproval. 'Look at you! It is past nine and you are still working. You will become the dullest creature imaginable if you carry on in this way!'

Rebecca laughed and reluctantly laid down her diamond scribe. She rubbed her eyes, which felt gritty from tiredness. 'I have to work. I need the money.'

Nan made a tutting sound. 'Not tonight. You are wan as a bowl of whey. Tonight you are coming out with me. It will cheer you up.'

'Not tonight, Nan,' Rebecca besought. 'Please! I am tired—'

Nan made a derisive noise. 'Then a change of scene is what you need to help raise your spirits.' Her face puckered. 'I worry about you, Becca, sitting here and working your fingers to the bone.'

'I hope it is not the Cyprians' Ball.' Rebecca could

feel herself weakening. 'I have not forgotten that you tried to persuade me to attend last year.'

'Of course it is not!' Nan looked virtuous. 'Would I take you to such an event? No, this is only a small, private affair. Besides, it is a masked ball, so no one will recognise you. It is taking place at Carlisle House. What could be more respectable?'

'Almost anything,' Rebecca murmured. She pushed her chair back from the workbench and got stiffly to her feet. The idea of going out was curiously appealing. She was tired of staring at the same four walls and enduring little but her own company. To go out amidst the bright lights and a crowd of people, to lose herself for one evening in noise and company and colour and *life*… Suddenly the idea seemed powerfully attractive. She had been living solitary for so long that she felt starved of fun. Yet a worry nagged at the back of her mind. There was something tense about Nan, as though she would brook no refusal; although her friend caught her glance and gave her a brilliant smile that seemed to contradict Rebecca's thoughts, still she felt vaguely wary.

'I have no suitable gown—' she began, looking for excuses, but Nan waved the objection aside.

'I have brought one with me.' She gestured to the fall of cherry-red silken stuff in her arms. 'It will become you exceedingly. I will do your hair. Now come along! We only have an hour. I do not wish to leave Bosham unattended for long or one of those dreadful Wilson sisters will snap him up. They have been waiting to pounce on him for months!'

Rebecca had no more chance to demur, for Nan was

already steering her towards the rickety wooden staircase and up to her narrow chamber. The room was
sparse but it had a dressing-table and a mirror, and
Nan appeared to have brought all the other items that
she required to transform Rebecca from ugly duckling
into, if not an elegant swan, precisely, then a seductive
siren. It was so contrary to Rebecca's normal style of
dress that, when she saw her finished reflection, she
almost choked.

After three-quarters of an hour, they were ready to
leave. Whenever Rebecca thought Nan wasn't looking
she would try to hoist up the front of the red silk dress,
which had a scandalously low *décolletage* and some
artfully cut lace that seemed to accentuate rather than
conceal the curves of Rebecca's breasts.

'Do leave the gown alone, Rebecca,' Nan scolded,
when she saw her. 'I do not know why you are fussing.
It is demure enough for a nun!'

'Only the sort of abbess who runs a Covent Garden
bawdy house,' Rebecca muttered. She wrapped her
black cloak about her, trying to cover the exposed bits.
Thank goodness for the black velvet mask with the
matching cherry ribbons. If anyone was going to recognise any part of her, it certainly would not be her
face.

It was only when they reached Carlisle House that
Rebecca began to suspect that she had underestimated
the nature of the party. Either that, or Nan had deliberately misled her by understating the case. It *was* a
masked ball, but in the style of a Venetian masque,
which had been popular in the previous century. A

crush of guests thronged the huge ballroom, which was lit by at least five hundred candles. The light reflected off the long, gold-framed mirrors, and it seemed that an endless parade of dazzlingly attired strangers circled in the dance. They were dressed in every costume imaginable, from pirates and highwaymen to shepherdesses and Roman goddesses, and some were rather more undressed than others. The scene was decadent, rich and glittering with vivid life. Rebecca felt as though she had stepped into another world, and one she was not sure she could deal with.

Nan squeezed her arm. 'I told you it would be fun, Becca,' she said smugly.

Rebecca had stopped on the threshold and now she almost choked at what was before her eyes. 'A small party?' she said faintly. 'Nan—'

Her mouth fell open even farther as she saw a young woman who was disporting herself with a couple of bucks. Her dress appeared to have lost its bodice and the rest of it was nothing more than a gauzy net about her legs. Not that the gentlemen were complaining as they chased her about the room with loud hunting cries.

Nan laughed. 'That is Miss Chudleigh making a fool of herself as usual. I declare her gowns get younger as she grows older! No wonder Lord Fremantle looks to find himself a new mistress.'

Rebecca gave her a sharp look, for Nan's words had penetrated her awed reaction to the spectacle of the masque. 'Lord Fremantle? Is he here tonight?'

Nan shrugged airily. 'Lud, who knows? We are all incognito. Is it not the most delicious fun?'

Rebecca was beginning to wonder. Nan, with her flimsy blue silk and lace dress, her outrageous peacock feathers in her hair, and her blue peacock mask, was already attracting plenty of male attention. No matter what she had said earlier, she did not seem at all inclined to find Lord Bosham in the throng and was giving her hand to a gentleman in harlequin's costume, who seemed intent on carrying her off. Rebecca felt a flutter of panic. She had not expected this and suddenly it seemed an alien world, dangerous and raffish, and she an innocent thrown to the lions.

'May I have the pleasure of this dance, madam?' A gentleman was bowing before her and, although he was costumed and masked, Rebecca had an absolute conviction that it was Lord Fremantle. He took her hand and her skin crawled. Behind the mask his eyes were a dead fish stare and his face a pasty white. Rebecca swallowed the repulsion in her throat.

'Thank you, sir, but I do not dance.'

The gentleman pressed a little closer. She could feel his hot breath on her neck. 'Indeed?' His flat, marble gaze appraised her from behind the mask, dropping to the neckline of her dress in insulting perusal. 'If you do not dance, what *do* you do?'

'What the lady means is that she is not at liberty to dance with you, sir, because she is promised to me,' a smooth voice interposed from behind them.

Both Rebecca and Fremantle spun around.

Rebecca's heart contracted. There was a gentleman standing directly before her. He was wearing a black domino and a plain black mask behind which his eyes glittered as he watched her. There was something both relaxed and dangerous in his stance, as though he was quite prepared for Fremantle to oppose him and knew precisely what to do if he did. Despite the disguise, Rebecca knew for certain that it was Lord Lucas Kestrel.

He stepped a little closer and she could tell from his eyes that he was smiling behind the mask. Had he recognised her? Rebecca felt a moment's alarm.

He was offering her his arm. 'Come, my sweeting. I am sorry to have left you alone for so long.'

Rebecca was torn. She wanted to escape Fremantle but she did not want to step into Lucas Kestrel's arms. In the heated atmosphere of the masque, that would be very perilous. Fremantle, sensing her reluctance, placed one fleshy hand on her arm.

'I cannot see that the lady is promised to you, sir, when there is no formality at such an event as this.'

'If there is no formality,' the black domino said, gently mocking, 'then you cannot object to me spiriting the lady away, sir.'

Fremantle bridled. 'I think the lady should choose for herself.'

'By all means,' the black domino agreed smoothly.

Rebecca made her choice. In truth, there was no real alternative, for she would accept Lucas Kestrel over Alexander Fremantle any day. The difficulty would be in preserving her disguise against Lucas and in getting away from him as swiftly as possible before he unmasked her. She felt quite hot and faint at the thought.

She dropped Lord Fremantle a slight curtsy. 'Excuse me, sir.'

Fremantle stiffened, then bowed abruptly. 'Very

well.' He turned back to Rebecca. 'A dance is a paltry matter, but I demand to be first in all else.' He walked away.

Rebecca released her breath sharply and turned to the black domino, who was still waiting, his head tilted quizzically. 'Thank you, my lord,' she said.

He took a step closer to her. 'My lord?' he questioned softly.

Rebecca smiled slightly. 'If I am a lady, sir, then surely you must be a lord.'

The black domino laughed. 'Do you imply that you are playing a part, madam?'

'We are all doing that tonight, sir.'

'So we are,' the black domino murmured. His breath stirred the ribbons that held her mask in place and Rebecca shivered. She yielded slightly as he placed his arm about her waist and drew her towards the ballroom. It was an intimacy, but one that did not seem out of place at a masque where the behaviour was already approaching, or even exceeding, the licentious. In fact, it felt more protective than dangerous, as though he had staked a claim and no other would be permitted to approach her.

'So which part do you play tonight, madam?' he asked. He looked across at Nan Astley, laughing behind her peacock mask as a gentleman whispered secrets in her ear. 'You are not the peacock or the shepherdess or the pirate queen…'

The pirate queen. Rebecca almost laughed aloud. The decadence of the masque was having a curious effect on her, as though she felt freed from the normal constraints she laid on her own behaviour. She felt reckless, lighter than air.

She met the shadowed gaze behind the mask. 'As I said, I am the lady tonight, sir.'

'Ah, I see. The lady. Respectable, virtuous and, oh, so untouchable…' His lips brushed her bare shoulder and the heat ripped through her with shocking intensity. It was all that she could do not to jerk away.

'And what is your role tonight, sir?' she asked, her voice a little breathless.

Once again she had the impression that the black domino was smiling. 'Can you not tell, madam?' he asked gently.

Rebecca shivered. 'The rake? The seducer?'

'You injure me,' the black domino said, and this time the laughter was clear in his voice. 'After rescuing you from Fremantle, do you not cast me as the protector of innocence, my lady?'

Rebecca shot a look at him from behind her mask. It was impossible to tell whether he had recognised her, for the mask hid everything but his eyes and their expression were unreadable. She felt her nerves tighten with a mixture of excitement and vivid apprehension. As though sensing the pulsing exhil-aration within her, his arm hardened about her waist and he drew her close against his body. She could feel the desire and the latent power in him and almost stumbled and fell.

It seemed that dancing was not his aim after all. He drew her into an alcove that was tucked away from the ballroom. It was draped with golden hangings and furnished with a gold brocade love-seat. The black domino seized two glasses of wine from a passing waiter and handed one to her, guiding her to the seat. Rebecca looked at her wine dubiously.

'I do not think this a very good idea, sir.'

'Why so?'

'The wine is remarkably strong and I am…' Rebecca hesitated '…I am tired.'

'I will take care of you,' the black domino said.

That was precisely what Rebecca was afraid of. He was sitting very close to her, his thigh pressing intimately against hers within the narrow confines of the seat. Suddenly the rub of the slippery silk against her skin seemed almost unbearably sensual. She shifted uncomfortably, aware that it had been her intention to escape him as soon as she could, yet even now she was contradicting her own good sense by lingering too long. Already she had no urge to break free.

'Tell me who you are,' the black domino said softly, persuasively, in her ear.

'Certainly not.' Rebecca turned her face away. 'There are no names at a masquerade, sir.'

He put a gloved hand lightly beneath her chin and turned her face to his. His touch was light, but it set her feelings blazing. That shadowed gaze scrutinised her with unnerving closeness.

'Hmm,' he murmured. 'Peerless blue eyes and a mouth made for kissing… I could almost swear that we had met before, perhaps even kissed before, my lady.'

Rebecca's breath caught in her throat. 'You seem very certain, sir.'

'Not so certain that I would not like to put my theory to the test. For then I would know…'

He was leaning forward to suit actions to words, but Rebecca eased herself from his grip and placed a hand against his chest to hold him off.

'Not so fast, my lord!'

'Such modesty at a midnight masque,' the black domino said, with a sardonic look at the couples that whirled past them in debauched abandon. He ran one finger thoughtfully down her bare arm above her glove. Rebecca could feel her skin responding to his touch, tingling beneath the caress.

'So who are you, madam, if not a lady of the night?'

'Did I say that I was no courtesan?' Rebecca said, a little huskily.

'You did not need to tell me, sweetheart.'

'Once again, you sound very confident, sir. You must have a great deal of experience of such matters.'

'I have enough,' the black domino agreed, 'and were I to kiss you, your innocence would be something else I could prove.'

'Then the matter must remain unproven,' Rebecca said.

The black domino smiled. 'So what is Lord Fremantle to you, madam?'

Rebecca's eyes narrowed. The more they spoke the more likely it seemed that he knew her identity. She definitely should not have lingered so long, nor engaged in this fascinating but ultimately dangerous conversation. She made to rise, but his hand on her wrist held her still and his imperative touch demanded an answer.

'He is nothing to me,' Rebecca said.

'He would like to be something.'

'His wishes are no concern of mine.'

'And my wishes?' the black domino mused. 'Do I have a chance of success where Fremantle has failed?'

'No more than any other man,' Rebecca said, although the desire that started to burn within her told a different story.

The black domino laughed. 'But no less?'

'It makes no odds.' Rebecca knew she sounded a little breathless. 'None of you has any chance.'

The black domino's gaze was inscrutable. 'So when Fremantle demanded to be first, what did he mean?'

Rebecca blushed behind her mask. 'I have no notion what he meant,' she said, 'but none of his wishes are likely to be granted.' She glanced sideways at him. 'I thought that you wanted to dance, my lord, rather than—'

'Rather than make love?'

The words hung in the air between them. Rebecca's breath caught in her throat. She felt the sensual languor sweep her blood. This was so out of character for her, and so perilous. Yet now she was embarked upon it, there was something compelling about the masquerade, about playing her part. It felt like an escape, almost as though she had stepped into another world, just for one night.

And there was also something about this man, who even now was shifting a little closer along the gold brocade sofa and raising his hand to stroke the soft skin on the nape of her neck. His glittering gaze held hers; his touch set her on fire. He leaned closer and his lips brushed hers. Rebecca sat as frozen as a statue whilst the warmth unfurled within her.

He was watching her face and now he laughed, a soft sound of triumph. 'You are nowhere near as cold as you pretend to be, my lady.'

He leaned forward again and the tip of his tongue touched the corner of her mouth lightly but deliberately. Rebecca's lips parted of their own volition. She could not help herself. A second later he had taken advantage, deepening the kiss, sending the ballroom and its dazzling, shrieking crowds spinning from her mind as she became consumed by the warm intimacy of his mouth moving over hers. It was sweet, intoxicating pleasure and she wanted to drown in it.

His lips left hers reluctantly. 'Have I persuaded you yet?' he whispered.

Rebecca tried to focus. 'I…no. I do not believe you have.'

He smiled. She could see it in his eyes. 'Still resisting me…'

But her resistance was weakening. In desperation, Rebecca got to her feet and held out a hand to him. 'Come, my lord. We have yet to dance.'

He got to his feet with languid grace and took her hand in his. Warm and strong, his fingers interlocked with hers.

If Rebecca had thought that to dance with him would provide some respite from the sensuality that flickered between them, then she swiftly realised her mistake. Their bodies seemed to burn at every point of contact. Together and apart, hands touching, his thigh brushing her skirt, his arm grazing hers as they moved through the slow steps of the quadrille… They were trapped in a sensual haze and each time Rebecca turned away from him she felt a frightening compulsion to turn back. She felt dizzy and helpless, weakened by feelings she did not understand, and she did not need to see behind his mask to know that he understood exactly what was going through her mind. The dance ended and she felt almost limp with exhaustion, breathing as though she had been running rather than dancing. The black domino tucked her hand through his arm and she had no thought to refuse.

'As a means of escaping what is between us, I have to say that that was remarkably unsuccessful, my lady,' he drawled.

Rebecca shivered. 'Escape…' she whispered.

He shook his head. 'It cannot be done, sweetheart. Whatever it is that burns between us cannot be denied and it will be there until we accept it and—'

'And?'

'And act on it.'

Rebecca stared at him. There was something about his stance and the predatory way that the dark eyes behind the mask swept over her with a gleam of desire that turned her throat to sawdust. She knew that he spoke the truth and she did not know what she was going to do. And as she hesitated, he took a very purposeful step towards her as though he were about to carry her from the ballroom and make love to her here and now.

'Here you are!' Nan's voice exclaimed. She did not sound pleased. 'I have been looking everywhere for you!'

Rebecca wrenched her gaze away from that of the black domino. She felt dizzy and disorientated. 'I beg your pardon, Nan. Were you wishing to leave?'

'Not at all,' Nan said. Her calculating gaze went from Rebecca to the black domino, who was watching them in quizzical fashion. 'I did not expect that you would throw yourself so wholeheartedly into the evening, however.'

She grabbed Rebecca's arm and dragged her away. 'What on earth do you think you are doing?' she hissed.

'I did not mean to become entangled with him,' Rebecca said miserably. She felt like a naughty schoolgirl. 'He… I do not know what happened.'

'I did not mean that!' Nan was dismissive. 'You may flirt with whomever you choose with my blessing. The only problem is that Fremantle is in a foul mood. He claims that you snubbed him for your black domino.' Her gaze sharpened on Rebecca's face. 'I do not blame you, my dear, for he looks a well set-up sort of a fellow, but is he rich, that is the question?'

'I do not know,' Rebecca lied, glad for once that the mask hid her reddening face. 'I did not ask…'

Nan tutted crossly. 'You have fallen for pretty compliments. It is a beginner's mistake, Becca. You *must* discover if a gentleman is well breeched before you promise him anything.'

'I am not beginning anything, nor promising anything,' Rebecca said rebelliously, ignoring the small voice in her head that told her she had both promised and given a great deal to the black domino and would have given much, much more had Nan not intervened.

Nan shook her head, frankly disbelieving. 'Another half-hour and you would have been in that gentleman's bed,' she said shrewdly. 'I saw the way he was looking at you.'

'Nan!' Rebecca felt aghast. Was the flagrant attraction she felt for Lucas Kestrel so evident for all to see? It appeared so.

Nan shrugged. 'And a good thing too, were it not—' She broke off whatever she had been about to say. 'Anyway, I need your help, Becca. My last partner was clumsy enough to step on a flounce of my skirt and I wondered if you would be able to pin it up for me?'

'Of course,' Rebecca said automatically. She flicked a glance over her shoulder as they started to climb the stairs. Lord Fremantle was watching them, but she barely spared him a glance. The black domino was still standing where she had left him and there was a quality of stillness about him as he stared at her that made Rebecca bite her lip.

No escape.

The thick carpet was soft beneath her slippers as they ascended. Nan hustled her into a small bedroom on the first floor, furnished opulently with a big four-poster bed and many gilt mirrors.

'This will do. There are pins in my reticule.'

Rebecca obediently knelt on the thick carpet and pinned up the torn hem of Nan's peacock dress. The rent was only small and took barely any time at all to mend. When she had done, Nan twirled in front of the mirror in self-satisfied admiration.

'Divine,' she said. 'Wait a moment for me here, Becca. I shall be back directly.'

She slipped out of the room and Rebecca hesitated, then sat down on the edge of the four-poster bed. It was draped in red damask that was slightly rough to the touch. Everything in the house was rich and fine, but Rebecca thought that there was nothing personal about it. Her artist's eye appreciated the colours and textures, but there was no stamp of personality.

A faint but unmistakable click from the door attracted her attention. She waited, expecting Nan to be coming back, but nothing happened. Puzzled, she got up and walked slowly over to the door, turning the knob. The door remained obstinately closed. Rebecca tugged on the handle, then pushed. Neither result elicited any response. The door was shut and she was locked within.

Rebecca was quick to understand then. There had been Nan's anxiety that she attend the ball, her deliberate dismissal of it as a small, private function, Lord Fremantle's anger when she had turned him down out of preference for Lucas, Nan's intervention and Fremantle watching them climb the stairs with his cold, zealous eyes.

Rebecca stood still with one hand resting on the panels and the doorknob cold against her palm. So Nan had betrayed her. She would never have expected it. She had thought that some loyalty bound her friend.

She rattled the lock. It looked flimsy, but it was too strong for her to break without some kind of weapon, and there was none. There was nothing at all in the room that could be used to aid her escape. She would have given a great deal to have brought her diamond engraving scribe with her.

She stood there, shivering in the red silk dress despite the heat of the room.

And then there was the sound of the key turning and Alexander Fremantle, stripped of mask and gown, stepped inside. He stood and looked at her, his greedy gaze drinking in every inch of her trembling body.

'Well, my dear,' he said, 'at last I have you where I want you.'

'My lord,' Rebecca said, attempting to eradicate the tremor from her voice, 'I do suggest that you reconsider—'

Fremantle was turning to close the door. He paused, looked over his shoulder at her with a gesture of disdain.

'And why should I wish to do that, Miss Raleigh?'

'Because once again, I fear that the lady is waiting for me and you are damnably *de trop,* old fellow.' Lucas Kestrel pushed the door open from the outside and strolled into the room. He had discarded the mask, but still wore the black domino. His lazy, incisive tones held just enough hint of amusement to make Fremantle flush angrily. He looked from Lucas's sardonic face to Rebecca's blank one and his mouth tightened into a thin line.

'That is impossible! I arranged—'

'You arranged for Miss Astley to entrap her friend on your behalf?' Lucas questioned, all amusement suddenly fled from his expression. 'I know. I saw you. Shame on you, Fremantle, that you cannot find a willing woman to take to your bed and have to resort to tricking a reluctant one.'

The bright red indignation mottled Alexander Fremantle's throat. 'It seems you have some need to play the knight errant, my lord. I assure you this lady has no need of your services.'

Lucas moved with predatory precision to stand behind Rebecca. Even before he touched her she could feel his presence, feel the tiny hairs stand up on the back of her neck, feel the goose pimples that tiptoed down her spine. His hands came to rest on her bare arms above the elbow and he drew her back against his body until they were touching. She could feel his chest against her back and the curve of his hip against her buttocks. He held her hard. She felt weak with relief and faint with anticipation.

'My apologies, Miss Raleigh,' he murmured, his breath tickling her ear. 'Once again it appears that you must convince his lordship that you prefer my company to his.'

Rebecca made an incoherent noise that, fortunately, sounded like assent. She could not have spoken had she tried. Lucas had bent his head and was feathering tiny kisses down the side of her neck. His lips drifted across her collarbone, igniting a fierce heat within her.

But Fremantle was still watching. Lucas raised his head and his eyes were cold and inimical.

'Need I remind you to go?' he asked coldly.

Fremantle was leaving, scarlet with repressed fury, muttering under his breath, but definitely leaving. The door closed behind him.

Lucas stepped away from Rebecca with exaggerated

care, as though he needed to make it clear that there was no price for his assistance. For a long moment they simply stared at each other whilst Rebecca felt a tumult of emotion batter her. She knew that if he had carried on making love to her she would not have resisted. Even here, even now, she wanted him. She could not deny it.

But there was no desire in the look that Lucas had turned on her now. She felt her own passion die beneath his scathing contempt and felt as though she was withering inside.

'You fool! What the *hell* are you doing here?' He snatched off her mask, the red ribbons coming loose and tangling in her hair, wrenching a small gasp of pain from her. The strength of his fury shocked her. His eyes glittered with rage. He looked murderous and, though he stopped short of touching her again, his fists were clenched as though he wanted to shake the life out of her.

'I cannot work out,' he said, 'whether you are wanton, stupid, or just plain mad.'

Rebecca's fury and misery balled in her chest. 'I was going to thank you, my lord,' she said coldly, 'but that was before I realised I had to endure your insults as well as your attentions.'

Lucas made a derisive noise. 'Make no complaints, Miss Raleigh. You have no idea what I *want* to inflict on you.' His gaze narrowed on her. 'Or perhaps you do, if you are the wanton you appear to be!'

Rebecca took a step back and he followed her, stalking her across the floor. His furious gaze held hers, and behind the anger she could see the unslaked desire and it scalded her hot and cold. She raised her chin proudly.

'You know that is not true,' she said, 'or you would not have stepped in to rescue me.'

Lucas made a repudiating gesture. 'I do not know why I did.'

The truth hung in the air between them. Rebecca did not need him to put it into words: *You did it because you were jealous... You did it because you wanted me for yourself...*

She swallowed hard. 'I should go home,' she said.

Lucas was looking at her moodily. 'I will take you back.'

Rebecca's heart jumped. 'No.'

This time he did grab her. His hands bit into her shoulders and she flinched. 'You still do not understand, do you?' He ground out savagely. 'They are out there—Fremantle and your so-called friend Miss Astley. If you simply walk away, they will know for sure that this was a sham and then how much chance do you think you will have of reaching Clerkenwell unprotected?'

Rebecca's humiliation made her cheeks burn. 'I had not thought—'

'Of course not. I do not believe you have done any thinking tonight.'

Rebecca gave him a look of intense dislike. 'You mistake, my lord. I thought enough about turning you down!'

For a moment she thought she had gone too far. She had wanted to explain to Lucas that the only reason she was at the masquerade at all was because she had been lonely. She had had a craving for light and company. She wanted to forget, for one evening only, that her life was so constrained and full of struggle. The desire to escape had overcome her common sense and she had ignored the warnings that her tired mind was trying to send her. Now she was richly rewarded, for she had lost Nan's friendship, if friendship it had been, and she had lost Lucas Kestrel's good opinion. She stared at him for a moment of frozen apprehension, wondering what on earth he was going to do, and then he laughed.

'So you did, Miss Raleigh. Upon which note we should end this charade.'

Rebecca scarcely saw the opulent gold-and-scarlet staircase as he swept her down to the front door. Lucas's arm was tight about her waist and he did not stop to speak to anyone. The music still played and the guests still danced, their behaviour even more unbridled than before.

In the hackney carriage she shrank within her cloak and curled up in the corner as far away from Lucas as she could. They did not speak. Rebecca watched the light flicker past the windows and listened to the reassuring beat of the horse's hooves on the road and wondered how matters could possibly get worse. For a few brief hours she had imagined herself as Cinderella, only to find herself banished back to the garret, her dreams in shreds. She could feel Lucas's gaze resting on her unfathomably. She could still sense his anger and frustration and beneath that something deep and elemental that made her shiver. She turned away and looked out into the dark, but she knew that his scrutiny had not wavered from her face. She could feel it and it stirred emotions that were barely beneath the surface.

Lucas had recognised Rebecca as soon as she stepped into the room. He had only attended the masque on a whim, for he was bored with the prospect of another night teaching Stephen to play snooker, or a gambling session at White's. Even worse was the thought of another dinner with Cory and Rachel Newlyn, glowing with happiness, making him feel like a frustrated outcast from a very exclusive club.

So he had gone to the masque and had felt the boredom and dissatisfaction grip him afresh at the sight of all that exotic and erotic excess, and then Rebecca Raleigh had walked into the room in her sinfully tight red silk dress and his heart had almost stalled. For a split second he had thought her to be the wanton she had always denied, and the hot disillusion and anger threatened to swamp all other feelings. Yet as he watched her he realised that there was something shocked and innocent in her demeanour as she stared at the licentious throng. And when he had seen her trying to refuse Fremantle's attentions, he had been sure of it.

He had not intended to see Rebecca again, for both their sakes. He had resolved that Justin should take over the investigation into the engraving. Yet the minute he laid eyes on her it had made mockery of his good intentions. He had forgotten his honourable resolve, his determination to disengage before matters spiralled out of control. Instead he had flirted with her and pushed her hard with a desire that was entirely unfeigned. She had played her part well, but with enough hesitation and innate modesty for Lucas to know that she was part afraid, part intrigued. He could tell that she felt the same irresistible passion that he did and that it confused her. The knowledge was the only thing that held him in check and prevented him from sweeping her into his arms and his bed. The strong protective urge that he felt for her had not diminished. When he had seen Fremantle about to lay his disgusting hands on her, he had almost given way to violence.

Now he looked at Rebecca curled up in a corner of the hackney carriage and his heart twisted with pity and the need to comfort her. She looked so small and forlorn. He wanted to chase those shadows from her eyes. The surge of feeling she stirred within him threatened to overwhelm him.

On impulse he put out a hand and touched her shoulder. She did not move.

'Rebecca…' his voice was gentle this time '…what were you doing at the masque?'

He caught the sheen of tears on her cheeks as she turned her head towards him and he pulled her into his arms. She came easily to him, curving against him.

'I wanted everything to be different,' she said softly, 'just for one night.'

Lucas pressed his lips to her hair. 'I understand,' he said, 'but did it have to be a masque?'

He felt her smile against his chest. 'There was nowhere else to go.'

Lucas's mind filled with images of all the places

that he would like to take her. She would enjoy the theatre, or an evening stroll through Vauxhall Gardens in the summer, when the sun was setting indigo and red and the lanterns were lit. Or a ball at Carlton House, or to visit the Royal Academy... There were so many places, so many treats that he wanted to shower upon her. Such matters were easy for him to arrange and he took them for granted. It was not the same for Rebecca, tied to earning a living, relentlessly working in order to survive. It made him feel oddly humble.

Rebecca shifted slightly in his arms and Lucas became instantly aware of the press of her body against his. Her cloak had slipped to reveal the bodice of the scandalously low red silk dress and the pale swell of her breasts above it. His body tightened in instinctive response to her luscious beauty and he bit back a curse.

'And the dress?' His voice sounded harsher than he had intended.

Rebecca snuggled closer to him, causing his body further agonies of self-denial. 'It belongs to Nan Astley.' She sounded a little sleepy.

'Of course it does.' Lucas, compensating for the tightness in his breeches that the dress caused, sounded pompous. 'And the flirting?'

'*You* flirted with *me*,' Rebecca said.

'And did you know it was me?'

There was a pause. 'Yes,' Rebecca sounded cautious. 'I...I thought it was you.'

'You *thought* it was me?' Lucas felt outraged. 'You

mean that you flirted like that with a masked stranger without knowing his identity for sure?'

Rebecca tried to sit up, but he held her tightly in arms that were suddenly as hard as steel.

'I was certain it was you,' she said. She sighed. 'Besides, I doubt you meant a word you said.'

'Every word,' Lucas said. 'I meant every word.'

Suddenly the silence between them was vivid with unspoken emotion. Rebecca struggled to free herself from him and even in the dark he could see the hectic colour in her face and the glitter of her eyes.

'Lucas—' she said.

'Hush.' He pressed his fingers to her lips. 'Rebecca.'

The hackney turned into the street and drew to a halt outside the silent workshop.

Lucas helped Rebecca down and turned to pay the jarvey. She heard the chink of coins and a mumbled word of thanks from the driver as he raised his whip and the carriage moved off. The night was cold and damp. Light no longer shone from the tavern and the street was silent.

Lucas waited whilst Rebecca unlocked the door. Her hands were shaking and it seemed to take her a long time, but it was not the cold that was making her tremble. The air between them was thick with sensual awareness. She felt as though she could touch it, taste it. She felt as though it was smothering her.

She stopped and turned to him. Behind her was the darkness of the workshop, the fitful moonlight lying in scattered beams across the floor. It was waiting for her—all the loneliness and the misery and the emptiness that had trapped her since her uncle's death had left her almost alone in the world. Yet before her was a man who could block out all that sadness and solitude, if only for a short while. He could hold her, give her comfort, turn the darkness to light for her.

Lucas did not move. She could not see his expression. She did not need to.

She put out a hand and her fingertips came up against the smooth material of his coat. Her fingers drifted across his chest and his own hand came up to imprison hers.

'What is it that you want, Rebecca?' he said. His voice was husky.

'You.' Rebecca spoke barely above a whisper. She knew nothing other than that the desire for him burned hotter than all else. Almost all...

The words *I love you* were blazed across her mind, so vivid she almost spoke them aloud.

'I need you,' she said. She tugged on his hand very gently and he followed her across the threshold. The door closed behind them with a gentle click and they stood in total darkness.

Time spun out between them. She could feel the tension emanating from Lucas's body. It felt almost as though he was about to turn and leave her. She could not bear for him to go now. She wanted to blot out the pain and the anguish and the unhappiness, just for one night.

'Lucas,' she said beseechingly, 'please...'

Then he closed the distance between them and took her mouth with his, and as he drew her into his arms, his kiss turned the darkness to light.

Chapter Five

Rebecca's head was spinning, her heart racing at the shattering sensations that were coursing through her. Lucas's mouth claimed hers again with a hungry demand and she responded with all the pent-up longing and loneliness and need in her soul. Her breasts felt full and heavy against the slippery silk of the ballgown and his hand slid up to cup her there. Rebecca shivered and pressed closer. It felt as though she had always known it would come to this. It had been inevitable from the moment that they had first met and now she wanted nothing more than to lose herself in him.

Her cloak fell to the floor in a pool of darkness, and then Lucas had swept her up off her feet and into his arms.

'Where is your room?'

'Up the staircase in the corner.'

They wasted no further breath on words.

The wooden stair was a narrow spiral, but it posed no difficulties for Lucas, who carried her as though she weighed nothing at all. Halfway up the stairs he stopped, and in the pulsing darkness, looked down into her face. Rebecca's lips parted as she stared up at him and he gave a ragged groan and swooped down to take her lips with his, his tongue darting wickedly to part them farther and invade the moist sensitivity of her mouth. Rebecca's senses reeled.

She had no memory of how she came to be on her bed in the tiny garret under the eaves. Lucas was leaning over her and she raised a hand to touch his lean cheek with a shy possessiveness, entranced to feel the roughness of his stubble beneath her questing fingers. There was a tender wonderment in her touch. Nothing had ever felt so good, or so right. She wanted to see him, but there was very little light in the room. Her other senses were heightened, drinking him in like water in the desert, the feel and the taste and the scent of him.

'Lucas,' she said.

His only reply was to slide his hands into her hair and find her mouth with his again. Rebecca was drowning in acute longing, waiting breathlessly in fevered, urgent desperation. He shed his clothes and hers too, their hands bumping impatiently as Rebecca sought to help and to rid herself of the constraining layers that came between them. She wanted to feel his skin against hers, but when they were naked together and she felt his hands on her body, she thought she would burn up with sheer, agonising need. He bent his head and nipped at her breasts, torturing her with his tongue and his teeth while Rebecca writhed beneath him and gave a low, wanton cry of total abandonment. She was driven to near madness by every sure, knowing stroke of his hands and his mouth on her. This was beyond anything that she had imagined.

She slid her fingers into the hair at the nape of his neck. He felt warm and strong, and she revelled in that strength. Her hands brushed the tousled hair from his forehead and slid over the hard, muscular perfection of his shoulders and down his chest, until he captured them and spread her arms wide apart on the mattress so that her body was open to him.

Rebecca shivered convulsively. Her mind was cloudy with heated desire. When he teased her thighs apart she shuddered, jerking and gasping as he found and traced the hot, intense centre of her. The exquisite sensations built and crashed about her, and wrenched a tormented gasp from her.

'Lucas, *please…*'

She was dimly aware of the urgency in his hands as he slid over her, then he plunged into her and the passionate invasion wrenched a sharp gasp of pain from her lips. He stilled in an instant.

'No! You can't be!' He sounded breathless and ragged.

Rebecca shifted slightly, utterly distracted by the tiny movements that were easing him all the way inside of her. It was impossible to concentrate and talking was the last thing that she wanted to do. 'I *told* you,' she said.

'Yes, but I thought…' Lucas sounded dazed.

Rebecca rubbed his arm in a gentle caress. 'Do you really wish to speak about it now, Lucas?'

His eyes came back to hers and she saw him register their situation, his expression darkening as he took in the tension and heat of her body wrapped about his in intimate conjoining. He gave a groan. 'No.'

'Then do not.' Rebecca wriggled a little and Lucas groaned again, bending to kiss her, ravishing her mouth with the same thoroughness with which he was now taking her body. He took his time now, building up the new and devastating sensations that had fled briefly from her when he had stopped. Raw desire possessed her again, whirled her up, mingled with the pounding surge of his body within hers. She was spinning, tense and tight and out of control, until the mindless pleasure burst like stars and tumbled her over the edge of a shattering release.

For a long time there was no sound but their breathing as it slowed and calmed, and then Lucas pulled Rebecca close to him and wrapped his arms about her. His mouth was against her hair.

'I am going to light a candle.'

Rebecca stiffened. It seemed too soon. Suddenly she needed the anonymity of the darkness. 'Please do not.'

'I want to look at you.' He sounded adamant.

Rebecca sighed with acquiescence. She heard him grope for the tinderbox and strike a light. The small flame flared, bringing the shabby garret into warm focus. Lucas lit the candle, set it down and turned to her.

'Now…' he said.

Despite the severity of his tone, there was gentleness in the way that he pulled her close to him once again, his arms going about her, drawing her against the hard, warm length of his body. Rebecca relaxed into his embrace. He smoothed a tender hand over her hair.

'You should have told me that I would be the first.'

Rebecca laughed. 'I told you several times.'

'You said that you were no courtesan.' Lucas hesitated. 'I thought you inexperienced, but I did not realise...' He sighed. 'I should have known.'

Rebecca gave a tiny shrug. 'I told you that I was virtuous.'

'Then why this—now?'

Rebecca turned her face against his shoulder. 'I told you that too. You said that you understood. I wanted to escape—forget everything—for a single night.'

Lucas took her chin in his hand and turned her face to his. His eyes were golden in the candlelight. 'Oh, Rebecca...' He sounded rueful and tender.

Rebecca kissed his shoulder, touching her tongue to his skin, inhaling his scent and tasting the faint tang of salt and sweat. She did not want to talk. She wanted to live in the moment.

She ran her hands down his body, exploring, learning as she went. His muscles felt tense and coiled and she wondered whether he was going to repudiate her, but after a moment he gave a soft sigh and she felt him surrender to her touch. Her mouth followed the path her fingers had taken. His skin felt hot and damp and as her hands drifted lower he rolled over and trapped her beneath him.

'That's enough...' His tone was rough and when she looked at him wonderingly he touched her cheek, his voice softening. 'I do not want to hurt you any more than I already have done, sweetheart.'

'You have not hurt me,' Rebecca said, ignoring the

slight ache of her body, 'and the morning is not yet here—'

Her words broke off as his fingers found the damp warmth that he had left only minutes before, and gently caressed and teased her into a state of shameless pleasure.

Fierce heat flowered in her and she pulled him close, arching against him, crying out as his mouth closed over her breast.

He nudged her legs apart and entered her again. This time was slow and gentle, a matter of small, exquisite movements and drugging sweetness that cast them adrift in sensuality until they finally and, oh, so slowly, slipped into pure ecstasy and from there to oblivion.

Rebecca woke to find that they were still intimately entwined. He was still inside her. She had *slept* with him like that. The shock ripped through her, followed almost immediately by a quivering leap of raw excitement at the shattering intimacy of it. She made a small sound, half-astonishment, half-pleasure, and as Lucas started to move she felt her body tighten once again into a slow, shimmering climax that went on and on. His hand slid up possessively from her stomach to her breast with a gentle, sleepy touch that made her want to press herself against him in sheer contentment. She was dazed and weak with the hot, endless pleasure, her mind as cloudy as her body was limp. Lucas kept her spread beneath him, shifting more firmly over her, lowering his head to take her nipple in his mouth so that the rasp of his tongue over her skin made her arch with desperation. He did not move within her but kept himself anchored deep, and she tautened like a plucked bow beneath his hands, his lips and his tongue, frantic for release whilst he played with her breasts. Finally she grabbed him to her, kissing him, lifting her hips in hopeless frustration until he could resist the temptation no longer and drove himself into her and the dizzying heat overtook them in endless waves.

When Rebecca woke again it was late. The damp grey skies of the previous day had given way to a fresh autumn day of blue promise. The pale sun dappled the floor of Rebecca's bedroom and lit up the dust motes that danced in its beams. Rebecca felt warm and dreamy and heavy with contentment. She knew that there was no likelihood of her working today, though when she did finally drag herself from her languor she wanted to continue engraving the kestrel glasses for Lucas. Lucas, who had taken all the passion she usually reserved for her work and transformed it into the most wicked, sensual and perfect night that she could ever have imagined.

She turned her head. The space in the bed beside her was empty, but the tangle of sheets and the dent in the pillow showed where Lucas had lain. She remembered waking at one point to find herself clasped tightly in his arms. She had lain quiescent and still, revelling in the close contact of his skin against hers and the warmth and intimacy of the embrace.

She knew she loved him.

Rebecca rolled on to her back and stared at the cobwebby ceiling. She did not feel guilty at what she had done. She did not feel embarrassed or ashamed or any of the other conventional responses that she might have expected to feel having given herself to a man with such passion and wild abandonment all through the night. It had been exquisite bliss. She wriggled slightly. So there was one thing that Nan Astley had been right about, after all. It had not been difficult in the end. It had been magical and far from the mercenary arrangement that Nan had advocated.

Rebecca got up very slowly and dressed with absent-minded movements, somehow managing to get herself down the stairs and into the workshop, where she threw open the windows and let the fresh air flood in. She could hear the scrawny stray cat mewing at the back door. She ignored it whilst she built up the fire—the wood that Lucas had purchased for her would last a good while longer—and set a light to the tinder. The flame caught and the studio immediately looked brighter, the light winking off the rows of engraved glass on the shelves. Rebecca's spirits were soaring and she hummed as she swept the floor. A servant had called to collect the last of her uncle's commissions the previous day, so at least she had been paid. She could eat.

And she would see Lucas again. Of that she was certain.

The mewing of the cat had become more insistent now, accompanied by a repetitive scratching that threatened to wear away the back door. Rebecca went through to the scullery. When she opened the door the cat shot in, accompanied by a blast of cold air that

Rebecca knew would make the chimney smoke. She was about to slam the door shut again when she saw the bag.

Her heart started to race. She bent down and picked it up. It had been wedged in a gap between the wall of the house and the drainpipe that ran down from the roof, which was even now emitting a sluggish stream of rainwater from the night before. The bag was made of oiled canvas and was slightly damp, but Rebecca could feel the shape of a small, folded piece of parchment inside—and the outline of golden sovereigns.

She took the bag into the scullery. When she pulled the drawstring, the sovereigns spilled out on to the table, dull in the darkness of the room. She ignored them and took the note across to the window, her fingers shaking slightly as she unfolded the thick parchment.

Dearest Rebecca,
I am sorry I have been away so long. Tovey will carry this message to you, but it is no recompense for not seeing you in person. I pray it shall not be long before we may meet again. In the meantime, I hope that these may make some small reparation for my absence.

Daniel

Rebecca sighed, refolded the note and stuffed it back in the canvas bag. Pleasant as it was to have fifty gold sovereigns, it was no compensation for her brother's absence. Nor had he indicated when she would see him again. Very likely he did not know. He was away at sea for months at a time and seldom knew in advance when he would make landfall again. He came to London even more rarely since it was too dangerous for him. It was close to a year since they had last met.

She scooped up the sovereigns, put them in the bag and placed it beneath the stale biscuits in the china crock, along with the money she had received for her uncle's commission. She had seldom had so much cash in the house. She should find a better hiding place.

Her heart ached with a sudden, fierce pain. She would give almost everything she possessed to have Daniel home. But she knew it could not be—not yet— and in the meantime she must make shift as best she could. She tried to feel better by telling herself that she would see Lucas again soon, but the feeling of warm intimacy had drained away and something colder had taken its place. It nagged at her—where was Lucas and why had he not left her any message? The day seemed suddenly pale and the sunlight dim. Rebecca poured herself a mug of milk and cut a piece of bread and cheese for her breakfast, then went back into the studio, sat down at her workbench and picked up her diamond scribe. If she could not see Lucas, then she could try to lose herself in her work, but somehow she could not quite shake off the creeping chill that told her everything was not well.

When Lucas awoke in his own bed, it was with a blinding headache. It was not alcohol induced, but the result of an over-active conscience, a conscience that had singularly failed to do its job and protect Miss Rebecca Raleigh from him the previous night. He lay still and stared at the ceiling. Last night he had behaved in the most dishonourable, disgraceful and discreditable way imaginable. It was the first time in his adult life that he had tried and failed to keep a measure of control. He had tried to do the decent thing. His mind recalled with perfect accuracy all the *indecent* things that he had done with Rebecca and the fact that he wanted to repeat them all again—and again. His body hardened into arousal instantly at the same time as he sat up and clutched his head in his hands with a groan. The fact that the night had been the most satisfying, exquisitely pleasurable and ultimately perfect experience he had ever encountered was beside the point.

He was a scoundrel.

He had awoken again just before dawn. Rebecca had been asleep, fragrantly, peacefully. He had seen her lying beside him and had felt the soft, tempting warmth of her body and had been overwhelmed by an emotion he had never previously experienced. He had felt awestruck and exalted and terrifyingly happy.

And then he had felt afraid.

He had eased himself out of the bed, dressed with speed and crept away, like a thief in the night. With each step away from Rebecca his heart had dropped like a stone into the depths. Fear and guilt had warred within him, smothering the contentment that had come to him when he was lying in Rebecca's arms. He had wanted her from the moment he had first seen her and now that hunger was not appeased, but raged within him with a dangerous intensity. Yet somehow that intimate lovemaking had unleashed far more than physical desire.

He felt angry and protective and *responsible*. He had never wanted to feel responsible for another person, preferring the independence that had been his way of life until the previous night. He had not wanted a woman to look on him with love. To see the same selfless devotion reflected in Rebecca's eyes that he had seen in his mother... It made him feel sick. His father had taken his mother's love and had twisted it out of all recognition through his endless infidelities. It had been a salutary lesson to all his sons, but it was Lucas who had felt it most keenly.

Yet now it was too late. He had seduced Rebecca Raleigh, had taken her body with a rapture that he would not previously have dreamed existed, and in the process had been given her love, her soul. A part of him wanted it most desperately, but the other part shrank away.

Lucas got slowly to his feet and stumbled across to the ewer on the chest of drawers. He bent over the bowl and poured the water directly over his head. The cold was refreshing, but the headache remained. He rubbed a hand across his hair, smoothing it down, scattering water droplets on his bare shoulders. He leaned both hands on the top on the chest of drawers and stared at his reflection in the glass.

There was only one solution—he would have to marry Miss Rebecca Raleigh.

No matter that he had sworn not to marry, no matter that he did not want the love of a good woman, no matter that he did not feel in the least worthy, he could not make a bad situation worse by behaving like a heartless seducer, taking her virginity and abandoning her after.

Oddly the decision to marry, so long avoided, soothed him. He felt immeasurably better, not only because it was the honourable solution, but also because it felt like the right one in some deeply satisfying way he did not care to analyse. He told himself cynically that this was because he had acted like a cad and was taking the only respectable course of action, albeit late in the day. He told himself even more cynically that once he was married to Rebecca he could experience that exquisite bliss every night. That was a decided benefit, one almost worth throwing away his freedom on.

His conscience, still tiresomely alert, told him that he was prevaricating and there was far more to his emotions than the satisfaction of honour and rampant desire. He told his conscience to be quiet.

He called his valet, dressed and made his way downstairs, stopping dead as he entered the breakfast room and found his elder brother already settled at the table, his meal complete, a cup of coffee before him and the *Morning Post* in his hand.

Lucas started forward. 'Justin! We were not expecting you until tomorrow at the earliest.'

Justin laughed, put the paper aside, got up and shook Lucas's hand. 'I received your letter, Lucas, and made what haste I could. I arrived late last night.' He shifted his broad shoulders against the chair back in an effort to get comfortable. 'I swear the roads get worse by the day. I feel as stiff as an old man.'

'What do you expect, at your age?' Lucas said, with an unsympathetic grin. 'Dukes approaching their dotage must anticipate such troubles.'

'Devil a bit,' Justin said cheerfully, raising his coffee and taking an appreciate mouthful. 'I have a few years left to me yet.'

He gestured to the coffee pot. 'Are you having some, Luc?' He was studying his brother closely. 'You're looking a little rough, if you will forgive me. Heavy night?'

Lucas hesitated. He looked with distaste at the litter of breakfast on the table. He had no appetite. 'It was a somewhat unexpected evening,' he said. He took a deep breath. 'Justin, there is something I feel I should tell you—'

There was a knock at the door. 'Tom Bradshaw is here, your Grace,' Byrne announced. 'Shall I show him in?'

Justin glanced at Lucas. 'Can it wait, Luc? I saw Bradshaw briefly last night and he had some information I wanted to discuss with you at the earliest opportunity.'

'Of course.' Lucas felt strangely on edge. It was he who had set Tom Bradshaw on to investigate and watch Rebecca Raleigh only a week before. It felt like a lifetime; a lifetime in which he had briefly forgotten the reason why he and Rebecca had met in the first place, so wrapped up had he become in all that had happened between them.

'Bradshaw tells me,' Justin said, folding his newspaper precisely, 'that Miss Raleigh has provided the engraved glass that the Midwinter spies have been using for their cipher—'

'It was her uncle who did the work,' Lucas said, without letting his brother finish. 'I do not believe that Miss Raleigh herself knows anything about it, other than that her uncle was fulfilling a commission for a client.'

There was a small silence. Lucas was very aware of Justin's gaze resting thoughtfully on him. He shifted uncomfortably on his chair. He knew Justin to be very shrewd. It would be well nigh impossible for him not to give his feelings away.

'I see,' Justin said, in measured tone. 'And the uncle himself?'

Lucas hesitated. He was aware of a very strong urge to say absolutely nothing at all. He wanted to protect Rebecca, not draw her into danger. And yet that was the precise reason that Justin was here.

He got up, thrust his hands into the pockets of his trousers and paced across to the fireplace. 'Her uncle was George Provost. He died recently. Miss Raleigh has carried on the work of the studio.'

Justin nodded. 'I imagine that she is in some financial difficulty?'

Lucas could feel the screws turning. Justin's line of reasoning was not difficult to follow. 'Why do you imagine that?' he asked expressionlessly.

'It cannot be easy for a young lady to carve out such a living if she is alone in the world. I take it,' Justin added, gently persistent, 'that she *is* alone?'

'I... Yes.' Lucas shot him a look. He was remembering the bare bedroom, pristinely neat, unmistakably poor, where *he'd* left Rebecca this very morning. 'She lives in some hardship, certainly.'

Justin gave him a long look. 'So it would be entirely possible that she might succumb to the lure of a job that paid very well, even if it were…illegal?'

Lucas met his eyes. 'It is possible in principle, but not in practice.'

'How so?'

'Because Miss Raleigh,' Lucas said, struggling with a temper that suddenly seemed incendiary, 'is no traitor, Justin. Besides, I have ascertained that no work has been commissioned for the Midwinter spies since the death of her uncle.'

Justin let that pass for a moment. 'I see,' he said pleasantly. 'But you do not deny that this mysterious client who places his orders with the studio might have instructed Miss Raleigh to keep the details of the commission secret?'

'She gave no such impression to me,' Lucas said, turning so sharply to look at his brother that he almost drilled a hole in the carpet. 'Indeed, she was very open about the type of work the studio had engraved for him.'

'So you believe her innocent of all this,' Justin said thoughtfully. There was a spark of humour in his gaze. 'In fact, you might just call me out if I imply otherwise?'

Lucas shifted uncomfortably under his elder brother's observant gaze. 'I believe she is entirely innocent, yes.'

'And her connection to the Archangel Club?'

Lucas could feel the tension stiff across his shoulders. 'Another commission, that is all.'

'Miss Raleigh,' Justin observed, 'has commissions from dubious sources.'

Lucas drew a sharp breath. He could hear the note of impatience in his own voice, the tell-tale edginess that gave his feelings away more clearly than any words. 'That is a co-incidence only.'

'You are hot in her defence.'

'I am.'

Their glances met and clashed like a sword thrust. Justin laughed.

'I see. So you see yourself as some sort of knight errant who wishes to protect Miss Raleigh from danger.'

'Hardly,' Lucas snapped. His conscience flailed him again. Of all the people who had placed Rebecca in jeopardy, he was the most culpable.

'Then,' Justin said shrewdly, 'your ill temper stems from a guilty conscience. You feel a scoundrel because you have deceived her as to your true interest.'

'I have and I do,' Lucas said, through shut teeth. He was within an ace of losing his coolness altogether. 'I have deceived Miss Raleigh in more ways than I wish to count and the damnable thing is that I am convinced she is innocent.'

Rebecca had been innocent in many ways until he had laid a hand on her. Lucas thought of her trust and her generosity of spirit and closed his eyes briefly.

'Would you prefer it if I were to go to Clerkenwell to interview her?' Justin asked mildly.

'No!' Lucas almost shouted. The thought of Rebecca learning of his perfidy through a third party was even more unendurable than the idea of telling her himself.

Justin raised his brows. Lucas took a deep breath and smoothed his hair down.

'I apologise, but Miss Raleigh must hear the truth from me, Justin. There is a particular reason for this. I wish to marry her.'

Lucas had not intended to announce his matrimonial plans in quite such a stark manner, but once the words were out he felt inexpressibly relieved. Justin, who had the reputation of being the coolest head in London, looked slightly winded. He opened his mouth to frame a response, but before the words were out there came a tentative knock at the door and Tom Bradshaw entered. From his apprehensive expression it was clear that he had heard the raised voices from behind the closed door.

'Your Grace, my lord...' He bowed. 'Would you prefer me to return later?'

Justin glanced at Lucas, who shook his head abruptly. Whatever Bradshaw had to report, it was better to learn it now.

'Take a seat, Bradshaw,' Justin said, nodding to the chair opposite. 'Lord Lucas and I may continue this...fascinating...conversation at a later time.'

Lucas went across to lean against the mantel. He had a disquieting feeling that the information Bradshaw was about to impart would not be to his liking. The servant was no fool either; his gaze went from one Kestrel brother to the other and his brows rose a little. Lucas could feel his tension balling in his chest.

He saw Justin's amused gaze on him, realised that he was almost dancing with impatience, and forced himself to calm.

Tom Bradshaw looked at Lucas. 'I have had Miss Raleigh's workshop under surveillance for the past week, as you are aware, my lord,' he began. He took a scruffy notebook from his back pocket and flicked the pages over. 'The lady has few visitors and seldom goes out, but yesterday she delivered a package to the Archangel Club.'

Lucas was aware of Justin's stillness and put his own construction on it. 'It was a commission for Lord Fremantle,' he said, 'on behalf of the Club.'

Justin nodded noncommittally. 'So I understand,' he said. 'Pray continue, Bradshaw.'

Bradshaw ruffled the pages of the book. 'Yes, your Grace. A servant called yesterday afternoon to collect the other commission that Miss Raleigh had waiting, the one for the collector.'

Lucas stiffened. 'Are you certain, Bradshaw?'

'Yes, my lord.'

Lucas felt his stomach knot. 'Did you overhear their conversation?'

'A little, my lord. He was not there for long. He paid Miss Raleigh two hundred guineas and left with a package—'

'Two hundred guineas!' Lucas could not stop himself. He was remembering Rebecca telling him that the market rate for six glasses was twenty guineas. Either she had provided a great many items for the mysterious collector or... The logic was obvious. Or he was paying her for more than the commission. For her silence, perhaps... Lucas shook his head sharply. He could not believe it. He simply did not believe it of Rebecca.

'Are you sure?' he said harshly.

'Yes, my lord.' Bradshaw looked nervous. 'I heard him say so himself.'

'It is a great deal of money,' Justin said mildly.

Lucas thrust his hand through his hair. 'Is there anything else, Bradshaw?'

'Yes, my lord,' the servant said. He swallowed. 'I followed the man when he took the package away.'

There was a silence.

'Where did he go?' Lucas asked.

Bradshaw looked up. 'To the Archangel Club, my lord,' he said.

Lucas and Justin exchanged a look. Lucas could see sympathy in his brother's eyes and it made him angry. The implication was obvious. Justin thought that he had been taken for a fool by Miss Rebecca Raleigh. He thought that he had lost his head and his judgement, and, to be fair, the evidence against Rebecca was strong. Yet instinct, deeper than any logic, told him that she was honest.

'Do you wish me to bring the servant in, your Grace?' Bradshaw was asking, cautiously. 'He rents a room in the Feathers in Cheapside.'

Justin shook his head. 'Nobody in the pay of the Archangel is going to talk to us. All it will do is raise the alarm. I shall go to the club and make the most discreet of enquiries, though I imagine I shall find precisely nothing. Lucas—'

'Yes,' Lucas said. 'I shall go to Clerkenwell and speak with Miss Raleigh.'

'She is all we have,' Justin said. Lucas could hear the pity that tinged his brother's voice. 'We need you to bring her here for questioning, Luc. Innocent or guilty, she has to help us.'

There was a sharp silence. 'If you do not care for the idea, then I shall go myself,' Justin added.

Lucas could feel Justin watching him, weighing him up, deciding if he could be relied on or not. He squared his shoulders.

'I should prefer to go,' he said quietly.

Justin nodded. He turned to Tom Bradshaw. 'Thank you, Bradshaw. You have done very well.'

'Thank you, your Grace,' Bradshaw said politely. He nodded to Lucas. 'My lord…' He backed hastily from the room when he saw the look on Lucas's face.

Lucas stared at the door panels after Bradshaw had left and silence had descended on the room. The connections that he had been too tired, too preoccupied to make, were clicking into place in his head.

'You knew where I was last night,' he said slowly. 'Bradshaw has already told you that I was with Miss Raleigh.'

Justin gave the ghost of a grin and waved the coffee pot at him. 'May I offer you some more? I am sorry there is nothing stronger.'

Lucas shook his head impatiently. 'Well?'

Justin shrugged. There was a twinkle in his eye. 'You put the poor fellow in the devil of a position, Lucas. After all, you had set him on to watch Miss Raleigh's premises in the first place, and then he finds himself spying on his employer's amorous entanglements! He left directly to preserve discretion.'

Lucas sighed. 'I did not even think of it.'

'It seems that there were a number of matters that you did not give consideration to last night.'

Lucas flung himself down onto one of the hard dining chairs. 'Miss Raleigh is no courtesan,' he said.

Justin paused in the act of pouring himself another cup of coffee. 'I never imagined for a moment that she was,' he said mildly. 'Indeed, your crisis of conscience this morning rather suggests that the reverse is true. I take it that you still wish to marry her?'

'Yes, I do.'

Lucas waited in explosive silence for the Duke to suggest that an engraver's niece was not a seemly match for one of the Kestrels. Instead Justin merely said,

'You still believe her to be innocent.'

'Certainly.' Lucas shifted on the seat. 'Nothing that I have heard from Bradshaw this morning changes my opinion.'

He saw a flicker of expression cross Justin's face and felt his temper tighten at the thought that it might be pity. His brother thought he had gone soft and lost his judgement. 'I may be suffering the pangs of guilt,' he said angrily, 'but I assure you that my reasoning is still sound.'

Justin made a pacifying gesture. 'I agree. My only concern is that you should not offer for Miss Raleigh out of a misplaced sense of chivalry. Something may be arranged.'

'You mean you will pay her off, as though she was

a harlot?' Lucas was on his feet before he even knew he had moved. 'I *told* you she was no courtesan—'

'Hold your peace,' Justin said, undisturbed. 'I meant no such thing. I merely do not wish you to tie yourself to a loveless marriage through a sense of honour. It is not fair for a man to spend his life paying for one mistake.'

Lucas understood what he meant. 'That is not why I am offering for Rebecca.'

Justin arched a disbelieving eyebrow. 'Then name your reasons.'

Lucas stared at his brother. It felt like a challenge to combat. In his mind were all of his own conflicting emotions; before him, Justin's implacability.

'I want her,' he said. 'I want to marry her.'

He saw Justin's expression shift as though his brother had read something in his face that he had not intended to be there.

Justin nodded. 'Then I wish you good fortune, Luc,' he said quietly.

It was only when Lucas had gone out that Justin raised his cup in mocking tribute to the oil painting of the previous Duke, whose portrait hung above the fire.

'So my little brother is in love at last, though he does not realise it,' he mused. 'Thank God you did not ruin everything for him, Father, with your endless infidelities.' His face sobered as he put the cup down. 'But of course Miss Raleigh may refuse him when she knows the truth. If she is half the woman I suspect her to be, I rather think she will.'

Chapter Six

Rebecca had been engraving for two hours when the sharp ache in her wrist reminded her that if she did not rest she would be unable to continue. With a sigh she laid down her engraving scribe and went into the scullery to make herself a pot of tea. Whilst the kettle sang on the hearth she leaned against the sink and thought about Lucas and the night before; of his hands on her body and his mouth on hers and the searing intimacy of sleeping with her body entwined in his. The room had filled with steam before she recalled herself to the present.

Back in the studio, the fire was already burning low, subdued by the wind that was drawing down the chimney. The sun had gone in and the room looked dark and cheerless. Rebecca went to fetch more candles. She had just lit two of them when the door banged and another blast of autumnal air swept into the workshop, blowing them out in a puff of smoke.

Rebecca swung round. Lucas was standing just inside the doorway, shaking the droplets of rain off his magnificent caped driving coat. Rebecca could not help herself. Her heart gave a huge leap of gladness and a smile burst from her that she had neither the means nor the will to control.

'Good morning, Lucas—'

She broke off. Lucas had not returned her smile and now he bowed very slightly. In the dim light his face looked tense and unyielding.

'Good morning, Rebecca.' He sounded strained. Rebecca's smile wavered slightly.

Lucas closed the door behind them with quiet deliberation.

A chill touched the top of Rebecca's spine and crawled down her back. She frowned slightly, looking at him. There was something dreadfully wrong. She could read it in his face. The fear began to crystallize about her heart.

'My lord?' she said warily. She jumped as Lucas shot the bolt home and reached behind her, groping on the desk for her diamond engraving scribe. Her hand grasped open air. Lucas, seeing the gesture, put out a hand to stop her.

'Do not be afraid. We need to talk, you and I, and I would prefer it to be uninterrupted.'

Rebecca searched his face, instinctively seeking reassurance, but there was none. His expression was as closed as a shuttered house. Rebecca felt fear and sheer disbelief swamping her like a tidal wave. Last night this man had held her in his arms and made love to her with single-minded passion. Now he wore the face of a stranger. The change from that man to this was almost too great to comprehend.

'I thought—' She broke off. 'Last night…'

She saw a bleakness come into Lucas's face, colder than the snow on the winter streets.

'Rebecca,' he said again, taking her arm and guiding her towards the *chaise-longue,* 'I need to speak with you.'

He spared neither of them. Rebecca listened in mounting disbelief and disillusion as he told the whole tale—that he was involved in a quest to discover and unmask a spy ring and the engraver who had been working for them, that he had set a man to watch her premises, that he had deliberately sought her out and set out to gain her confidence. She started to tremble. Her hands were so cold she could barely feel them. She wrapped her arms about herself, but it could not quell the shaking. The fearful discovery that Lucas had betrayed her from the very start cut to the very heart of her.

'Last night...' she said again. She stopped and cleared her throat, wanting to hide the worst of her pain from him. 'You need not have taken your masquerade so far, my lord.'

Lucas put out a hand and she flinched away from him. She saw the hurt in his face and it lacerated her own pain. So he had some feelings for her after all, just not enough to have told her the truth from the start.

'That was no pretence,' he said, in a hard voice. 'Rebecca, I care for you. I want to marry you.'

Rebecca stood up violently. Rage, fierce and primeval, stormed through her. '*Marry?* You wish to marry a woman you do not even *trust?*'

Lucas rubbed his brow with exasperation. 'Rebecca,

it is not that I do not trust you. I never believed you to be a part of the espionage.'

Rebecca made a sound of disgust. 'Of course not! You merely chose to keep from me the fact that you were here with a secret purpose!' Her voice broke and she swallowed hard. 'Oh! You are detestable, Lord Lucas! I despise you!'

Lucas's face was white and tense. 'I understand that you are upset to know the truth, Rebecca—'

'You have no notion how I feel!' Rebecca said, as white as he. 'How could you imagine that I would ever accept your proposal? I do believe that one of us is run mad here, and it is certainly not me!'

Lucas got to his feet. 'What else could I do?' he said. 'If I had asked you to marry me first and then told you the truth, would I have stood a better chance?'

Rebecca gave him a look of contempt. 'No. My response would be exactly the same as it is now. I will never marry you.'

Lucas drove his hands into his pockets. 'You have no choice, Rebecca.'

Rebecca stared at him in outrage. 'I beg your pardon?'

'You have to marry me,' Lucas enunciated, with great care. 'I seduced you last night.'

'Oh, do not be so ridiculous!' Rebecca said, her temper soaring again. 'I seduced *you!* I needed you last night.' She squashed down the misery that threatened to swamp her as she remembered the way that she had turned to Lucas with unquestioning love and trust. 'I wanted what happened,' she finished starkly.

Lucas's face was set hard. 'Nevertheless, I took

your virginity and you may be carrying my child. Under the circumstances I must insist that you marry me.'

'I would as lief take poison!' The words were out before Rebecca could prevent them. It felt as though some huge, destructive power was rampaging through her blood, turning all the pain to anger and cruelty. She took a deep shuddering breath and tried to regain her self-control.

'I beg your pardon,' she said with constraint. 'That was unnecessary. But I cannot marry you, Lord Lucas. I will not let *your* belated sense of honour place *me* in a situation I do not want.'

Lucas came to her and took both her hands in his. 'Rebecca, you responded to me last night,' he said softly. 'Would it really be so bad?'

Rebecca could not bear his touch, nor the treacherous part of her that whispered that in another life, another time, to marry Lucas would have been the height of her most tender dreams. She wanted to throw herself into his arms and make all well again. Except that it was too late; it had always been too late. She moved a little away, determined to take refuge in practicality and block out the pain.

'Since it is information that you want from me, my lord,' she said, 'you may as well ask me now.' She seated herself on the sofa and looked at him with cold expectancy. 'Well?'

Lucas looked slightly bemused. 'Rebecca—'

'The questions, my lord,' Rebecca repeated tonelessly. 'You say that you are investigating a spy ring. In what way may I help you with your enquiries?'

She saw Lucas hesitate and for a moment her perfidious heart hoped that he would override her coldness and take her in his arms, murmur the words of love that surely should accompany a proposal of marriage, the words she had secretly longed to hear…

Instead he sat down slowly. 'Are we not to speak of our marriage any more?' he enquired, with studied politeness.

Rebecca shook her head. For a second the tears obscured her vision and she blinked them away fiercely. 'I think it better not. You will ask whatever it is that you wish to know and then you will leave.'

Lucas paused on the edge of saying something, then appeared to change his mind. Rebecca's heart shrivelled. So there was to be no declaration of love, no putting right of the wrong. Instead, Lucas put a hand inside his jacket and extracted a folded piece of parchment. He held it out to her.

'I am here on the authority of the Foreign Secretary,' he said. 'Read it—please.'

Rebecca unfolded the paper, trying to keep her hands from shaking. It was short and to the point. The warrant gave the bearer permission to question any person appropriate about certain treasonable activities that were focussed on the villages of Midwinter in the County of Suffolk. She was to give full cooperation to the enquiry.

Rebecca read the name of Suffolk and almost fainted. The paper fell from her hand to the floor. She could hear a buzzing in her ears and put a hand to her forehead to try to ward off the dizziness that was washing over her. She heard Lucas move and felt his fingers cool against her cheek.

'I will fetch you a glass of water,' he said.

She wanted to tell him not to do so. She hated the thought that he had been in the studio before and knew where to find all the simple things—the pots and pans in the scullery, a beaker of water… It felt like the greatest intrusion now that she knew he had had another purpose for seeking her out. The fact that he knew so much about her and her life was almost as distressing as the fact that she had had the poor judgement to give herself body and soul to a man whom, it seemed, had betrayed her. She started to think about all the things she had confided in him, all the words she had spoken, all the intimate moments they had shared. It had seemed so precious. Now she felt sickened.

Lucas had returned within moments and pressed a cold beaker into her hand. She wanted to dash the contents in his face. She wanted to smash every item of glass she could lay her hands upon. Instead, she took a deep, steadying breath and accepted the water with a brief word of thanks, whilst she locked the anger and the hurt and the violation deep inside. She took a sip of the cool liquid and gave Lucas a look of defiance.

'I know nothing about this, my lord.'

'I did not believe that you did,' Lucas said easily. 'However, you will not object to answering a few questions?'

Rebecca shrugged ungraciously. 'If you wish.'

'Thank you.' Lucas resumed his seat. He picked up the small package that he had brought with him and unwrapped it quickly. Rebecca's eyes widened as she saw the contents. It was a small sherry glass, engraved with a picture of a half-moon.

Lucas was watching her closely. 'You recognise it?'

'Of course. It is a piece of my uncle's work.'

Lucas leaned forward. 'You are certain of that?'

Rebecca met his eyes. 'Yes. His style is very distinctive.' She could not read anything from his expression.

'Do you know for whom the order was made?'

'Not without checking the order books,' Rebecca said.

Lucas nodded. 'You have a client who is a major collector?' he asked.

'You know that I do.' She did not have to make it easy for him. She saw his look of resigned amusement as he realised that fact.

'What is his name?'

Rebecca frowned. 'I believe he is called...Mr Johnson.'

Lucas raised his brows in patent disbelief. 'Is that his real name?'

'How should I know? I have never questioned otherwise.' Rebecca gave him a faintly contemptuous look. 'I have never queried that you are, in fact, Lord Lucas Kestrel, although there are a great many other things that I could call you.'

Lucas inclined his head. *'Touché.'* He shifted. 'So yesterday Mr Johnson's manservant collected a commission from you?'

'He did.'

'And paid you two hundred guineas for your uncle's work.'

Rebecca's eyes narrowed. 'How did you know that, my lord?'

'That is nothing to the purpose. Is it correct?'

'It is.'

'Why so much? Had you completed a very large piece of work for him?'

Rebecca set her jaw. 'If you know how much he paid, then I would wager that you also know the package was of modest size.'

Lucas laughed and took a leaf from her book in the brevity of his response. 'I did know that.'

'Then why try to trick me?' Rebecca asked sharply. 'You know that the parcel was small, you know that I told you a set of six engraved glasses cost twenty guineas.'

'And I know he paid you two hundred.' Lucas was watching her with the intentness of a hawk. 'Why should he give you so much money, Rebecca?'

'Because he owed payment for three consignments of work,' Rebecca said.

There was a silence, then Lucas nodded slowly. 'I see.'

'So simple an explanation.'

'So it would seem.' The lines around Lucas's mouth deepened as he smiled and Rebecca's wayward heart missed a beat. She was furious with herself. How was it possible to hate a man so much and yet long for his touch with a yearning that owed nothing to hatred? In the heat of the night she had loved this man. Now it was daylight and it was raining and she was still in love with this cold stranger who had misused her trust. She despised her own weakness.

'Is that all, my lord?' she said starchily.

'No, it is barely the beginning.' Lucas looked at her. 'I should like to see details of all orders placed by Mr Johnson and all transactions bought and paid for.'

Rebecca stared. 'That will take hours!'

'You do have the information?'

'Of course. It is in the account books, but—'

'Yes?'

'I am sorry, but I must ask why you require to see it.'

Lucas waved the document under her nose. 'Johnson is known to consort with spies, Rebecca. They are using your uncle's engravings as the cipher on which they base their coded letters to the enemy.'

Rebecca drew in a sharp breath. Her first reaction was one of relief. This was nothing to do with Daniel at all. She felt a little colour come into her cheeks.

Lucas was watching her closely. 'You do not seem surprised.'

Rebecca suddenly realised her danger. In her relief for Daniel she had probably greeted the news with a calmness that made her appear guilty.

'On the contrary,' she snapped, 'I am astounded.'

Lucas gave a short laugh. 'A cunning plan, is it not?'

'Very clever. But not original.'

'How so?'

'The Jacobites used engraved glasses to communicate their coded messages last century,' Rebecca said. 'The most famous case was that of the Bolingbroke crystal, which was engraved with symbols relating to a plan to overthrow the government. The glasses were passed between the members of the conspiracy as a means of making contact.'

'And you did not know that the Midwinter spies were using the same trick?'

'Certainly not. I have already told you that I know nothing of the Midwinter spies and I am certain that my uncle knew nothing either. He took the commissions and did the work in all innocence.'

Lucas's scrutiny dwelled on her face and Rebecca felt herself blush beneath it.

'You are very cool,' he murmured. 'One might almost say professional.'

'Professional at what?' Rebecca asked sharply. 'The only thing I am, Lord Lucas, is a professional engraver. You should know that now—after last night.'

Their eyes met and held, Rebecca's hard with dislike, Lucas's expression more equivocal. Rebecca saw a hint of colour come into his face. His jaw set hard. 'Rebecca, if we could leave that aside for a while—'

'How like you,' Rebecca said with contempt, 'to wish to leave aside any matter that would trouble the conscience of any decent man.'

She saw Lucas's hands clench and the expression flare in his eyes, and she felt a savage satisfaction that she could vent her anger on him and provoke a response. Yet even now he was in control of his feelings, smoothly pushing aside her fury as though it was of no account. Perhaps it was not, to him. Rebecca's nails dug into her palms as she thought of the extent to which she had given of herself; generously, freely, openly, as though modesty and convention and reserve were of no concern. She had been lost in passion whilst he…he had been playing a part. Or perhaps that was too harsh. He had said that he cared for her. He had offered her marriage in a declaration that half the débutantes in London would no doubt kill for. It was her misfortune that he was offering for all the wrong reasons and she was refusing for all the right ones.

Lucas was watching her expressionlessly. 'Did you know that Johnson's servant delivered your commission to the Archangel Club?'

Rebecca was startled at that. 'No, I did not.'

'You did not know Mr Johnson's direction?'

'He has always sent his servant to place orders and collect the work. I do not believe we know his direction.'

Lucas grimaced. 'But what if he had not paid his bills?'

Rebecca's gaze mocked him. 'Then I should have starved—as I almost did.'

Their gazes held for a long moment.

'You must concede that it is a coincidence,' Lucas said.

'What is?'

'That both your recent commission and Mr Johnson's direction should be connected to the Archangel Club.'

'It is,' Rebecca allowed, 'but if it is more than chance, I am not aware of it.'

Lucas stood up. 'If you could fetch me the account books, please?'

'Of course,' Rebecca said, with scrupulous courtesy. She was very conscious of him as he followed her into the tiny office that led off the engraving studio. His presence seemed to fill the room. She felt over-whelmed and suddenly dangerously vulnerable. The anger that had kept her hurt at bay was ebbing now, leaving her with a feeling of emptiness and disillusion greater than she had ever imagined. To have loved so briefly and been so swiftly betrayed was difficult to comprehend. Yet there was already a formality be-tween them as though the man who had held her and loved her was quite different, and this cold stranger someone else entirely…

She tried to concentrate. She needed this year's book of accounts and the last one. She would give them to him and then he would go and she need not see him again. She grabbed the dusty, leather-bound tome in which her uncle had recorded the previous year's transactions. Her hands were unsteady and the corner caught the china biscuit jar in which she had placed the money. For a second it teetered on the edge of the shelf and then, with a terrifying finality, it tum-bled to the stone floor and smashed into shards. The money spun across the floor in a tumble of dull gold. And Daniel's note…

Rebecca pounced on the paper, but Lucas was a second too quick for her. He plucked it from her fin-gers and she was left grasping nothing.

'Just a moment,' he murmured.

Rebecca made a grab for the paper. 'That is private! Give it to me!'

Lucas held the paper infuriatingly out of reach and grabbed her with his other hand. 'So frightened, Re-becca?' he drawled. 'Whatever can it be?'

'Beast!' Rebecca said. 'It is no concern of yours! It is nothing to do with this!'

'Then you will not mind my reading it,' Lucas said smoothly. He unfolded the paper and scanned it quickly. She saw him pale slightly. 'Who is Daniel?'

Rebecca thought quickly. 'He is my brother. That is a personal letter. Give it back!'

Lucas ignored her, reading the letter again. 'You did not tell me that you had a brother,' he said slowly, without taking his eyes from the text.

Rebecca wrenched her arm from his grip. 'There are plenty of things that I did not tell you, and a good thing too, since this is how you have repaid me!' she stormed, thoroughly angry now. 'I trusted you, Lucas Kestrel! I *trusted* you! You are a heartless scoundrel and I hate and detest you for the villain you are.'

Lucas gave no indication that he had even heard this diatribe. He dropped the letter onto the table and pulled her around to face him. 'Why did you not wish me to read this?' he asked.

'Why should you?' Rebecca demanded, her face flushed with fury. Her temper was soaring and it felt good to give in to the fury at last and be damned to self-control. 'It is private and you have intruded in my business quite enough under false pretences.'

'What does your brother do? What is his profession?'

Rebecca's heart raced. This was becoming very dangerous. She could feel her pulse pounding beneath Lucas's fingers and she knew he could feel it too. He could tell she was nervous and it was making him curious. She tried to breathe more deeply and calm herself. 'He is at sea,' she said. 'That is why I do not see him often.'

'What ship does he serve on?'

He had assumed that Daniel was in the Royal Navy. Rebecca did not correct him. She shrugged.

'I do not know. I never paid much attention.'

Lucas's eyes narrowed. 'I find that difficult to believe. What happens if you need to contact him?'

'I don't,' Rebecca said shortly. 'He comes to see me when he is ashore.'

'Or sends a messenger.' Lucas looked from the note to the scatter of sovereigns on the floor. 'And rather a lot of gold.'

Rebecca shrugged again. 'He gives me money when he can.'

'I see. From his Navy pay, I suppose?'

'I imagine so. I do not ask.'

Lucas smiled mirthlessly. 'You seem very incurious all of a sudden, Rebecca. I do believe that I should try to trace this brother of yours...'

Rebecca felt a fugitive rush of amusement. She had given so much of herself away, but at least there was one secret she had kept. *You can try...* She almost spoke the words aloud.

Lucas was still watching her closely. 'If, of course, he is your brother. You might well have been spinning me tales from the very beginning.'

Rebecca's palm itched to slap him. 'Oh, no, my lord,' she said with acid sweetness. '*You* are the one who has been spinning the tales, commissioning pieces of glass that you do not want, professing an interest that you do not feel, seducing me to order. What were you hoping for—that I would give away secrets in my sleep?'

Lucas's attention snapped back to her and she almost flinched to see the anger in his eyes. 'Are you implying that I made love to you simply to further the course of this investigation?'

'Of course!' Rebecca felt reckless with fury. 'You took your duty very seriously, did you not, Lord Lucas, and I, poor fool that I was, was quite misled by your attentions! I thought—' She cut off the words before she betrayed her innermost anguish. 'I loathe you,' she said precisely. 'You are the worst sort of deceitful devil and I never want to see you again.'

She saw Lucas recoil and tried to crush down the soaring pleasure it gave her to inflict pain on him. It was so difficult to keep it bottled up; she wanted to vent all her torment on him and hurt him as much as he had hurt her.

'It was not like that,' Lucas said. His voice was rough. He ran an impatient hand through his hair. 'Devil take it, I never intended this to happen in this way.'

'And yet you must have had me under suspicion from the moment you met me.' Rebecca held her breath, hoping that he would contradict her, tell her that he had not known until that morning, that he had never intended to deceive her. Then she saw the conflict in his face and her hopes tumbled.

'You knew all along,' she repeated tonelessly.

'Not precisely.' Lucas looked hunted. 'Rebecca, I never believed you guilty! I thought all along that you must have been in ignorance of the work your uncle had done.'

Rebecca shook her head blindly. 'Yet you hid your true purpose from me and then you come here asking questions…' She looked at him. 'I do not believe that there is any way you can make amends for the way that you have behaved, Lord Lucas.' She thrust the account books at him. 'Here you are. Take them and begone, and this time do not even think to return them yourself. Send a servant, or the door will be barred to you!'

Lucas took the books and put them under his arm. 'Thank you. There is one other matter remaining, however.'

Rebecca did not bother to try to conceal her impatience. All she desired now was to see him gone. 'Which is?'

'You,' Lucas said. 'You are coming with me.'

Chapter Seven

'Come with you?' Rebecca repeated, appalled. 'Surely you jest? I would not go to the end of the street with you, let alone anywhere else!'

Once again she saw the flash of vivid emotion in Lucas's face before it was wiped blank. 'I regret that I must insist,' he said.

'Why on earth would I accompany you?' Rebecca said, hands on hips. She started to laugh. 'You ask far too much, my lord.'

'You are the only person who can recognise your uncle's work,' Lucas said. 'We need you to come to Midwinter to help trap the spy.'

Rebecca shook her head. 'You have a fine way of trying to persuade me, Lord Lucas. I will not come!'

Lucas took a step towards her. 'I must ask you to reconsider.'

Rebecca shook her head. 'You would have to abduct me first!'

Lucas smiled mirthlessly. 'I will if I must.'

Rebecca spread her arms wide in defiance. 'Then pray do so, for it is the only way I will help you.'

She was utterly unprepared for what happened next. She had not believed he would do it, but then, she had consistently misjudged Lucas Kestrel.

He moved so quickly that she had no time to think. He swept her off her feet and up into his arms with insulting ease. He reached the door of the studio in three strides and kicked it shut behind them, freeing one hand briefly to turn the key in the lock.

It was bright again out in the street, with a fresh breeze. Rebecca had a blurred impression of cold sunlight and the astounded expressions on the faces of the vintner and the silversmith before she was bundled unceremoniously into the waiting carriage. Lucas threw the account books onto the seat beside them and slammed the door, and the vehicle immediately moved off.

Rebecca struggled upright, but Lucas already had an arm about her, clamping her close to his side.

'Let me go!' she gasped, but he merely shook his head.

'If I do, you will cry for help or throw yourself bodily from the coach. I do not trust you.'

'That is all too apparent,' Rebecca said. She knew it was pointless to struggle. He was far stronger than she was. The hard muscles of his arms beneath her fingers argued a man in prime physical condition, which she knew already anyway. She relaxed and immediately felt Lucas's cruel grip ease.

'That's better,' Lucas said.

Pressed against him as she was, she could feel the pistol in his belt. It shocked her to think that he had come to her studio armed, as though she were a dan-

gerous criminal. Logic told her that it had been the
sensible thing for him to do. He had suspected her to
be a traitor and had to deal with her accordingly. She
was too hurt to be interested in logic.

Quick as a flash she stole her hand inside his jacket
and wrenched the pistol from its holster, pulling away
from him at the same time. 'Stop the coach!'

She saw Lucas tense; saw the rapid calculation going on behind his eyes as he decided what tactic to
take. She did not wish to hurt him—she shut her mind
to the noise and the blood and unpleasant mess that
firing a pistol in an enclosed space would provoke.
She was so angry that all she wanted was to get out
of the carriage and be free to walk home and forget
everything that had happened. She was furious and
humiliated and distraught, and to escape from Lucas
was the only thing that mattered now.

'Do you know how to use that thing?' Lucas asked,
his eyes on the barrel. 'Hold it steady or you will never
hit your target. Which you will not anyway, since the
pistol is not loaded.'

Rebecca hesitated for a split second and in that moment Lucas caught her wrist in a vicelike grip and she
cried aloud. The pistol fell to the floor, skittered away
and went off with a loud report, burying a bullet in
the cushions of the seat. Lucas pulled her beneath him,
sheltering her body with his as the interior of the coach
filled with smoke and pieces of velvet and stuffing
rained down on them.

Rebecca sneezed. 'It was loaded,' she said.

'Of course it was,' Lucas said. 'What use is an
empty pistol?'

Rebecca felt another pang of misery. 'I wonder how long it will be,' she said bitterly, 'before I learn not to trust a word you say.'

She tried to sit up, but Lucas held her still, ruthlessly trapped beneath him.

'I should be obliged if you would allow me up,' she said.

'I will only let you up if you promise not to pull any more tricks like that one,' he said. 'You could have killed both of us. What did you think you were doing?'

'I wanted to go home,' Rebecca said. Her lip trembled and she bit it viciously, turning her head aside so that Lucas could not see the tears in her eyes.

She felt him brush the tumbled hair away from her face very gently and shuddered at his touch. It undermined every single barrier she was determined to erect against him.

'Stop fighting me, Rebecca,' he said.

Rebecca looked at him. 'I did not believe you would abduct me.'

Lucas gave her a faint smile. 'I gave you fair warning.'

Rebecca turned her face away. She had underestimated him. She would have to be a great deal more careful in the future. How had she made such a serious error of judgement with Lucas Kestrel? The self-loathing threatened to swamp her. No one had ever hurt her so much.

She struggled to sit up and this time he allowed her. She turned a shoulder to him and stared out of the window of the carriage, determined not to show any weakness.

'I cannot simply leave my workshop,' she said. 'This whole matter is preposterous!'

Lucas sounded unconcerned. 'I will have someone keep an eye on the place for you,' he said.

'But my commissions—'

'You told me that you had no work at present.'

Rebecca cursed herself. How many more unguarded remarks had she made to him that he had stored away and would use against her when the time was fit?

'That is true,' she said bitterly. 'I do have a half-finished set of glasses that you ordered, but as you never actually wanted them—'

'That is not correct.' For the first time, Lucas sounded angry. 'I should be delighted to have some of your work.'

'As a souvenir, perhaps,' Rebecca said.

Once again, Lucas did not rise to the provocation, and after a moment Rebecca sighed. 'I cannot afford to close my business,' she said.

'We will pay you for each day you are away from your work,' Lucas said. 'Ten guineas a day.'

Ten guineas a day. It was a fortune to Rebecca. She set her jaw. 'I will not accept it. I will not work for you for money, my lord.'

She remembered him touching her hand when he offered words of comfort over her uncle's death. She remembered him taking her in his arms and the blissful pleasure of his kiss. She remembered thinking that if one was obliged to take a lover, there would be no one preferable to Lord Lucas Kestrel, and discovering that those wanton thoughts had indeed been perfectly true. The shame and anger swept through her again at the way he had betrayed her and she had betrayed herself.

'In fact, I do not want to help you at all,' she said, driven by bitterness.

She felt Lucas shift slightly. 'Rebecca,' he said, with weary patience, 'I appreciate what you must think of me—'

'I doubt it!' Rebecca snapped.

'But I must ask you to put aside personal animosity for a moment to consider the greater good.' Lucas continued. 'The Midwinter spies are putting thousands of lives at risk with their treasonable work. They have already killed a man and are quite ruthless enough to kill again if they see the necessity.' He took a deep breath. 'They have to be stopped and you are the only one who can help us get to them.'

Rebecca was silent.

'Please,' Lucas said again. 'If you would not help us because I ask it of you, Rebecca, then do it for your country.'

Rebecca turned away. If only he knew her complicated pedigree then he would think twice about putting such an argument to her. She wondered what Lucas would say if she told him the truth: *My lord, my ancestors travelled to the New World before they returned to settle here in England. There is very little English blood in me.*

Yet she had lived in England all her life and was fiercely attached to this country, and she knew she owed it her loyalty. So she had no real choice. If only it was not Midwinter...

She sighed. 'Very well. I do not think I have a choice.'

Lucas gave her a searching look as though he was not entirely sure he trusted her, then she saw him relax.

'Thank you,' he said. He took her hand and kissed it. 'You are a very good person, Rebecca.'

Startled, Rebecca whipped her hand away. It tingled from the touch of his lips. 'I am doing this for loyalty and not for liking,' she warned. 'I trust you will keep your distance in future, my lord.'

Lucas grinned at her as though he sensed her weakness. 'I regret that I cannot oblige you, Rebecca. If you are to help us, then I am sworn to protect you. These are dangerous men—and women—and I must keep you safe.'

They stared at one another.

'Does it have to be you?' Rebecca said wearily. 'Why not another?'

Lucas's smile deepened. 'It has to be me because I want it to be.'

'And I do not want it,' Rebecca argued. 'I detest you, Lord Lucas. You have behaved as no gentleman would. To be obliged to spend more time in your company merely adds insult to the injury of your behaviour.'

Lucas shrugged. 'I regret that you see matters in that way. You should know that I still mean to marry you.'

Rebecca raised her chin haughtily. 'I do not believe

that we need to discuss this, my lord. It is all academic now.'

'You mistake, Rebecca,' Lucas said softly, and though he did not touch her his tone felt like a brush against her skin. 'I intend to persuade you to accept me.'

Rebecca drew in a short breath. 'You are clearly deluded, my lord. You have as little chance of persuading me as I have of swimming the English Channel.'

'You have consented to spend some time in my company,' Lucas pointed out. 'I intend to use it well.'

Rebecca was shaking her head in disbelief. 'It is impossible, my lord. I shall not change my mind.'

'We shall see.' Lucas smiled slightly. 'I do not expect you to make it easy for me, Rebecca.'

His implacable confidence shook Rebecca to the core. 'But why?' she wailed. 'Just because of what happened?'

Lucas was shaking his head. 'Not just because of that. I want you, Rebecca. I find I want you very badly. And the only way I may have you with honour is through marriage. So...'

Rebecca swallowed hard. She could not trust him. How could she, after the way in which he had deceived her? And yet there was a part of her that longed for him, longed for his touch and the comfort of his arms. It had felt absolutely right to give herself to Lucas and that fundamental rightness had not changed, overlaid as it was by disillusion and disappointment. If she fought his will, she would be fighting a part of herself as well, and she was not sure that she was

strong enough to do so. She looked at Lucas's unyielding face and shivered slightly. He had said no
words of love to her; even in the heat of the night
when he had uttered words of sweet tenderness he had
not spoken of love. Must she compromise on that too?
She could not believe that she had entertained the idea
for even a minute. She was angry at her own weakness.

She raised her chin. 'I still do not accept your proposal,' she said.

Lucas smiled. 'I did not for one moment expect that
you would,' he said, 'but I have every intention of
making you change your mind.'

'You have no notion how stubborn I can be,' Rebecca said.

'I have some idea,' Lucas contradicted, 'and I can
be very determined.'

'I am aware,' Rebecca said. She smiled bitterly.
'We shall see, my lord. You have limited time and a
difficult task.'

Lucas took her chin in his hand and turned her face
to his. Her skin heated beneath his touch. 'And you
are fighting on two fronts,' he said softly, 'against me
but against yourself as well. So you are weakened before you start.'

Rebecca jerked her head away, but not before she
had felt the tell-tale quiver of desire through her whole
body. 'Damn you!' she said bitterly.

'For telling the truth?'

'For being insufferably conceited!' Rebecca said.

And for making me want you, she added to herself,
for despite her furious resistance and the ache in her

heart, there was no denying that she still loved Lucas Kestrel and she was afraid that she always would.

When they reached the house in Grosvenor Street, Lucas took no chances on Rebecca refusing to cooperate and practically carried her out of the coach with one arm tight about her waist. He bundled her through the front door as though she were an awkwardly shaped parcel and finally let go of her when they were standing in the entrance hall.

Smoothing down her cloak, Rebecca glared at him. 'If this is your persuasion, my lord, I have to tell you that you waste your time!'

She fell silent as the butler glided out to greet them, determined, despite the misery inside, that she should not show how shaken she was.

'Good morning, Byrne,' Lucas said, as though it were a common occurrence for him to be manhandling a young woman through the front door of the house, 'has the Duke returned yet?'

'Yes, my lord,' the butler said expressionlessly. 'He is waiting for you in the small salon, with Lord and Lady Newlyn.'

'Thank you,' Lucas said. He turned to Rebecca. 'May I ask you to wait in the drawing room, Miss Raleigh? We will not be above a moment.'

'Very well,' Rebecca said. She waited pointedly whilst Byrne opened the drawing-room door and Lucas ushered her inside.

He looked at her. 'Pray do not climb out of the window and run away or I shall have to go to the trouble of bringing you back.'

Rebecca gave him a disdainful look. 'You would not find me.'

'Don't try me. Do I have your word?'

Rebecca sighed. 'Would you accept it if you did?'

'Of course. Well?'

'Then you have it.'

'Thank you,' Lucas said. There was a smile deep in his eyes. Rebecca saw it and blushed. She hated that she was still so susceptible to him. The thought that he would be close to her, guarding her life, was well-nigh intolerable. She deliberately turned her back and walked over to the window, staring out over the neat, green garden. Suddenly she felt very tired.

The door opened again and a girl of Rebecca's age entered the room. She had wide brown eyes and a friendly expression. She came forward, smiling. 'Miss Raleigh? I thought that I would come and keep you company. My name is Rachel Newlyn.'

Rebecca came away from the window with a sigh and sat down on the sofa. 'Did Lord Lucas not trust me sufficiently to leave me on my own, Lady Newlyn?'

Rachel's eyes widened at Rebecca's tone, but she answered levelly enough, 'I have no notion. It was my own idea to join you, but if you prefer to be alone I can leave.'

Rebecca immediately felt churlish. 'I am sorry to be so rude,' she said. 'I do not know what is wrong with me today.'

'I do.' Rachel came and sat beside her and, to Rebecca's surprise, smiled warmly. 'You have been deceived by someone you trusted and snatched from your home and delivered to a bunch of strangers. It is quite enough to spoil one's whole day!'

Rebecca was forced into a reluctant laugh. 'When you express it like that...'

Rachel made a slight gesture. 'That is how it is. So if there is anything I can do to make amends, Miss Raleigh, then you must tell me.'

'I do not believe that you are the one who should be doing that, Lady Newlyn,' Rebecca said bleakly.

Rachel sighed. 'You mean Lucas, I suppose. I assure you, Miss Raleigh, that he feels his betrayal very keenly.' She hesitated. 'I have never seen Lucas quite so irritable before. Usually he is the most even-tempered of men. I think his conscience is giving him trouble. He told my husband Cory a full week ago that he knew he was behaving like a scoundrel.'

Rebecca felt slightly surprised. 'Did he truly? I thought he believed me a traitor!'

Rachel laughed. 'I cannot believe that such a thought would endure more than a minute in your company, Miss Raleigh. It is manifestly absurd. I am persuaded that Lucas knew you could not be directly involved.'

Rebecca could feel a dangerous inclination to ask more questions about Lucas but forced herself not to do so. 'He has acted very badly,' she said coldly.

Rachel sighed again. 'And yet he is the one arguing for the others to trust you,' she said, 'which proves that he has faith in you.'

Rebecca looked at her sharply. 'Lord Lucas is *defending* me?'

'Certainly,' Rachel said. 'His brother the Duke is

taking a little convincing that we should trust you enough to take you with us to Midwinter, given the damage done to his best carriage!'

Rebecca grimaced. 'That was foolish,' she admitted.

'But understandable, given the provocation,' Rachel said.

Once again, Rebecca resisted the urge to confide. It was easy to warm to Rachel Newlyn and her uncomplicated friendship, but it was too soon.

'I cannot be surprised at the Duke's reluctance,' she said. 'There is no reason for him to believe that neither I nor, I am convinced, my uncle knew that the work he was doing was treasonable.'

'No reason other than Lucas's belief in you,' Rachel said smiling. She touched Rebecca's hand lightly. 'I heard that your uncle and aunt died recently, Miss Raleigh. I am sorry.'

Rebecca looked at her and realised that she meant it. There was genuine sympathy in Rachel's eyes. Rebecca rubbed her forehead dispiritedly.

'I have tried to keep the workshop going. I am persuaded that it is what my uncle would have wanted. But it is very difficult and I am very tired.' She rubbed her eyes. 'Excuse me. I do not normally complain like this.'

'Of course not,' Rachel said. 'You sound most dauntless, Miss Raleigh.' She squeezed Rebecca's hand. 'Do you know, I have travelled all around the world and gone to places and done things that others would never dream, and yet I have never been alone? I think that is the more difficult part.'

Rebecca looked at her. 'All around the world?'

'My parents are antiquarians—' Rachel sighed '—and I travelled with them before I married.'

'How wonderful,' Rebecca said. 'And now you are married to Lord Newlyn, who is a most notable explorer.'

Rachel laughed. 'Fortunately, Cory has shown no inclination to travel farther than Cornwall of late,' she said. 'Which suits me. Do not worry about going to Midwinter, Miss Raleigh. We shall take care of you.'

'You are going as well?' Rebecca asked.

Rachel nodded. 'My parents live in Midwinter Royal. I have not seen them for several months. This is a good opportunity for a visit.' She smiled. 'My good friend Lady Marney also lives nearby. Her sister is married to Lord Lucas's brother Richard, but they are on their honeymoon at present. Nevertheless you will find a warm welcome in Midwinter, Miss Raleigh. We shall strive to make you feel at home.'

Rebecca bit her lip. This kindly welcome was so far removed from the cold isolation that gripped her heart. It threatened to undermine her already, when she had promised herself that she would go to Midwinter and return as quickly as possible and let nothing, least of all Lucas's presence, touch her.

'I wish,' she burst out with sudden fierceness, 'that matters had not fallen out this way! I would have helped—of course I would—but now I feel deceived and coerced against my will. When Lord Lucas came to the studio today—' She broke off. It was impossible to tell Rachel what had happened the previous night and how the pain of Lucas's duplicity had been magnified by what had happened between them.

Rachel touched her hand. 'I do not suppose that Lucas dealt with the situation very well,' she said dolefully. 'Men seldom do. He would not have thought to apologise first and try to explain properly.'

Rebecca laughed. 'No, indeed he did not.'

Rachel shook her head sadly. 'I suppose that was because he could not think about more than one thing at once.'

'I have observed that before in men,' Rebecca agreed. 'It is very vexing.'

'Lucas told us that it is his most ardent wish to marry you,' Rachel said, 'but that you were not inclined to accept his suit. One cannot wonder at it.' She saw the look on Rebecca's face and added quickly: 'Have no fear—he told us none of the particulars, but he wanted us to understand how matters stood.' She touched Rebecca's hand. 'I am sorry that everything has fallen out so badly, Miss Raleigh. Is there any chance that you might forgive Lucas in time?'

Rebecca was silent for a moment. 'I do not believe so, Lady Newlyn,' she said reluctantly.

Rachel sighed. 'I see. Well, you may count me your friend if ever you need one, Miss Raleigh. And you must call me Rachel since we *are* to be friends.' She smiled. 'If I may call you Rebecca?'

'Of course,' Rebecca said, and she felt a little warmer. It would be very easy to accept Rachel's friendship and to sink into this half-remembered opulence of aristocratic living. Once, long ago, she had taken such things for granted. If she were not careful she would start to feel that she belonged, but then what happened when it was all over? The empty studio in Clerkenwell would feel all the more lonely…

The door opened and a fair-haired man stuck his head into the room in a somewhat informal manner. 'Rachel? Miss Raleigh—' he gave Rebecca a warm smile '—how do you do? I am Cory Newlyn. We are ready now, if you would be so good as to come through to the salon.'

Rebecca looked at Rachel, who stood up and held out a hand. 'Come along. As I said, we shall look after you.'

Rebecca stood up and smoothed her skirts in a nervous gesture. Her heart was suddenly racing so much that it was difficult to breathe; it was not the prospect of meeting the Duke of Kestrel that disturbed her, but more the thought of facing Lucas again. For how was she to resist him when she clutched at every small suggestion that he was an honourable man? Yet in her heart of hearts she knew that honourable or not, she could not marry Lucas without an offer of love, and that was the one thing he had not given her.

Lucas was standing by the window when they entered the room. He turned to look at her, an indecipherable look, then came forward to draw her into the room. 'Miss Raleigh, may I introduce my brother Justin, Duke of Kestrel. Justin, Miss Rebecca Raleigh. I see that you have already met Lord and Lady Newlyn.'

Justin Kestrel had got to his feet as Rebecca entered the room and now she found herself subjected to a searching scrutiny from his very dark eyes. He was a formidable man, in every way. An inch or two taller than Lucas, he was also broader and a good few years older. His face was thin and bronzed, almost hawklike in its predatory good looks, and the expression in his eyes was very shrewd. Rebecca felt a *frisson* of apprehension.

'Good morning, Miss Raleigh,' the Duke said. 'I understand from my brother that you are responsible for a bullet hole in the upholstery of my best carriage.'

Rebecca raised her chin and held his gaze. 'That is correct, your Grace. I was aiming at your brother, but unfortunately I missed.'

She heard Cory Newlyn stifle a laugh and saw Justin Kestrel's lips twitch. 'Despite that,' he murmured, 'Lucas assures me that you have agreed to help us.'

Rebecca glanced at Lucas. His face was quite impassive. 'I have, your Grace.'

Justin nodded. 'Thank you, Miss Raleigh.' He gestured Rebecca to a seat. 'We have been most remiss. May I offer you some refreshment?'

Lucas passed her a cup of tea and the plate of biscuits. Rebecca, for whom breakfast seemed a long time ago, was surprised to discover she was ravenous.

'Lucas will have told you the reason we are all here, Miss Raleigh,' Justin Kestrel said, smiling as he watched her demolish five biscuits in succession. 'I will leave it up to him to brief you further on the situation in Midwinter. We thought that for the purposes of the visit to Suffolk, you should pose as Lucas's fiancée.'

Rebecca put the plate down with a clatter. She knew that this had to be Lucas's idea and she needed to spike his guns immediately.

'No!' She flushed, and glanced at Lucas, who was looking studiously blank. 'I beg your pardon, your Grace,' she amended, 'but I cannot agree to acting the part of Lord Lucas's betrothed. I should never be able to convince anyone.'

Justin Kestrel raised his brows. 'It would not be for very long, Miss Raleigh.'

'No,' Rebecca said again. She felt panic rising in her throat at the thought of acting out the role of Lucas's fiancée. That would bring him far too close. It was too intimate. She had to keep him at arm's length now, at all costs, or she would never be able to resist him.

Lucas came across to her chair. 'We could make it a marriage of convenience,' he said. His tone was bland, but there was amusement lurking at the back of his eyes. 'Then you would not be required to show me the slightest degree of affection.'

Rebecca blushed again and looked away. 'I cannot,' she said. 'It would be too difficult. Why do we need to pretend anything of the sort?'

'We need a reason, Miss Raleigh,' Lucas said persuasively. 'I am sworn to protect you and therefore we need a reason to explain why I shall stay as close to you as a lover.'

The air in the salon seemed suddenly highly charged. Rebecca was trapped by the look in his eyes, which conjured up the heated images of the previous night.

'No,' she said for a third time, but this time it came out as a whisper.

'I think,' Rachel Newlyn said, breaking the fraught

silence with a tactful clearing of the throat and throwing a look at her husband for support, 'that we might consider some other solution, Justin. How would it be if Miss Raleigh was to be a cousin of yours—a distant one?'

'Good idea,' Cory Newlyn said at once. 'You have so many cousins, Justin, that no one would remark on it.'

Justin nodded slowly. 'It might serve. What do you say, Miss Raleigh? You are a distant cousin whom Lucas has met again for the first time in years and he is quite *épris*.' A smile lurked at the corner of his mouth. 'You, alas, are not in the least smitten by him.'

Rebecca felt swamped with relief. Once again, she caught Lucas's quizzical look and glanced hastily away. He made her feel as though her defences were as fragile as glass.

'I am content to agree to that,' she said cautiously, 'as long as I do not have to pretend to any degree of fondness for Lord Lucas.'

'Capital!' Justin Kestrel said, smiling broadly. 'I shall leave the two of you to work out the details of our family connection and tell the rest of us how it stands. Keep it as simple as possible. You will wish to spend some time with Miss Raleigh after luncheon, Lucas?'

'I shall,' Lucas said, with disconcerting promptness.

'Then we shall travel to Midwinter tomorrow morning,' Justin Kestrel concluded. 'I shall send a message ahead to Kestrel Court. Is there anything else?'

Rachel Newlyn raised a point of her own. 'We are

going to need some time to arrange suitable attire for Miss Raleigh,' she said.

Everyone looked at her, including Rebecca. She had not given any thought to clothes. She seldom did.

'I can go back to Clerkenwell to fetch my belongings,' she began, but Lucas shook his head.

'In the first instance, it is too dangerous for you to return there until this matter is settled,' he said, 'and in the second, I doubt you have anything suitable for this masquerade.'

Rebecca glared at him. She knew that she was being trivial, but it was good to have an excuse to argue. 'I assure you, Lord Lucas, that I have some very attractive gowns. It is simply that I do not wear them.'

'Lucas is in the right of it, Miss Raleigh,' Justin interposed smoothly, 'although he could have expressed himself much more diplomatically. No one will believe that you are our cousin unless you are suitably attired.'

Rebecca looked around the rose salon at the simple but expensive furnishings and the understated elegance of her hosts. She deflated slightly. 'Oh, very well! But I require the minimum of items. I cannot believe my stay will be a long one and there is no point in wasting the money.'

She saw the brothers exchange a look and wondered just what Lucas had told his brother about her. 'Just so, Miss Raleigh,' Justin Kestrel said. 'We shall be most frugal.'

Even so, it soon transpired that the Duke's idea of frugality and Rebecca's own did not accord particularly well.

'This cannot be right,' Rebecca said hopelessly, gazing at the mountains of clothing and accessories that were piled up in all corners of the blue bedroom by the middle of the afternoon. 'I cannot possibly need all of this! I have not ordered the half of it!'

'No, I did,' Rachel Newlyn said calmly. She gestured to the piles in turn. 'You have gloves over there, Rebecca, stockings there, various undergarments there—I shall not put you to the blush by itemising them!—nightgowns and robes, handkerchiefs and scarves, hats to choose from there—oh, and shoes, of course.'

Rebecca pressed both hands to her hot cheeks. Never had she imagined setting eyes upon such a selection of fashionable and expensive clothes, much less being able to purchase them. Yet there was no possibility of refusal on her part. Rachel had accompanied Rebecca to Bond Street, for a bewildering array of items Rebecca had not even realised she needed. In addition to all her clothes there was a selection of glass cosmetic bottles and a very beautiful set of silver-backed brushes. Her head ached with the opulence of it all.

The day dress she was wearing became her well. It was rose pink and suited her complexion perfectly. On the bed was a huge selection of gowns—walking dresses, riding habits, ballgowns, spencers, pelisses… She had no notion when she would have the opportunity to wear them all. When she had first tried on the rose-pink gown she had stared at herself in the mirror for quite five minutes, for it had utterly transformed her appearance. Her thick chestnut hair, which

normally she wore tied back or pushed hastily under
a lace cap, was loose about her face in a dark cloud.
Her eyes were a vivid blue. It felt odd to be a dressed
as a lady of fashion, but she knew she looked pretty.
She hesitated to use the word for it had not had much
currency in her world, but it was true.

'You look lovely, Rebecca,' Rachel said warmly,
watching her with amusement. 'It is a shame that we
have had to buy your gowns off the peg, but you are
fortunate to have found things that fit you well.'

'I had no idea what I was choosing,' Rebecca admitted, still turning surreptitiously to view the gown
from all angles in the mirror. 'I was looking at colour
and cut.'

'You have a flair for it,' Rachel agreed. 'It must be
the artist in you.'

'It feels strange,' Rebecca admitted. 'I never wear
clothes like this.'

'Do you like them?' Rachel asked, her eyes twin-
kling at Rebecca's poor attempts to conceal her pleasure.

'Oh, yes,' Rebecca admitted with a little sigh.
'Rather too much! It will be a pang for me to give
them up when the masquerade is at an end.'

There was a knock at the door. 'Come in!' Rachel
called, before Rebecca could say anything.

Lucas Kestrel walked in. 'I am come to see how
much longer the security of the nation must wait on
the demands of fashion—' he began, then his eyes fell
on Rebecca and he stopped.

She stood somewhat self-consciously before him

whilst his astounded gaze travelled over her. There was a long moment of silence.

'Good God, Rebecca...' Lucas said. He sounded stunned.

'Try for something more coherent, Lucas,' Rachel said, a spark of amusement in her eyes. 'Does Rebecca not look fine?'

Lucas seemed to recollect himself. 'It is extraordinary what one can achieve with good grooming,' he said. 'I am come to ask Miss Raleigh when she will be free to discuss our plans.'

'We shall not be much longer,' Rachel said. 'Rebecca may join you in the garden shortly, as it is a fine day.'

Lucas went, with one long, backward look at Rebecca, who had gathered the nearest piece of material to her—a riding habit—and was holding it defensively at her breast, despite the fact that the pink gown was all that was demure.

'How rude he is,' she said breathlessly. 'Good grooming, indeed!'

Rachel laughed. 'He was only rude because he was shaken,' she said shrewdly, 'and if you can do that to Lucas, who is accounted a man of experience, I'll warrant you will have the whole of Midwinter falling at your feet, Rebecca!'

Chapter Eight

When Rebecca joined Lucas in the garden some twenty minutes later, she was wearing a warm pelisse over the pink day dress and therefore felt a great deal more prepared to face him. Her confidence lasted precisely thirty seconds—until he took her hand in his to guide her to the wooden seat that overlooked a pretty little ornamental fishpond.

'Are you sufficiently warm out here?' he asked. 'We may talk inside if you prefer.'

Rebecca shook her head. At least out here in the open air she felt free. The thought of being shut away privately with Lucas was enough to make her breathing constrict.

'It is a pleasant day and I have not been outside much of late,' she said. 'I am content to stay here.'

'Very well.' Lucas sat down beside her, crossing his long, elegant legs and giving her a sideways appraising look.

'So we are to be cousins, Miss Raleigh,' he said softly. 'I rather like that, although I could ask for a closer relationship.'

'Even this is too close,' Rebecca said. 'We are not kissing cousins, my lord. If you recall, you have succumbed to a *tendre* for me but I, alas, wish for none of it.'

'Kissing cousins...' Lucas said. The corner of his mouth lifted in a smile. 'I rather like that idea.'

'Pray disregard it,' Rebecca said sharply. 'You are supposed to be acting as though you suffer unrequited love, rather than planning a conquest.'

Lucas's smile deepened as it rested on her face. 'It would not be in character for me to ignore a challenge, Miss Raleigh.'

Rebecca's pulse fluttered and was ignored. He had already told her that he would do all in his power to convince her to accept his suit. This, then, was the confirmation.

'I believe we are intended to be discussing my aristocratic antecedents,' she said, 'rather than wasting our time. To which branch of your illustrious family do I belong?'

Lucas laughed. 'You are to be a very distant cousin on the distaff side. We have so many cousins that no one will think anything of it.'

'And the reason that I have come to visit you?'

'We thought to stick as closely to the truth as possible,' Lucas said. 'The relatives with whom you lived were recently carried off by fever and so you are on a protracted visit to us whilst Justin, as head of the family, decides what is to become of you.'

'How very convenient,' Rebecca said, her lips thinning. 'Not only does it have the ring of authenticity but it would be a cruel person indeed to question me when I have been in mourning.'

'Indeed so,' Lucas said. 'It also explains why you have not been in society.'

'But not why I never had a season or made an advantageous match,' Rebecca said. 'I am scarcely a débutante, my lord, so what is the explanation for that? Were we too poor?'

'No,' Lucas said. 'That would make Justin look ungenerous for failing to sponsor you.' He put his head on one side. 'I think, Miss Raleigh, that you must have been disappointed in love.'

Rebecca raised her brows. 'That will not require a great leap of imagination, my lord,' she said bitterly.

Their gazes clashed. 'And I am pledged to make you forget,' Lucas said softly, 'which is why I dog your footsteps like a suitor.'

'I prefer to think of you as a faithful hound,' Rebecca said, shifting away from him along the seat. 'Mutely devoted. Then I need not have to tolerate your conversation.'

Lucas's smile was genuinely amused. 'You certainly have the wit to carry this off, Miss Raleigh.'

'Thank you. I am not entirely sure that you have the charm to do so.'

'We shall see. I can play your devoted lover with a great deal of conviction, I assure you.' He gave her a quizzical look. 'There is one other thing, of course.'

Rebecca looked enquiring.

'You will have to call me Lucas, and I will call you Rebecca. A greater formality would cause suspicion.

Now I need you to tell me a little of your family history, Rebecca.'

Rebecca looked at him suspiciously. 'Why?'

Lucas sighed. 'Why do I always have the feeling that you are withholding something from me? Because we need to stick to the truth as closely as possible and keep matters simple. And as your cousin, I will necessarily know your history.'

Rebecca nodded reluctantly. She did not want to tell Lucas anything but she could see the point of what he was saying.

'I was born in Somerset and lived in that county for the first eight years of my life,' she said. 'My father was in the army and he was killed in India. My mother went into a decline and died later the same year. Daniel—my brother—joined the navy and I was sent to live with my mother's cousins, the Provosts. The rest you know.'

It was true, as far as it went.

'A succinct history,' Lucas commented. His hazel eyes were keen. 'It must hide a multitude of experience for you, however. It is a difficult thing to lose both parents so young and be uprooted from your home.'

Rebecca felt a treacherous rush of affinity for him and crushed it down. It was not fair that Lucas understood her so well and that his sincerity could undermine her already shaky defences.

'It was,' she said, unconsciously twisting her hands together in her lap, 'but I was very happy in Clerkenwell.'

There was a strained silence, then Lucas dropped

his hand over her clenched ones and for a moment she did not free herself.

'I can see no reason why we need to change your past history to suit our purposes,' he said, 'other than to suggest that you have been living quietly in the country until the death of your aunt. In Somerset, say, to add authenticity.'

Rebecca nodded. 'Very well. And perhaps I could have been betrothed to a curate who felt it his mission to travel to the Indies and subsequently died of fever, leaving me inconsolable.'

Lucas's smile deepened the lines at the corners of his eyes. It would be difficult to imagine anyone who looked less like a sickly curate, Rebecca thought.

'Is that the sort of man who would attract your enduring love?' he asked.

Rebecca looked at him. She felt unseasonably hot as he kept his eyes on her face.

'I have enduring love for nothing other than my engraving,' she said.

'I thought so.' Lucas nodded. 'One cannot imagine a fever-stricken curate inspiring the sort of passion that features in your work, or indeed that we experienced last night.'

Rebecca's eyes kindled. She had been afraid that he would raise the subject once more, and that her reactions would betray her. She snatched her hands away from his. 'Pray make no mention of that, Lord Lucas. You are no gentleman even to think of it.'

Lucas stretched, reminding her all too vividly of the lithe body beneath the elegant clothes. 'I fear that you cannot prevent me from doing that, Rebecca,' he murmured. 'Or, more accurately, you cannot prevent me from remembering every last moment of it.'

'Then if you cannot control your own unruly thoughts, pray do not seek to provoke mine,' Rebecca snapped. 'I have no wish to remember.'

'And I am pledged to remind you,' Lucas said. 'Such affinity as we achieved, Rebecca, happens rarely. It was the single most sweet and passionate experience of my entire life—'

'Stop it!' Rebecca said, the pleading note audible even to her own ears. 'It was false pretences.'

'It was no such thing.' Lucas leaned forward. 'I wanted you, Rebecca, and you wanted me, and if we are to marry—*when* we marry—I suspect that it will become even more pleasurable.'

Rebecca put her hands over her ears. She was scarlet, mortified to feel herself aroused by his words and by the heated memories of the previous night that flashed across her mind in a series of shockingly explicit pictures. How was it possible to dislike someone—to be so angry with them and feel so disillusioned—and yet long for their touch? Would she ever cure herself of the love she held for Lucas Kestrel? In the cold light of day, with the truth and its betrayals clear between them, she still loved him and it was hopeless to deny it.

She could feel her body warming, melting, the excitement growing in the pit of her stomach, and when Lucas gently touched a finger to her bottom lip she almost gasped aloud.

'You see…' his eyes were bright with desire '…you feel it too. Why deny it?'

He was leaning forward to kiss her and every instinct in Rebecca's body urged her to meet his embrace and lose herself in that blissful, sensuous pleasure. When his lips were a bare inch from hers she finally found the strength to draw away.

'I think not.'

She saw the admiration in Lucas's eyes and knew also that he saw her resistance as a challenge. It seemed that to deny his advances only served to increase his determination and she could see no way past that. He smiled at her and she felt the warmth of it tingle through her entire body.

'You are a very strong-willed woman, Rebecca Raleigh,' he said. 'It is one of the many things that I like about you.'

'Whereas I sadly cannot compile a long list of things I like about you, my lord,' Rebecca said untruthfully.

'Not even my kisses?'

'I can live without them.'

'We shall have to change that,' Lucas said, with a look that made her tremble.

Rebecca caught sight of Rachel and Cory Newlyn lurking in the window of the drawing room and studiously pretending that they were not watching them. She sighed.

'What we have to change, my lord, is my ignorance of the Kestrel family and this business of espionage. I have much to learn and little time. Please enlighten me.'

But as Lucas complied and started to lay out the complex history of the Midwinter spies, Rebecca

found that her most difficult task lay not in learning
but in concentrating on the information he was im-
parting rather than on Lucas himself.

When Lucas came down for dinner that evening he
found Rebecca already ensconced in the drawing
room, dressed in a scandalously attractive gown of
aquamarine crepe that seemed to hint at every curve
of her figure without doing anything so vulgar as making them obvious. Making a mental note that Rachel
Newlyn had done her job rather too well for his peace
of mind, Lucas took a glass of wine and, rather than
joining Rebecca, went across to the window alcove,
the better to observe her. She was sitting with Stephen
on one side of her and Rachel on the other and, for
the first time since she had arrived in Grosvenor
Square, she looked happy and at ease. Stephen, for his
part, was clearly smitten. There was an eager light in
his eyes and his ears were bright pink with excitement
as he exerted himself to entertain Rebecca. Lucas was
obliged to admit that Rebecca looked flatteringly
pleased with his company, encouraging his conversation with exactly the right degree of friendliness without flirtation. It was very different from the wary dislike in which she held him. Lucas felt a violent surge
of envy towards his younger brother, which both
amazed and disconcerted him. It was not so much the
fact that he had never been possessive of a woman
before, for he had already established that Rebecca
Raleigh could do things to him that no one else was
capable of doing. What shocked him more was that
Stephen, whose innocuous admiration of Rebecca was

so very innocent, should be the victim of his own indiscriminate jealousy.

'Rachel has played Pygmalion very successfully, has she not?' Cory Newlyn said in his ear. 'Miss Raleigh looks every inch the ducal cousin. Not,' Cory added thoughtfully, 'that a great deal of work was required in the transformation. Miss Raleigh has a certain natural assurance.'

'Yes,' Lucas said. He had been giving some thought to Rebecca's antecedents, based on the meagre information that she had given him and the poise she had unexpectedly shown. 'Her father was in the army. I wonder... If he was a commissioned officer and the son of a gentleman, then there may once have been family money.'

'She has not told you?' Cory asked.

'Miss Raleigh would not willingly tell me anything now,' Lucas said, with an expressive lift of his brows.

Cory smiled broadly. 'Ah. You have your work cut out, then.'

Lucas watched as Stephen offered Rebecca his arm into dinner and she laughingly accepted. She glanced across at him and their eyes met, the brimming laughter in hers dying away and being replaced by a chill edge. Had it only been that morning that he had arrogantly thought he did not wish for the responsibility of seeing love for him reflected in Rebecca's eyes? He would have given a great deal already to see that cold disdain replaced by something warmer. He thought he had not wanted her love. Now that he had her anger instead, he realised how empty it made him feel.

* * *

Dinner felt like a huge test. Rebecca had not experienced such a long and formal meal for years and was obliged to dredge up every memory of etiquette that she had ever possessed to get her through the meal without mishap. She knew that everyone was watching her; Justin and the Newlyns were assessing how well she could carry off the role of the duke's cousin, whilst Lucas's eyes were upon her frequently and he attended to her every need with disquieting promptitude. It put Rebecca on her mettle and she carried off the evening with the gracious authority of a duchess. Only Stephen's shy admiration and Rachel's friendship helped to ease the situation, and by the time that the ladies had withdrawn and tea had been taken, she was utterly exhausted. When she went up to bed she had no time to dwell on the extraordinary developments of the day, but, rather to her surprise, succumbed immediately to a deep and dreamless sleep.

Downstairs in the Duke of Kestrel's study, Justin and Lucas were sharing a nightcap and a desultory game of chess.

'I have not yet had chance to ask how you fared at the Archangel Club this morning,' Lucas commented. 'Any progress?'

Justin grimaced. 'Very little. I had a glass of very fine port with that unpleasant fellow, Fremantle. He offered me membership of the Club, but declined to tell me the names of any other members. So we have no notion for whom Miss Raleigh's parcel was destined.' He frowned. 'Miss Raleigh puzzles me, Lucas. She shows remarkable confidence for one not raised in this style of environment. And I have never yet met a woman who insisted on frugality in her dress! She is a rare enigma.'

Lucas smiled ruefully. He had already observed how much detail of her childhood and upbringing Rebecca had chosen not to tell him.

'I was watching her at dinner,' he said. 'Such assurance comes only with a privileged background.'

'I doubt that your scrutiny was as objective as mine,' Justin said drily, 'but I agree with your conclusions. What did she tell you of her family?'

'Very little,' Lucas said. 'Apparently she grew up in Somerset. Her father was an army man who died in India and after that her mother fell into a decline. There was no money, so Rebecca went to live with relatives who had a trade.'

Justin was frowning. 'It is a curious story.' He broke off, deep in thought, then turned his head sharply to look at his brother. 'What do you think, Luc?'

Lucas sighed. 'I think,' he said carefully, 'that everything that Rebecca has told me is true but that for reasons of her own she has omitted some of the facts.'

'And the reason for that omission?'

'The same reason that prompted her nervousness this morning,' Lucas said. 'She is protecting her brother.'

'The mysterious Daniel Raleigh,' Justin said, as there was a quiet knock at the door. 'When you told me about him this morning, I instructed Bradshaw to make a few enquiries. Unless I miss my guess, that will be him now.'

Sure enough, it was Tom Bradshaw who slipped

into the room. Both Justin and Lucas looked at him expectantly.

'There is no Daniel Raleigh on the Navy List, your Grace,' Bradshaw said.

Justin looked expressively at Lucas. Lucas sighed. 'Somehow I did not expect that there would be.'

'He could be a merchant sailor,' Justin pointed out, toying with his brandy glass. 'Which ship did Miss Raleigh say that her brother sailed on?'

'She claimed not to know,' Lucas said.

'And you do not believe her.'

Lucas shifted. He disliked speaking of Rebecca like this when all his instincts told him that she was fundamentally honest. Her silence spoke of family loyalty rather than treachery, but even so it frustrated him that she would not tell him the truth. He drained his brandy glass, acknowledging to himself that it was in fact a miracle that Rebecca told him anything at all when he had treated her so badly.

'I trust everything that Rebecca has told us, with the exception of the information about her brother,' he said tentatively. 'I do not believe her to have been in the confidence of the Midwinter spies, I do not think her uncle was aware of the nature of the work he was undertaking and I trust Rebecca to do everything in her power to assist us. But in this…' He shook his head. 'She is keeping secrets. She knows which ship her brother sails on, but she is trying to safeguard him.'

Justin tilted his head thoughtfully. 'Why would she do that?'

'I have no notion. Or rather,' Lucas corrected himself, 'I have an idea but no proof.'

Justin looked at him. 'Construe.'

'I think,' Lucas said slowly, 'that Daniel Raleigh is involved in something illegal. His sister knows it and wishes to keep the truth from us.'

'Something to do with the engravings and the spy?'

'I doubt it. On that score I think Rebecca is all she seems.' Lucas stared into the fire. 'When I was questioning her this morning, she was very cool and composed, because she knew she was innocent and was telling the entire truth. But when I found the letter from her brother she became very agitated. It was the only time during the interview that she appeared shaken. She also pretended to know nothing of his whereabouts.' Lucas smiled with betraying tenderness. 'She is a poor liar, for she is not practised at it. She gave herself away many times over.'

'Perhaps he is a petty criminal and Miss Raleigh is simply worried that we will find him,' Justin suggested.

Lucas shook his head. 'He is definitely at sea. That much is true. The sea features prominently in many of Rebecca's engravings—anchors, seagulls, sailing ships… There is a most beautiful vase on the windowsill of her studio with a picture of a privateer ship. It is exquisite—' He broke off as Tom Bradshaw gave an exclamation. 'What is it, Bradshaw?'

'A privateer, my lord,' Bradshaw said excitedly. He grabbed his pencil and scribbled a few names. 'Raleigh, Drake, Hawkins…'

'Is this some kind of guessing game?' Justin enquired drily.

'No, your Grace.' Bradshaw pointed his pencil at Lucas. 'Lord Lucas mentioned privateers and I thought of Raleigh and Drake.'

'A little harsh,' Lucas said. 'I am sure our brother Richard would defend them as great, patriotic sailors rather than pirates.'

'Indeed, my lord,' Bradshaw said. 'The point that I was trying to make was that Daniel Raleigh does not exist amongst the ranks of his Majesty's Navy, but he may well exist as a different sort of sailor—a privateer—and one who may not even be called Raleigh...'

There was a silence.

'That is very ingenious, Bradshaw,' Justin admitted. 'I can see why Lord Newlyn values your code-breaking skills so highly. You think outside the normal span of things.'

Bradshaw shrugged self-deprecatingly. 'It is merely a thought, my lord, and one that could be quite mistaken, but I can explore the possibility. I will start with Miss Raleigh's uncle, George Provost, and see if I may discover more about the family.'

'How long will it take you to find out?' Lucas asked.

Bradshaw scratched his head. 'Two days, three maybe, my lord, if the information is hard to find.'

'Then you had best bring your results to us at Midwinter,' Justin said, 'for we travel there tomorrow.'

'There is one more thing that you might like to look into, Bradshaw,' Lucas said slowly. 'On the windows-ill in Miss Raleigh's workshop is a magnificent vase with a family motto engraved on it. *Celer et Audax.* Swift and bold.' He sighed. 'It may well be that if you find the family to whom the motto belongs, you have found Miss Raleigh's rightful ancestry and the identity of her brother. I leave it to you.'

Bradshaw bowed and went out and Justin Kestrel turned his thoughtful, dark gaze upon his brother.

'A useful piece of information,' he commented. 'Tell me, Luc, how stands your current relationship with Miss Raleigh?'

'Poorly.' Lucas was betrayed into a rueful smile. 'She will have none of my suit.'

'Hmm.' Justin moved a chess piece with precision on its marbled board. 'And how do you think that our enquiries into Miss Raleigh's identity will affect that?'

'I imagine it will make an already parlous situation ten times worse,' Lucas said crisply. 'However, I would rather know the whole truth than be left with any uncertainty. Besides, I shall persuade Rebecca to accept me in the end.'

'You sound very certain,' Justin said, with a twitch of the lips.

'I am,' Lucas agreed. He looked at his brother. 'She is my match in every way and now, having found her, I shall never let her go.'

The journey to Midwinter, in the Duke of Kestrel's second-best carriage, the first being out of commission for repairs to the upholstery, seemed long and arduous to Rebecca.

The weather had turned colder, with a clinging fog that made progress slow. Justin Kestrel had elected to ride, but Lucas had chosen to accompany her in the carriage, much to Rebecca's annoyance. She wished that he would not persist in speaking to her when she had made it clear that she wanted nothing to do with him. Throughout the journey he had been quick and unobtrusive in attending to her comfort. There had been rugs and hot bricks to warm her feet, food and drink at the hostelries. Every so often he would point out something of interest on the road—a stately home behind high gates, or a model village, or a curious inn sign swinging in the breeze. Lucas was knowledgeable and interesting and, little by little, Rebecca found herself unbending towards him and chatting with animation, only to fall silent when she remembered once again that she did not like him and was determined not to fall for his charm a second time. Instead she fell asleep, waking a little stiff and totally mortified to find herself with her head on Lucas's shoulder and his arm gently holding her to him.

Despite her reticence, when she saw the sea for the first time in sixteen years, Rebecca could not help but give a little exclamation of excitement. It was late in the afternoon by now and the dusk was starting to fall. The mist that had dogged their journey had lifted and, beyond the high hedges and lofty pines, she saw the glimmer of silver on the horizon. The carriage had slowed now and was trundling down a sandy track. Rebecca found herself sitting forward and searching for glimpses of the sea that ran like a pale-blue ribbon beyond the trees.

'Oh! It is so beautiful, my lord.' She turned spontaneously to Lucas. 'I had no notion that Suffolk was so pretty a county. I thought it flat and empty...'

'It is both of those things,' Lucas said, smiling at her enthusiasm, 'but in a very beautiful way. When you stand on the seashore the sky seems huge, like a great dome above one's head. But you must have seen the sea before,' he added, 'for so much of your engraving contains the imagery of ships and seabirds.'

Rebecca felt surprised that he had noticed. 'I... Yes, we lived near the sea when I was a child,' she said.

'In Somerset?'

'Yes. At Watchet, on the north Somerset coast. But it is many years now since I have been to the seaside.' She remembered that it had been part of Lucas's job to observe her and to notice things like the images on her engraving, and her spirits dulled a little. She had to remember that this was no holiday, but a business trip with a serious purpose. When she had fulfilled her part of the bargain she would be away back to Clerkenwell. In the meantime she would do well to give Lucas as little information as possible, not for her own sake, but for Daniel's. Never had she been in a position to do him more harm than she was at this moment.

'That road takes you to Midwinter Royal,' Lucas said, pointing to a track that peeled away through the woods. 'Rachel and Cory will be staying there with Rachel's parents. And this...'

The carriage swung through resplendent wrought-iron gates. 'This is Kestrel Court,' Lucas said. 'Welcome to Midwinter, Miss Raleigh.'

The drive was a long one between stands of tall limes interspersed with the dark green of oak. The parkland beyond looked verdant in the dusk. Beyond the high wall to the east, Rebecca could see the roof of a smaller building, a miniature manor house.

'Saltires,' Lucas said, following her gaze. 'That is the dower house to the Court and currently home of Lady Sally Saltire.'

Rebecca remembered the brief summary that he had given her of the Midwinter villages and their occupants.

'Lady Sally, whose husband was a great friend to your brother the Duke?'

'That is correct.' Lucas's gaze rested on the quaint beamed exterior of the manor. 'Justin gave the lease on the house to Stephen Saltire after he and Lady Sally were married. She was widowed eight years ago and Justin has held a candle for her ever since.'

Rebecca was startled. The Duke of Kestrel seemed too self-contained a man to suffer the pangs of unrequited love. She felt a certain curiosity to meet the woman who could have so profound an effect on such a formidable man.

Kestrel Court came into view now at the end of the lime avenue. It was a beautifully proportioned building, tall, classical and elegant.

'It is one of Justin's smaller properties,' Lucas said, and Rebecca laughed. If anything was going to remind her of how far she had stepped out of her class in undertaking this venture, it was this opulent world. Once she had lived on the edges of it, but that had been a very long time ago. She felt as though a whole lifetime had passed between then and now.

The carriage stopped at the edge of a flight of shallow steps and Lucas helped her down himself, escorting her up to the door and into the entrance hall. A glass cupola scattered light across the stone floor. A wide iron staircase climbed to the first floor. It was very beautiful and really rather frightening. Rebecca's hand tightened unconsciously on Lucas's arm and he gave her a reassuring smile.

'You will find it easy to take your place in Midwinter society, Rebecca. You have already shown great self-assurance.'

A maid showed her up the broad flight of stairs to a well-appointed room on the second floor. Rebecca stood by the window, one hand resting on the thick pale-blue velvet curtains, and looked out across the formal gardens, over the roof of the dower house of Saltires, which looked positively diminutive beside its grander neighbour, and out to the sweep of Kestrel Bay. The sun was a great red orb sinking fast into the ocean, and opposite it a tiny sliver of moon climbed into the darkening sky. Rebecca stood still and watched as a pale smudge on the horizon seemed to draw closer and take shape before her eyes; a schooner, its tall masts dark against the inky horizon, its white sails furled. It glided across Kestrel Bay, the sea carved into ripples by its wake, and then it slipped stealthily from her sight beyond the curve of the shore.

Rebecca sighed. Never had she felt closer to Daniel and never had she felt more alone. A part of her cried out to Lucas. She wanted the comfort and the protection of his arms. She wanted to tell him the whole truth, but she could not.

She stepped back and drew the curtain against the approaching night.

Chapter Nine

'Welcome to Midwinter, Miss Raleigh,' Lady Sally Saltire said, her green eyes sparkling as she shook Rebecca warmly by the hand. 'Curious, but I had thought I knew every relative that Justin possessed!' Her speculative gaze moved from Rebecca to the tall figure of the Duke of Kestrel, who was chatting to Lady Benedict across the other side of the ballroom.

'Nevertheless, it is a pleasure to make your acquaintance,' Lady Sally continued. 'We are always delighted to have new company in the Midwinter villages.'

'Thank you, Lady Sally.' Rebecca was quite dazzled by their hostess, who had drawn her away from Lucas's protective presence with a skill that argued great social aplomb. Lucas was currently standing some twenty feet away and looking as though he did not quite dare step in to rescue her. Rebecca found it rather amusing that Lady Sally Saltire appeared to have all the Kestrel brothers neatly under control.

Lady Sally had followed the direction of her gaze

and was now eyeing Lucas's impatient figure with interest.

'It seems to me, Miss Raleigh, that Lord Lucas Kestrel is another who has been delighted to be reacquainted with his cousin,' she observed. 'He looks as though he would much prefer a closer relationship with you, however. He has scarce strayed from your side since you all arrived. His interest is most conspicuous.'

Rebecca found herself blushing and was surprised and vexed. She knew she would never be able to carry off her role if she was so conscious of Lucas's presence. Yet it was difficult not to be aware of him. Over the last few days they had driven out together several times, attended the assembly in Woodbridge, joined a picnic of Lady Benedict's devising and generally drawn as much attention to themselves as possible. It had been part of the plan to involve Rebecca in Midwinter society as quickly as possible, but it had also thrown her into Lucas's company almost all the time, and he had been quick to take advantage of their proximity.

Rebecca had found herself enjoying his company far too much for her own comfort, taking pleasure from his conversation and easy companionship. Yet beneath Lucas's measured courtship ran other feelings that could not be ignored. Dangerously, she felt as though she was starting to like as well as to love him. Slowly but surely, she was being drawn into an intimacy she could not avoid, did not want to avoid. The protectiveness that Lucas showed towards her was both tender and terrifying. It made her want him all

the more. Worse, he never touched her other than to
hand her into the carriage, or accompany her in the
dance, and conversely, Rebecca found herself desperately wanting him to take her in his arms. She ached
with the memory of his lovemaking. It broke her sleep
and left her trembling to remember the feelings he had
evoked. And she knew that Lucas could sense how
she felt, for often she caught him watching her and
saw the flash of desire in his eyes, desire held under
supremely tight control, that left her shaken and longing for his touch.

Lady Sally eyed her high colour shrewdly. 'I beg
your pardon for mentioning it, but perhaps you are not
indifferent to his admiration, Miss Raleigh? One must
congratulate you, for I always thought Lord Lucas the
most dangerous of the Kestrel brothers because he appeared never to have a heart to lose…'

'Well, he need not lose his heart to me,' Rebecca
said, giving herself a mental shake and assuming the
role of the indifferent object of Lucas's affections. 'I
have no desire to be the subject of Lord Lucas's rakish
attentions.'

'You disapprove of rakes, Miss Raleigh?' Lady
Sally said, smiling. 'Many ladies deplore them—
whilst secretly hoping, of course, to be seduced by
one!'

Rebecca stifled a laugh. 'If Lord Lucas wishes to
behave like a rake then that is, of course, his own
concern,' she said, 'as long as he does not seek to
practise on me. I am not susceptible to his charm since
I was betrothed to another.'

'I heard that you buried your heart along with your

fiancé,' Lady Sally said sympathetically. She touched Rebecca's hand. 'I feel for you, my dear Miss Raleigh. However, you may find that Lord Lucas's regard is the very balm that you need for your wounded feelings.'

'I suppose that he is considered quite a catch,' Rebecca said, watching as Miss Chloe Ducheyne from Woodbridge artlessly drew Lucas's attention and inveigled him into private conversation.

'I assure you, Miss Raleigh, that ladies would wade across the Winter Race for a chance to engage Lord Lucas's interest,' Lady Sally said, and they laughed together.

'I hope that you will join my reading group whilst you are staying with us?' she added. 'It is rather fun, although you may find it another opportunity for the Midwinter quizzes like myself to question you shamelessly about your cousin.'

Rachel Newlyn had already told Rebecca all about Lady Sally's reading circle and Lucas had encouraged her to take part if invited, pointing out that it was the ideal way to mingle with the ladies of Midwinter. Rebecca was not averse, for she had taken a liking to Lady Sally and thought that the chance to read and discuss books would be rather a novel and exciting luxury for her.

'You are no quiz, Lady Sally,' she said, laughing, 'but, yes, I should be delighted to attend the meeting of the reading group.'

'Capital!' Lady Sally said, smiling broadly. 'We are currently studying *The History of Miss Harriot Montague*. Are you acquainted with it, Miss Raleigh?'

'I fear not,' Rebecca said. 'Is it a morality tale?'

'Of a kind.' Lady Sally flicked her fan. Her eyes were amused. 'Truth to tell, it is an improbable story of a prosy girl who suffers endless hardships and conquers them all through her virtue. I find it dull, but the more impressionable ladies in the group enjoy the drama. I will lend you my spare copy and you may tell us what you make of it, Miss Raleigh. A fresh opinion is always welcome.'

The Duke of Kestrel was approaching and Lady Sally turned to him with a swish of green silk. 'Justin, my dear! I was telling your charming cousin that we will look forward to her attending the next meeting of the reading group.'

'Splendid,' Justin Kestrel said. He smiled at Rebecca, but she noticed that his gaze warmed still further as it returned to Lady Sally's piquant face.

'May I claim your hand for the quadrille, Sally?' he asked smoothly.

'Certainly you may,' Lady Sally said, throwing him a sparkling glance. 'I think I half-promised it to Mr Lang, but will gladly allow you to pull rank, Justin!'

'I do believe that my brother is intending to ask you for this dance, Rebecca,' Justin Kestrel said, offering Lady Sally his arm. 'Do you think that you could try to be kind to him just this once?'

'I fear not, your Grace,' Rebecca said sweetly. 'I should not like to give him false hope.'

'So cruel,' Justin said, shaking his head ruefully.

'And so wonderful to see Lucas hoist by his own petard,' Lady Sally said cheerfully. 'Bravo, Miss Raleigh!'

Left on her own, Rebecca took the opportunity to study the rest of Lady Sally's guests and see if her own impressions matched the descriptions that she had been given by Lucas. Miss Lang and Miss Ducheyne were both young, flighty and utterly over-excited by the fashionable company in which they found themselves. Rebecca thought it likely that Miss Ducheyne might spontaneously combust if she smouldered any harder in Lucas's direction. The sight of the girl hanging on Lucas's arm should have amused her but it did not, so she turned away and studiously considered the other guests. Miss Lang's brother Caspar, whom Lady Sally had just snubbed in order to stand up with the Duke, was a young man with a very good opinion of himself. Sir John Norton likewise, although he was not such a young man and rather florid, running to fat. He was paying a great deal of attention to Lily, Lady Benedict, whom Lucas had said was an old school friend of Lady Sally. Despite Sir John's fulsome interest it seemed that Lady Benedict would have preferred the compliments of Cory Newlyn, who was so wrapped up in his wife that he scarcely noticed her... Rebecca sighed, wondering why it was that the unobtainable was so attractive.

Lucas, meanwhile, seemed quite content to stay by Miss Ducheyne's side rather than claim his supposed cousin for a dance. Rebecca found herself trying to look at him objectively. By anyone's standards he was a good-looking man, and within Lady Sally's glittering and sophisticated social circle he appeared carelessly confident and at ease. Rebecca had never been shy herself, but she had found stepping into this rank of society to be quite a difficult task. Lucas's casual assurance made her feel unsophisticated and out of her depth.

'Miss Raleigh?' Sir John Norton was at her elbow, claiming her attention. He smiled at her with an unpleasantly speculative twinkle in his eye. 'If you are not engaged for the next, I should be honoured were you to promise it to me.'

Rebecca smiled, though her heart was not in it. 'Thank you, Sir John, I should be delighted—'

'Have you forgotten that that honour has already been granted to me, Rebecca?' Lucas drawled, materializing at her side. 'I should be desolated if you preferred Sir John's company over mine!'

'On the contrary,' Rebecca said coolly, 'I thought you very well consoled by Miss Ducheyne, Lucas. Besides, surely cousins do not need to stand on ceremony with each other if there is an offer more attractive?'

Sir John Norton smirked. 'You heard the lady, Kestrel!'

There was a spark of devilment in Lucas's gaze as his eyes rested on Rebecca's face. She felt a shiver of anticipation along her nerves as he smoothly took up her challenge.

'I did indeed,' he murmured. 'However, you and I know, Sir John, that a lady will often say quite the reverse of what she is thinking in order to make her erstwhile suitor all the more devoted.'

'You delude yourself, Lucas,' Rebecca said sweetly. 'Or perhaps it is your conceit that deceives you. You certainly have enough of it. Enough for two men, in fact!'

Lucas's smile held a wicked glint. 'My dear Rebecca, why pretend? You know you are not indifferent to me!'

'I believe that we were discussing Sir John's invitation to dance, rather than my feelings or lack of them,' Rebecca said sharply. She turned to Norton. 'I fear that we have already missed this opportunity, Sir John, but I should be delighted to dance with you later in the evening. The country dance after supper, perhaps?'

Sir John shot Lucas an unsubtle look of triumph. 'Enchanted, Miss Raleigh,' he murmured. 'Perhaps you would also like to drive with me one day next week? I could show you my yacht—'

'That would be splendid,' Rebecca said hastily, as Lucas looked as though he were about to make an abrasive remark. 'Thank you, Sir John.'

Sir John took her hand and kissed it gallantly, allowing his lips to dwell rather too long. Rebecca was sincerely glad that she was wearing gloves.

'Your cousin will soon tire of your attentions if you are so pressing, Kestrel,' Sir John said with a sneer as he released her. 'Not your usual style, eh?'

Lucas took Rebecca's hand and tucked it through his arm in a gesture of possession. 'Where my cousin is concerned I do not conform to my usual mode of behaviour,' he said smoothly.

'Nor, indeed, to any style at all,' Rebecca added.

Sir John gave a crack of laughter and strolled away, pleased with himself, and Lucas held on to Rebecca a little tighter.

'Rebecca, my sweet,' he said in an undertone, 'if

you wish to cross swords with me I suggest that you do so in private in future, or you may find yourself in the most compromising position of being kissed in a ballroom full of people!'

Rebecca tried to draw her hand away, but he held her firmly.

'I was merely trying to add a little colour to our supposed relationship,' she said coolly. 'I am sorry you did not care for it.'

Lucas was looking dangerous. 'Two can play at that game,' he said. He put an arm about her waist in a hard grip and drew her towards the window embrasure. The alcove afforded some privacy from the curious gaze of Lady Sally's guests, but Lucas's highhanded behaviour did not go unnoticed. A little ripple of scandalous excitement fluttered through the ranks of the assembled ladies as they watched him.

'If you wish to lend colour to the deception, I am at your service,' Lucas said. He had not released Rebecca, but stood with his back blocking the ballroom from view. Rebecca felt breathless and slightly nervous, a reaction that was only heightened by the unrelenting grip of his fingers about her wrist. He moved closer, until his body just brushed against hers.

'I shall match you step for step and the money will be on me to overcome your scruples and make you my bride.'

Rebecca caught her breath. Although he was referring to the show they were putting on for society, his words echoed precisely their own, secret situation. Lucas had sworn that she would accept his declaration and she had rejected him out of hand. Yet with each day that passed her will to oppose him grew weaker, and now, with the insistent pressure of his body against hers, she felt utterly incapable of resistance.

'You are mine, Rebecca,' Lucas said. 'Do you think that if I cannot have you I would permit anyone else to even touch you?'

Rebecca gave a gasp at the undisguised intimacy in his voice. 'Permit?' she said. 'You presume too much, Lord Lucas. It is scarcely your place to permit or forbid.'

'By all means believe that if you wish.'

Rebecca's eyes narrowed. 'You do not have the right to dictate my behaviour!'

'Whilst you are in Midwinter you are my responsibility.'

'I can take care of myself; once this is all over, we shall not meet again.'

They were standing stiffly now, like combatants. Lucas caught her wrist and jerked her close to him, so close that she could feel the staccato beat of his heart against the bodice of her gown.

'I will not let you go,' he said softly.

Rebecca was trapped by the look in his eyes. It spoke of possession and demand, and it heated her blood with sparks of fire. The ballroom, the guests, the curious glances cast their way…all were as nothing compared to the raw claim that Lucas was staking to her.

'Lucas,' Justin Kestrel said from beside them, and his voice cracked like a whip, 'I am persuaded that you would not wish to draw any further attention to Miss Raleigh in such a public place.'

They both jumped and Lucas released Rebecca's wrist.

'I beg your pardon,' he said. His gaze still smouldered. He backed away and sketched a bow. 'You will excuse me. I shall be better off in the card room.'

Justin Kestrel offered Rebecca his arm. 'I believe,' he said smoothly, 'that Lucas is finding the experience of unrequited love more trying than he had imagined, Miss Raleigh.'

'I am also finding it rather difficult, your Grace,' Rebecca retorted, trying to quell her shaking.

Justin laughed. 'Lucas can be very determined when he wants something sufficiently.'

'As can I,' Rebecca said. 'I have not forgotten that once my stay here is complete I shall be returning home.'

She had not forgotten, but she was finding it increasingly difficult. The more time that passed the easier it seemed to believe that she belonged here and, worse, that she belonged with Lucas. She had to hold on to the truth at all costs, and the truth did not include a future with Lord Lucas Kestrel. It was as simple as that.

'So, Miss Raleigh,' Lady Sally said, 'what do you think of *The History of Miss Harriot Montague?*'

The eyes of the reading group were fixed on Rebecca. It made her a little nervous. Although Rachel Newlyn and Olivia Marney had both been extremely friendly to her, Chloe Ducheyne and Helena Lang were, as far as Rebecca could tell, gossiping quizzes in the making, and Lily Benedict was without a doubt the most spiteful creature that Rebecca had ever had the misfortune to meet. She clutched the handsome brown morocco edition in her hand and tried not to feel as though she were back in the schoolroom.

'I find it improbable,' she said. 'So many abductions and kidnappings, and adventures and pirates! I doubt that anyone could survive so much excitement.'

'I fear you are of distressingly practical disposition, Miss Raleigh,' Lily Benedict said, smiling her feline smile and regarding Rebecca through half-closed eyes. 'I suppose you do not believe that such brigands truly exist?'

'I am sure that they do,' Rebecca said crisply, 'but that they are nowhere near as romantic as the heroes of literature.'

Lily Benedict gave a tinkle of laughter. 'I am certain that no dyed-in-the-wool villains could withstand your sternness, Miss Raleigh. They would wither beneath your pitiless regard!'

'Surely Miss Raleigh's point is correct,' Rachel Newlyn interposed. 'In literature one may allow one's imagination full reign, whereas in life—'

'In life one never gets swept off one's feet by a handsome hero!' Lily Benedict said. She tittered. 'Oh, but of course that was exactly what happened to you, Lady Newlyn! I forgot! And to Miss Raleigh herself, if Lord Lucas Kestrel has his way! Will he have his way with you, Miss Raleigh?'

There was a sharp intake of breath around the circle. Some, such as Rachel and Olivia Marney, were looking disapproving of Lily Benedict's blatant malice. Others were looking intrigued.

'I have a very cousinly regard for Lord Lucas, Lady Benedict,' Rebecca said. 'However, I assure you that it is no more than that.'

'You looked extremely close, if not cousinly, at Lady Sally's ball,' Lily Benedict said. 'And I must confess that it is difficult to see Lord Lucas as anything other than a very attractive man.'

'Even attractive men have mothers, sisters—and cousins,' Rebecca said drily.

'Lily,' Lady Sally interrupted, 'much as I enjoy a good gossip, I do believe we are here to discuss Miss Harriot Mon-tague's romantic trials and tribulations rather than those of anyone else.'

Lily Benedict waved one white hand dismissively. 'I merely ask what everyone else wishes to know, Sally—is Lord Lucas Kestrel caught in a parson's mousetrap? If so, it would be a good joke for the man who has broken half the hearts in London!'

'You exaggerate, Lily,' Lady Sally said calmly.

'I beg your pardon. A quarter of the hearts in London, then.'

'That woman is as unpleasant a creature as one could ever find,' Rebecca fumed as she and Rachel walked back to Kestrel Court after the meeting of the reading group. 'I cannot believe that we are engaged to dine at Midwinter Bere this evening! Justin and Lucas seemed anxious to fulfill the obligation, whereas I fear every morsel of food will stick in my throat!'

Rachel nodded sympathetically. 'It is only because they hope for the opportunity to search Midwinter Bere house,' she pointed out. 'Lady Benedict rarely entertains because her husband is an invalid, and since

Sir John Norton does not appear to have the engravings in his possession, suspicion inevitably falls on her.'

'The idea is foolish,' Rebecca said shortly. 'What, is Lady Benedict to entertain us to dinner with her engraved crystal sitting on the table? Surely even she would not be so arrogant as to parade it when she must know she is under suspicion?'

Rachel grimaced. 'She is intolerably proud and it may well be that arrogance that brings her down.'

Rebecca kicked in vicious and unladylike fashion at a pile of autumn leaves drifting down from the bank. 'It cannot be too soon for me!'

Rachel smiled and tied the ribbons of her bonnet more securely beneath her chin. 'You seem most put out by Lady Benedict's spite, Rebecca,' she observed. 'I know that she is a wicked scandalmonger, but I wonder whether her barbs have upset you because they have so much truth in them?'

Rebecca cast her a sideways glance. There was nothing but concern in Rachel's face; none of the curiosity that she had encountered from the ladies of Midwinter, none of the envious speculation.

'I am sorry,' she said, with difficulty. 'You have been the kindest of friends to me, Rachel, and I know that I am very bad at confiding.'

Rachel gave a little elegant wave of the hand. 'You need confide nothing if you do not wish, Rebecca. Once before I said that I would stand your friend if you needed me; I merely wanted you to know that the offer still stands.'

Rebecca nodded. 'Thank you, Rachel. You are most

kind.' She sighed. 'I suppose I *am* a little liverish because I am finding it difficult to remember that I dislike Lucas Kestrel. He is very good at making me forget it.'

Rachel laughed. 'Oh, dear—must you keep reminding yourself?'

'I think so,' Rebecca said. 'He did deceive me.'

'And has been most sincerely repentant on the subject.'

'And I am supposed to be spurning his advances.'

'As part of a pretence, perhaps, but in real life?' Rachel frowned. 'If you like Lucas, Rebecca—if you can forgive him—I would suggest that you give him a chance to redeem himself. It is a melancholy thing to punish both of you when you might be happier together.'

Rebecca clasped her gloved fingers together tightly. 'It is not so simple, Rachel. I love Lucas. I loved him even when I was angry with him. In fact…' Rebecca hesitated '…I was probably so angry because I loved him so much, if that makes sense.'

'Perfect sense,' Rachel said sagely. 'I see. You love Lucas, but you are not certain if he loves you too.'

Rebecca shrugged dispiritedly. 'I know that there are those who hold that love is not essential for marriage, but I am not amongst them.'

'Nor I,' Rachel said. 'It is a melancholy thing to settle for second best.'

'So I believe,' Rebecca said. 'Which is why it is easier for me to keep Lucas at arm's length.'

Rachel looked unconvinced. 'I do believe that Lucas

cares for you a great deal, Rebecca. One only requires
to watch him with you to realise that.'

Rebecca blushed. 'Liking and wanting someone are
different from loving them, Rachel.'

'I understand that. What I am unsure of is whether
Lucas does.' Rachel glanced quickly at Rebecca.
'Please do not misunderstand me. Lucas has not confided in either Cory or myself. Having known him for
a little, however, I would say that he has been caught
off guard by his feelings for you, Rebecca, and may
not yet have realised quite how important they are.
Men,' Rachel said, with a little sigh, 'can be rather
slow in recognising these matters.'

They had reached the place where the path to Midwinter Royal split from that to Kestrel Court.

'I will not come back for a cup of tea,' Rachel said,
'for Mama is expecting me back to help catalogue
some artifacts she has found in the burial field. We
shall see you tonight at Lady Benedict's dinner, Rachel.'

Dinner at Midwinter Bere was every bit as bad as
Rebecca had anticipated it would be. Lily Benedict
had elected to place Justin Kestrel on her right and
Lucas on her left, putting Rebecca at the very bottom
of the table between her husband and John Norton. It
was extremely unusual for Sir Edgar Benedict to be
present at any social occasion and he sat in his Bath
chair, a huddled figure smelling strongly of old, musty
clothes and cloying illness, and said not a single word.
Occasionally his hooded gaze would sweep the assembled throng like a malignant crow until he would bend

his head over his food once again, speaking only to the assiduous servant who was by his side throughout.

That left Rebecca to the tender mercies of Sir John Norton, who seemed delighted to be squiring her for the evening and told her many, protracted tales of his Arctic exploration and his sailing prowess. Rebecca listened and smiled in all the right places and noted that the crystal on the table was very fine, seventeenth-century Dutch workmanship, but that it certainly was not the glass engraved by her uncle for the Midwinter spies.

It was later, when the ladies withdrew after dinner, that she saw something that made her heart leap into her throat and made her wonder whether there was, after all, someone in the Benedict household with a closer connection to her uncle than she had supposed. On a pedestal in the shadowed alcove by the library door was a tall glass vase with an exquisite engraving of a sailing ship on it. It was certainly the work of George Provost's workshop. Rebecca's heart started to race. She could not see the detail of the vase clearly in the dim light, but it roused her curiosity and made her wonder whether there were any other pieces in the house.

She allowed the other ladies to stroll on ahead of her, then slipped unseen into the library. It seemed as good a place as any to start. It was a gloomy chamber that seemed to fit all too well Sir Edgar's melancholy personality, and whilst there were various pieces of sculpture on plinths about the room, there were no other pieces of engraved glass. Rebecca, aware that she could not be missing for too long, heaved a sigh and retraced her steps into the hall. She looked again at the engraved vase. It was most definitely her uncle's work, which meant that someone in the household must have placed a commission for work with George Provost at some time. She had no recollection of it having been made, but that was not extraordinary. In her uncle's heyday the engraving workshop had been inundated with orders.

Deep in thought, Rebecca rounded the corner of the corridor and walked straight into Lucas. He grabbed her above the elbows and held her hard. He looked absolutely furious.

'I have been searching for you everywhere. What the *devil* do you think you are doing, Rebecca?'

Rebecca was stung by his tone. 'What do you think I was doing? I was *trying* to find the engraved glass. I thought that to be the purpose of our visit!'

'You do *not* go off wandering about on your own!' Lucas shook her slightly. 'Good God, Rebecca, have you understood nothing? This is dangerous work!'

Rebecca was shaken by the savage undertone in his voice. 'I am perfectly aware of that, Lucas,' she said, with dignity, 'and I do not think it adds anything to the secrecy of our situation for you to stand upbraiding me in the corridor. Anyone might hear you!'

They stood glaring at one another. There was the sound of a door closing, footsteps, raised voices. Rebecca tried to move away but, quick as a flash, Lucas's arms went around her hard and his mouth came down on hers in a ruthless kiss.

Rebecca could not move, could not break free, and

did not want to. The moment Lucas had touched her she was lost, knowing this was what she had wanted through the long, lonely nights when she had lain alone in her bed, tormented to know that Lucas was so close to her and yet so far away. Her body trembled and went soft with acquiescence and the kiss eased at once. Lucas bit down gently on her full lower lip then rubbed it with the tip of his tongue, teasing, dipping inside her mouth and then retreating. It melted her and made her reach blindly for him. In return he moved his mouth over hers with a thoroughness that had her sighing. She had forgotten about their audience until there was the sound of gentle laughter close at hand and Lady Sally Saltire spoke from out of the shadows.

'I do believe,' she said, and the amusement was clear in her voice, 'that your cousin has overcome her indifference to Lord Lucas, Justin!'

Rebecca jumped as though scalded, but even then Lucas was slow to let her go, releasing her with every sign of reluctance. Justin Kestrel and Lady Sally were standing a mere ten feet away, Lady Sally looking speculative and Justin looking quite blank. Rebecca could not tell whether he approved or not.

Lucas drew her close to his side. It was difficult to resist the reassuring protectiveness of his gesture.

'I wondered,' Justin said in measured tone, 'whether you were ready to depart, Miss Raleigh? It is a shame to cut the evening short, but I think it wise not to tax Sir Edgar's strength too much.'

The journey back to Kestrel Court was conducted in simmering silence. As soon as they were through the door, Lucas murmured an apology to his brother, caught Rebecca's arm and bundled her though the door of the drawing room.

'I do not believe that we had finished our conversation,' he said pleasantly.

'No!' Rebecca spun around. She was feeling edgy and vulnerable. 'You will not use kissing me as…as an excuse for loitering in corridors, Lord Lucas!'

'You were the one who was loitering,' Lucas said, a gleam in his eyes. 'I could not be certain who was about to come across us and needed to provide a good reason as to why we should be standing in the shadows outside Lady Benedict's library.'

'You are inexcusable!'

'I am sorry that you should think that.' Lucas strolled over to the mantelpiece. 'I confess I forgot my original motive within a few seconds. Kissing you was long overdue, Rebecca.'

The tension between them spun out and thickened until it was almost tangible, then Rebecca shook her head impatiently. 'You make me forget… What I really needed to tell you was that Lady Benedict has a glass vase that was engraved by my uncle.'

Lucas's gaze had sharpened. 'You are positive?'

'Certain. There can be no mistake. The style is slightly different from the glasses the spies have been using, but I recognise his work. Someone at Midwinter Bere had commissioned the piece from my uncle.'

Lucas let out a long sigh. 'Yet Bradshaw has searched both Midwinter Bere and Sir John Norton's house and neither has yielded a sign of the glasses.'

'Which leads one to the only conclusion—that the glasses are kept elsewhere.'

Lucas nodded. Unexpectedly he caught her hand. 'Thank you, Rebecca.'

Rebecca was startled. 'For what?'

'For helping us. I understand that there are many reasons why you might not.'

Rebecca tugged gently to free her hand, but he held her tight. He gestured to the sofa.

'Rebecca…I need to speak with you. Will you hear me out?'

After a moment Rebecca sat down. Her heart was hammering and her legs trembling so much she had no choice.

'I know that I deceived you badly over my original motive in coming to your workshop,' Lucas said. 'I hurt you. It was very wrong of me and I regret the way that I behaved.'

'You were doing a job,' Rebecca said. Her throat ached.

Lucas did not take the excuse. He came to sit beside her. 'That is true, but it is no justification. My instinct told me to trust you and I ignored it. That was my mistake.'

Rebecca did not argue the point. She was achingly aware of his presence beside her although he had made no attempt to touch her. He was making it very difficult to resist him. He had made no excuses; made no attempt to deny that he had hurt her very badly. Silence fell and lingered. Lucas put one hand over her clenched ones.

'I would never injure you again, Rebecca. I swear it. I want you to marry me. I want it very much.'

Rebecca shivered. He was watching her intently and

she was almost unbearably aware of his touch on her hand. His softly spoken words were so persuasive.

'I cannot.' The words were wrenched from her.

'You are still angry with me,' Lucas said, watching her. 'I understand that. What happened between us—'

Rebecca made a sharp movement. 'I cannot blame you for that. I asked you to stay. It was my choice.'

Lucas ran one finger in a silken caress along the line of her jaw and tilted her chin to look down into her eyes. His own were smiling. 'I admire your candour, Rebecca, but I cannot let you take that responsibility. I could have refused. Knowing what I did, I should have refused.' His hand lingered against her cheek. 'But I wanted you too. I needed you…'

Admire. Need. Want…

Rebecca closed her eyes for a second. She had asked Lucas to stay with her that night because she had been seeking escape, but she had chosen him because she already loved him. Yet he had never pretended that love was what he was offering her. She met his dark, hungry gaze.

'I love you,' she said with deliberation. 'That is why I cannot marry you. Because I have made enough mistakes and I cannot accept second best.'

She saw the stupefaction in his eyes as he took her words in and for a few endless, fragile seconds she waited, knowing that she was hoping for the words she wanted to hear. They did not come. Lucas got to his feet and took several steps away from her.

'It is not second best.' His voice was rough. 'I *need* you, Rebecca.'

Rebecca shook her head. The disappointment and despair threatened to swamp her. She got to her feet and made blindly for the door. 'No, Lucas...'

He was there in two strides, easily blocking her way. 'Do not fight me, Rebecca. You want me as much as I want you.'

It was true, but Rebecca's mind stubbornly told her that it was not enough. 'You mistake,' she said. 'I want none of this.'

Lucas's face was white with strain. 'Let us see, shall we?'

He kissed her with hunger, need, and a blistering passion that shook her to her soul. She did not know if she was strong enough to withstand this onslaught.

'How much more proof do you need?' he demanded when he released her.

'It proves nothing!' Rebecca said. For a long moment she stared into his eyes. And then she wrenched herself out of his arms and ran away.

Chapter Ten

Lucas stayed quite still for several minutes after the slam of the door had died away. He felt tense and heated and strangely disoriented.

'I want none of this,' Rebecca had said and, although he had proved otherwise in a physical sense, she had still remained obstinately aloof from him. It was as though there was a part of her that he could not reach, a part that stubbornly refused to accept what was between them no matter how he tried to convince her.

Lucas thrust one hand through his hair in a gesture of extreme frustration. He wanted to reach that corner of Rebecca's mind that she withheld from him. He wanted all of her. She was meant to be his. They both knew it. He loved her...

He stopped dead. It was not a conclusion that he had reached logically, by rational thought. It had burst into his head with the sudden explosion of a shower of fireworks and yet he knew without a doubt that it was true. He loved Rebecca Raleigh. He had done so

for a long time. He had been monstrously slow to recognise his own feelings. He was a fool.

There was a knock at the door and Justin stuck his
head around. 'Tom Bradshaw is here, Lucas. Do you
wish to join us in the study?'

For a moment Lucas could not even remember who
Bradshaw was, let alone why he was there. Then he
recollected that they had asked the man to look into
Rebecca's antecedents and in particular to investigate
the motto he had seen on the engraved glasses. At the
time he had felt uncomfortable at this latest, small betrayal. Now he felt it was even more distasteful. He
did not want to know. And yet he had to know. He
had to know everything. He followed Justin slowly out
of the drawing room.

'Well, Bradshaw?' Justin said expectantly, when
they were settled in the study. 'Do you have information for us?'

'Yes, your Grace,' Bradshaw said. He ran a hand
over his hair, looking slightly nervous. 'I apologise for
the delay. It took me longer than I had expected to
find the information you required.'

'Cut the courtesies, Bradshaw,' Lucas said. His
nerves were strung as tight as a bow. 'What is your
news?'

Bradshaw looked at him and Lucas felt a lurch of
fear as he saw the expression in the man's eyes. Justin
was silent.

'My lord—'

'Spit it out.'

'Yes, sir.' Bradshaw cleared his throat. 'The motto,
my lord—'

'*Celer et Audax?*'

'Yes, my lord. Swift and bold. It is the family motto of the Pearce family. The current head of the family is a Sir Gideon Pearce, a country gentleman whose seat is at Bowness in Westmorland.'

Justin looked as blank as Lucas felt. 'Never heard of him.'

'No, your Grace.' Bradshaw shuffled his feet. 'There is no real reason why you should. Sir Gideon lives quietly and, as far as I am aware, there is nothing notable about him at all.'

'And Miss Raleigh is related to this paragon?' Lucas questioned.

'Distantly, my lord. Very distantly.' Bradshaw took a deep breath. 'Bear with me, gentlemen. The Pearces are an old gentry family. During the English Civil War they were split, like many at the time. The father and elder son were for Parliament, but the younger son, Richard Pearce, fought for the King. He went into exile with Charles II after Worcester.'

Bradshaw ran a hand over his hair. 'He met and married a French Huguenot girl whilst he was in exile and changed his name to hers as a sign that he repudiated his father's allegiance and all it stood for. He wrote to his father that the only thing that he was keeping was the family motto because he was the only one who deserved it. His father disinherited him as a result.'

'A man after my own heart,' Lucas said, with a grin.

'Indeed, my lord,' Bradshaw said. His face was still strained. 'Richard Pearce did not return to England after the restoration of King Charles II. Instead he and his wife went to America and became very wealthy and prominent in New York society.' Bradshaw consulted his notes. 'The family supported the British during the Revolutionary Wars, lost all their money and were obliged to flee the country as a result, returning to England nearly thirty years ago. Miss Raleigh's father, James, became a soldier. For a few years his family lived at Poyntz Manor in Somerset.'

'Miss Raleigh told me this. She said that her father was killed in India.' Despite the fact that Bradshaw's tale bore out Rebecca's meagre information about her childhood, Lucas still felt uneasy. There was something that Bradshaw had not yet told them, something bad. He could feel its approach with an inevitability that chilled him.

'He was indeed, my lord. His son Daniel, then fourteen, joined the Navy and his daughter went to London to live with a distant cousin of her mother's.'

'George Provost,' Lucas said thoughtfully.

'That is so. Glass engraving,' Bradshaw added, 'was one of the professions of Miss Raleigh's Huguenot ancestors.'

'It all seems perfectly straightforward and blameless,' Justin said, his eyes narrowed shrewdly, 'so what is it that you have not told us, Bradshaw?'

Bradshaw took a deep breath. 'When Richard Pearce changed the family name in 1652 it was not to Raleigh, your Grace. That is a much more recent fiction. Since the seventeenth century that family name has been De Lancey. Miss Rebecca Raleigh was born Miss Rebecca De Lancey. Her brother is Daniel De Lancey, smuggler, pirate and suspected French spy.'

There was a silence in the Duke of Kestrel's study.

'Good God,' Lucas said softly. He was remembering all the little details that came together to create the
damning whole: the way that Rebecca had told him
the truth of her childhood whilst leaving out the most
important aspect—her name and identity. He thought
of all the images of the sea that lived in her engravings
and decorated her studio, he remembered her panic
when he had found the note and the money from her
brother, and the way she had pretended to know nothing of Daniel De Lancey's ship or current whereabouts. He let his breath go in a long sigh. He was
not sure if he was angry or disappointed or merely
disillusioned, but he knew now that Rebecca had never
completely trusted him and that his hopes that matters
might change between them were based on sand.

'What is Daniel De Lancey's history?' Justin asked
quietly.

'He left the Navy at the age of nineteen, your Grace,
and for a while there was no word of him,' Bradshaw
said quietly. 'He first came to the government's notice
as a privateer some five years ago when he captured
a French ship off Calais. These days he sails the east
coast between Kent and Suffolk. There have been
countless attempts to catch him. All have failed. It is
rumoured he deals in smuggled goods and piracy, and
also that he is a French spy.'

'Is there any foundation to that rumour?' Lucas
questioned sharply. He could not help himself. 'Given
his family's previous loyalties to the Crown, it seems
unlikely.'

Bradshaw shrugged. Lucas could tell that he thought

he was clutching at straws. A privateer sold himself and his services indiscriminate of loyalty.

'With De Lancey there is never anything firmer than rumour, my lord,' he said. 'There is also a tale that he passes information to the Admiralty when it suits his purposes and for that reason they have not tried too hard to catch him of late.'

'That, at least, may be corroborated,' Justin said, reaching for pen and ink. 'I shall send to the Admiralty immediately.'

Lucas rubbed his eyes. The facts were stacking up in his mind like dominoes, one leading inexorably to the next. 'This fits rather too well to be coincidence, does it not?' he said bitterly. 'We have French spies smuggling information abroad. We have a privateer lying off the coast, we have a glass engraver who has provided the cipher and…' he sighed '…now I have brought Daniel De Lancey's sister to Suffolk!'

Justin raised his brows. 'I do not believe you should jump to any conclusions, Luc—' he started, but Lucas cut him off.

'It is not a question of jumping,' he said bitterly, 'more a matter of stumbling blindly over the truth. Miss De Lancey has played me royally for a fool. She and I will have settlement over this. Now.'

He ignored Justin's measured suggestion that he should wait a little as though he had not heard it, and took the stairs to Rebecca's room two at a time. He could hear the low murmur of voices from behind the closed door and when he flung it open without ceremony or even the courtesy of knocking, Rebecca's maid scuttered away like a terrified mouse.

'Lucas?' Rebecca was sitting at her dressing-table. She had already undressed for the night and was in a silky peignoir of a deep plum colour that made her hair look rich and coppery. Lucas looked at her. She looked puzzled and innocent and very, very desirable. His insides twisted.

'Tell me about your brother,' he said. He saw a flicker of bewilderment cross her face—and saw the tiny flicker of fear grow.

'I have told you before—' she began.

'No, you have not,' Lucas said. 'Tell me about Daniel De Lancey.'

Rebecca did not deny anything. She put down her silver-backed hairbrush very slowly and met his eyes in the mirror. 'How did you find out?' she asked.

'Tom Bradshaw has a way of discovering these things.' Lucas had thought his feelings in turmoil, but now he found that he was furiously angry. He gripped her by the shoulder, forcing her to her feet. She yielded with a little gasp.

'Lucas—'

'Were you ever going to tell me?' Lucas demanded.

Her eyelashes flickered down. 'I thought about it.'

'And?'

'And decided probably not. It was not my secret to tell.'

Lucas's hands tightened. 'Do not give me that! This has all been a huge conspiracy from the start, has it not?'

Rebecca's eyes widened with what appeared to be genuine shock. 'I do not know what you mean.'

'Come now! Your uncle did the engraving for the

Midwinter spies,' Lucas spat out. 'Your brother is a privateer, no doubt in the pay of the French. And you—'

'Yes?' Her gaze defied him. 'What about me?'

Lucas let her go with a gesture of repudiation. She stumbled back and almost tripped over the stool. Her vulnerability just made him all the more angry. 'You knew all along, and played me like a fool,' he said.

'Did I?' Rebecca swept away with an angry swish. 'How strange. I thought that it was *you* who deceived *me* in order to gain information from me rather than the other way around.'

'And, in fact, all along it was you who has deceived me to *keep* information from me,' Lucas countered. 'So we are equal, sweetheart.'

Rebecca looked disdainful. 'Oh, no, we are not, my lord! The only reason I omitted to tell you about this was to protect Daniel.'

Lucas strode across to the window, moving with a repressed fury. She seemed so honest and yet he could not be taken in by any more of her lies. Was it only a half-hour before that he had realised he loved her? It felt like a whole century.

'Next you will be telling me that it is mere coincidence that brings you here to Midwinter!' he said bitterly.

'No!' Rebecca's eyes flashed. She drew the peignoir close about her throat and Lucas could see that her hands were shaking. 'It was you who brought me here to Midwinter, Lord Lucas. I did everything in my power to avoid it.'

'Because you did not wish to draw danger to De Lancey?'

'Exactly.' Rebecca stood braced as a bow. 'I am no traitor who schemed with my brother in order to come to Midwinter as part of our treasonable plan, my lord! I told you from the start that I knew nothing of the spies!'

Lucas spun around. 'You told me some things and neglected to tell me many others. Why should I believe you now?'

He saw Rebecca whiten though the look in her eyes was still defiant. 'So you do not trust me,' she said.

'You have not answered my question.'

In reply she came very close to him, so close that he could smell the scent of jasmine on her skin and see the pale violet shadows beneath her eyes.

'You should believe me because I have done everything I could to help you since I have been here,' she said.

It was not enough. Lucas held her gaze, his eyes hard. 'Have you been in contact with your brother since you came to Midwinter?'

'No!' Rebecca's expression was as clear and honest as it always had been, but there was a spark of anger burning in the depths of her eyes as she searched his face.

Lucas broke away. He felt a white-hot anger for her, but in some odd way he felt even more angry with himself and out of the depths of his despair and his misery he dragged the words.

'I am wondering,' he said, 'just what you would have been ready to do to keep me from the truth. You invited me to bed with you. You even told me you loved me. There were not many things that you were not prepared to do, were there, Miss De Lancey?'

Rebecca turned so pale that he thought she would faint and he instinctively put out a hand to steady her, but she knocked it aside.

'You disgust me, Lord Lucas,' she said between shut teeth. 'Get out of my room. I never wish to see or speak with you again.'

He went.

It took Rebecca ten minutes to dress again. She did not call the maid. She had never needed one. Her first inclination—to walk straight out of Kestrel Court, never to return—had not withstood the obvious conclusion that the Kestrels would never let her go. There was only one thing to do and that was to take the fight to the enemy.

Even so, it took every ounce of her courage to go down the stairs and knock on the door of the study. There was the low murmur of voices from within but, to Rebecca's inexpressible relief, when the door opened it was to reveal Justin Kestrel talking to a man she had never seen before. Of Lucas there was no sign. Rebecca felt almost faint to be granted such a respite. She had only managed to get this far by blocking all thoughts of Lucas and his final words from her mind, and she knew that once she started to think of him she would be completely lost.

'Miss Raleigh.' Justin Kestrel did not seem particularly surprised to see her. He turned to the man at his side. 'Thank you, Bradshaw. We shall speak again.'

'Your Grace.' The man gave Rebecca an unmistakably curious glance as he went out. Justin gestured Rebecca to a seat.

'Were you looking for Lucas, Miss Raleigh?'

'No!' Rebecca said. She gulped a steadying breath. 'I wished to speak to you, your Grace.'

Justin gave her a flicker of a smile. 'Then may I offer you a glass of brandy? You are looking somewhat shaken.'

Rebecca accepted and sat down a little abruptly in the chair that Bradshaw had vacated. Justin did not speak whilst he poured for her and topped up his own glass. When she took it from him she was surprised to see that she was trembling. She took a grateful sip and felt the brandy warm through her limbs, strengthening her. She gave a little sigh. 'That is good.'

'It should be,' Justin said. 'Your brother runs it.'

Rebecca almost choked. She put the glass down. 'Your Grace—'

'Miss Raleigh?' Justin was not making it easy for her but then, Rebecca acknowledged wryly, why should he? She was the one who had some explaining to do. She sat up a little straighter.

'I came to tell you that it is true that I am Rebecca De Lancey,' she said. 'I know that there must be a connection between the Midwinter spies and my uncle's work, but I swear to you that I am not that link. Everything that I have told you is true. I am no traitor and—' her voice warmed '—I cannot believe that Daniel is in the pay of the French either.'

Justin Kestrel let that one go. His face was grave. 'I cannot offer an opinion on your brother, of course, but I must tell you, Miss Raleigh, that I never imagined that you were playing us false. Anyone who knows you at all well should surely realise that you are no spy.'

Rebecca stared. 'But I thought… Lord Lucas assumed…'

'Ah, Lucas,' Justin said. He smiled at her. 'Lucas always was impulsive and I am afraid…' he sighed '…that he is also labouring under strong emotion, which is never conducive to making a man see clearly.'

Rebecca bit her lip. Honesty prompted her to admit that Lucas's reaction was scarcely surprising, although the intensity of his anger had stunned her and the cruelty of his words hurt her deeply.

'I concede that the facts looked damning against me,' she said with a little shiver. 'I cannot explain the connection between the Midwinter spies and my uncle, other than to repeat that it is nothing to do with me.'

'The facts do indeed look damning,' Justin agreed, with the ghost of a smile. 'Lucas was angry and disillusioned to learn the truth, Miss Raleigh, but he may realise his mistake if you grant him a little time.'

'There is no more time for us,' Rebecca said bleakly. 'Lord Lucas and I never could quite trust one another sufficiently to make matters work and now we never shall. I wish to go back to London immediately, your Grace.'

Justin nodded slowly. 'A pity, but I understand your sentiments. If that is what you desire then it shall be so. However, I must ask you to wait a couple of days more, Miss Raleigh.' He saw her instinctive gesture of denial and went on, 'We move against Norton and Lady Benedict the day after tomorrow. We cannot risk any change of plan before then or it may alert suspicion. After that, you are free to return home whenever you wish.'

Rebecca stood up. She knew that it was the best she could hope for and that under the circumstances Justin was being more than generous. It was only the inevitability of seeing Lucas again that made her heart ache so fiercely she was not sure she could bear it. Between them they had destroyed all the fragile trust that had grown up against the odds, and they had hurt each other beyond measure. She bore the responsibility for that as much as Lucas, for although he had deceived her first, she had never trusted him sufficiently to tell him the truth about Daniel, and now it would never be possible to gain his love.

Chapter Eleven

It was odd to behave as though everything were as normal and yet to know that everything had in fact changed. Rebecca had been tempted to remain in her room for the whole of the following day, but she hated to be confined; she had also agreed to go shopping in Woodbridge with Rachel Newlyn. Lucas and Cory were to accompany them, but Lucas elected to ride and did not acknowledge Rebecca's presence with more than a nod when they met in the hall. There was not another look or a word or a touch that passed between them. Rebecca knew that Rachel had noted this new coldness, but fortunately she asked no questions, and when the carriage rolled into Woodbridge and the gentlemen went off to the gunsmith's, Rachel headed towards the bookseller's and Rebecca pleaded a headache and told her friend she would await her on the quay, where she hoped that the fresh sea air might help quell the blue devils.

It was a misty morning and the sea fret hung about the boats, muffling sound and casting a grey pall across the water. The quay seemed quiet but for the

scrape and hammer coming from the shipwright's
yard. An old man was sitting in a wildfowling boat,
sorting methodically through nets and floats and whis-
tling soundlessly through his teeth as he did so. He
raised his head and greeted Rebecca as she walked
slowly by, touching his cap to her before he went back
to his work. Beside his tiny boat gleamed Sir John
Norton's yacht, *Breath of Scandal,* and Rebecca was
halfway past it before she realised with a sinking heart
that Sir John was actually on board and had seen her.
It seemed unfortunate. Her spirits were lower than the
tide, her heart and her thoughts were full of Lucas and
the last thing she wished for was to fend off Sir John's
bluff gallantry. Remembering Justin Kestrel's words
the previous night, she felt a *frisson* of fear. This was
dangerous company in which to linger.

However, it was too late. Sir John had seen her and
now jumped down on to the quay with every expression of delight.

'Miss Raleigh! Well met, ma'am! I was wondering
when I would have the pleasure of showing you my
craft.'

'It is a trim yacht,' Rebecca agreed, dredging up a
smile and giving the boat's shining lines a look of
approval. 'Do you go out today, Sir John? It seems an
inclement day for a sail.'

Sir John looked over his shoulder at the sea mist
pressing on the shore. 'This will lift shortly,' he said
dismissively. 'The sun is already breaking through.
Perhaps you would care to come for a cruise with me
later?'

Rebecca smiled. 'Thank you for your kind offer, but

I fear I shall not have the opportunity today. Some other time, perhaps?'

Sir John did not appear particularly cast down. There was a flicker of calculation in his blue eyes as he watched her. 'At the very least, permit me to show you the trophy I won in this year's Deben Yacht Race,' he suggested. 'I am sure that you will appreciate the workmanship, Miss Raleigh. It is a marvellous piece of engraved glass.'

'Engraved glass?' Rebecca said unwarily. Her gaze shot up to meet his, but Sir John was looking bland. She cleared her throat. 'That is…I know little of such matters, Sir John, but I should be delighted to see the trophy, of course.'

'Splendid!' To her shock, Norton put one arm about her waist and practically carried her over the side of the yacht, guiding her down the companionway and into the cabin below before she could even protest. Gasping, ruffled and confused, she put out a hand to steady herself on the table—and heard the stealthy click of the cabin door behind her.

Rebecca jumped, trying to sound no more put out than any young lady who had been manhandled aboard a yacht and was now in danger of having the vapours. At all costs she had to seem no more than Justin Kestrel's slightly feather-headed cousin.

'Good gracious, Sir John, you are importunate!' she exclaimed. 'What on earth can you be doing—'

'A moment,' Norton murmured. 'I have it here.'

The neat wooden cupboard under the bulkhead was slightly ajar, and through it Rebecca could see the gleam of light on glass. There was indeed a magnificent engraved rose bowl, but next to it on the shelf was a set of smaller glasses and they looked suddenly and shockingly familiar. There was the one with the engraved sun, the seagull, the anchor, the half-moon…

Rebecca stared as the ideas slowly slotted into place. Of course. How foolish of them to have thought that either Lily Benedict or John Norton would keep an incriminating set of engraved glasses on display in their homes for all the world to see. The Midwinter spies were arrogant, but they were not stupid. Here on the boat was the perfect repository for their master code, the boat that Norton used for his illicit meetings with his French spymaster…

'Superb, is it not?' John Norton's voice sounded loud in her ear. 'Allow me to show you the detail, Miss Raleigh. I am sure that a connoisseur such as yourself will appreciate the magnificent craftsmanship involved.'

Rebecca shook herself out of her reverie. Her nerves were jumping and she was suddenly aware of the extreme danger of her situation. She looked at Sir John, but his face betrayed nothing but its usual good-humoured bonhomie.

'I am scarce an expert,' she said lightly, 'but I should be delighted to see the trophy, Sir John.'

Norton bent to extract the rose bowl from the cupboard. His voice was muffled.

'You should not be so deprecating, my dear Miss Raleigh. Who could be more qualified than you to judge the merit of a piece of engraving?'

Rebecca's throat dried. She started to edge backwards towards the doorway but Sir John Norton straightened quickly, empty-handed.

'Not so keen now, eh, Miss Raleigh?' His bluff red face had flushed to an even redder hue. 'What a pity that your faithful protector is unaccountably absent on the one occasion when you require his aid—'

He broke off and stiffened as the boat shifted slightly under the weight of someone coming aboard. There was a thud, the sound of voices and then Lily Benedict burst down the steps and into the cabin. Her bonnet was askew and she looked flustered and distraught.

'John, what is happening?' she demanded. 'Edgar said that the girl, Miss Raleigh, had come this way.' She broke off as her gaze fell on Rebecca. Her eyes narrowed in calculation. 'Oh! Then you already have her.'

'Tell Edgar to cast off,' Norton said without taking his eyes from Rebecca's face. 'Quickly, Lily! We must get away before the Kestrels come looking for her.'

Lily Benedict looked from the half-open cupboard to Rebecca and back again. 'I see,' she said slowly. 'Edgar!' She turned on her heel. 'Cast off! We must make sail at once.'

In a desperate, unthinking effort to escape, Rebecca made a dash for the doorway, but Norton reached her within two strides and caught her about the waist, pulling her brutally backwards. Her hip caught the edge of the table; all the breath was knocked from her and she bit back a gasp of pain.

'Do nothing foolish, my dear.' Norton murmured, his breath hot against her ear. 'There is so little point.

We had always planned to leave for France today and all is prepared. Your presence merely complicates the matter slightly, but I do not suppose that you shall be with us for long.' There was a threat beneath the words that was impossible to ignore.

Rebecca struggled and was held hard. 'I do not know what you are talking about—or what you think you are doing!' There was no need now to pretend to fear. It was clear in her voice. She could hear the sound of the ropes being released and the anchor chain clinking. It would take only a matter of moments to get the boat ready to sail. Norton, as he had said, had had it all prepared. Rebecca's mind raced as like a trapped rat. She could not get off the boat and Norton knew her identity. There could be no pretence any longer.

He laughed now and tightened his grip. 'Silly chit, thinking you could come here and ruin all for us. A little engraver's girl with delusions of grandeur.' He pushed her in front of him up the steps onto the deck. 'Edgar recognised you straight away. He was a member of the Archangel Club and he commissioned the glass from your uncle and no one ever knew. No one guessed the truth.'

Edgar, Rebecca thought. For a moment her mind was blank, and then she remembered the huddled figure of Sir Edgar Benedict, skin papery yellow, sitting in his Bath chair at the dinner, a sinister figure racked with pain... Sitting in his chair and watching her to see if she really was George Provost's niece come to expose the truth. They had never even considered him as one of the conspirators. He had fooled them all.

As Norton dragged her up the companionway, the cold sea air hit Rebecca's face and helped to clear her head a little. She could see Edgar Benedict now, working the sails, as hale and hearty as the vigorous man he had evidently been all along. Already the yacht was halfway out into the middle of the estuary, but it was not that which concerned Rebecca so much as the shifting banks of mist that she could see curtaining the entrance to the harbour. She stared in horror.

'Surely you are not intending to take her out in this?'

Norton gave a snort of derision. 'What would you know of sailing, engraver's girl? Best stay below if you are going to have a fit of the vapours!'

He pushed her back down the companionway and Rebecca fell in a sprawling heap on the floor below and heard the cabin door slam shut and the key turn in the lock.

Lucas had completely failed to find anything he required in the gunsmith's, which was no surprise since he could not even see what was in front of his eyes. All he *could* see was Rebecca's white face as she pleaded her innocence, an innocence he had not been prepared even to consider. Burning with anger, he had gone out into the night and walked around until his head had cleared a little. Then he had lain awake for the entire night whilst he sifted the facts in his mind, weighing and discarding the evidence. All the indications were that Miss Rebecca De Lancey was as guilty as sin, yet all the evidence of his own intuition told him once again that she was true. He was not accustomed to acting on intuition and he did not like it. Yet now he was obliged to admit, at last, that where Rebecca was concerned his instinct had never let him down. He had loved her before he even knew it. He loved her still. And now he wanted her back, and no secrets or misunderstandings would ever part them again.

'Lucas?' Cory's voice cut through his thoughts. 'It is clear to me that you are never going to make your choice, so why do we not rejoin the ladies—'

The door of the shop swung open violently and Rachel Newlyn ran inside. Cory broke off and grabbed his wife by the arm, but it was Lucas whom she addressed through panting breaths.

'Lucas! Hurry! Rebecca is on *Breath of Scandal*.'

'What?' Lucas focussed abruptly. 'She has gone with Norton on his yacht? What in the name of thunder was she doing—?'

'No time for that,' Rachel said, gulping air and dragging them both out on to the pavement. 'They have just this moment set sail. I saw her on deck and then Norton pushed her below. Quickly!'

She did not need to tell him twice. Lucas had already abandoned Rachel in Cory's arms with more haste than chivalry as he raced towards the harbour. The air tore in his lungs, clammy and thick. Norton had taken his yacht out in this? It seemed suicidal.

He reached the edge of the jetty to see the yacht in the middle of the channel, already drifting into the sea mist. Beside him on the quay Benbow, the wildfowler, calmly sorted through his nets, humming beneath his breath as though he had not a care in the world. Lucas turned to him.

'Benbow, Sir John Norton's yacht...'

'Aye, m'lord?' The man's eyes were an incurious pale blue.

'Has he been preparing it for long?'

'Aye, m'lord. Said they were to sail today.'

'They?'

'Him and the Benedicts. Took the girl as well, of course,' Benbow added, shaking his head. 'Poor little missy.'

'You mean he kidnapped her?' Lucas's stomach churned. A small, doubting part of his mind had wondered whether Rebecca had gone of her own free will. Now he doubted no longer.

'Aye,' Benbow said, shaking his head. 'Kidnap, right enough. Saw her struggling with him in the cabin.'

Lucas resisted the urge to shake him into urgency. 'We must go after them.'

'Aye, m'lord.' Benbow sounded unmoved. He gazed across the misty harbour. 'Powerful bad day to take a boat out.'

'That can't be helped,' Lucas snapped. He was already starting to untie the wildfowling punt. 'Come on, man! I need your help.'

'Never catch them up,' Benbow opined gloomily. 'Not in a punt.'

Lucas stared in frustration. 'There is no wind. They are practically becalmed! We will catch them.'

'Aye, m'lord.' The fisherman scratched his head. 'No harm in trying, I suppose.'

Lucas was already reaching for the punt pole when the first rustle of breeze across the water caught the sails of *Breath of Scandal* and the yacht turned and headed towards the harbour mouth.

'Quickly, man,' he urged Benbow, who was reaching ponderously for the other punt pole. 'Damn it, we need oars.'

'Need more than that,' Benbow muttered under his breath, but he took the second pole with a will and started to steer them out in the direction the yacht had gone whilst Lucas found himself praying hard and fervently for the sort of miracle he was desperately afraid could never occur.

The yacht was making good headway, picking up the ripples of breeze that were guiding it gently but surely out of harbour. Rebecca could hear the footsteps of her captors on deck overhead. She knew that she had to work quickly for it could only be a matter of minutes before they came below to check on her. To check on her or to dispose of her. Her hands shook as she rummaged in her reticule. Where was it…? She always carried it with her… Her hand closed reassuringly around her diamond engraving scribe and she scrambled across to the porthole. There were three screws that held it closed and each was twisted tight, but with a few deft turns of the scribe she was able to loosen then sufficiently to push out the little pane of glass. She knew she was a good swimmer and that with the mist she might just be able to get away from them, but the mist was also her enemy as well as her ally for she would not necessarily be able to tell the harbour from the open sea. Crushing down her fears, she put out a hand and was about to push the porthole open when the boat juddered to a sickening halt. There was a scrape along the keel like claws on wood.

Rebecca froze. The boat lurched and stuck again with a grating roar this time. Overhead the footsteps and voices became frenzied and urgent as the little yacht started to cant at a crazy angle. Rebecca's porthole rose high out of the water whilst on the other side she could see the boat settling lower on its side and the glassy grey of the sea lapping at the window. Her breath caught in her throat. There was no time to waste. With one sharp move she punched the porthole open and dragged herself through the gap.

The mist pressed all around her like a shroud and the sea was pale and almost unnaturally calm. The fear pawed at her, but she took a deep breath and jumped, and in the same moment there was a shout from the decks and a scream and then the entire boat tipped over in one swift and frightful movement so that its painted hull pointed to the sky like a tomb.

Rebecca cast one hasty glance over her shoulder, then struck out strongly away from the terrible wreck that was even now settling down on its grave of shingle. And then the mist was ripped aside in the strengthening breeze and she looked up in astonishment and saw the ship coming for her.

Lucas had never been so afraid in his entire life. As *Breath of Scandal* disappeared into the mist it felt as though it was taking every last vestige of his hope with it. They were out in the harbour mouth now and the wind was fresher here and the mist hung like ragged curtains. Every so often a gust would blow the fret briefly aside, giving a tantalising glimpse of *Breath of Scandal* fleeing before them. The punt was quick, but the yacht was picking up speed now as the wind started to fill her sails. Benbow leaned on the pole and wiped the back of his hand across his forehead. The mist pressed in around them, smothering all sound.

'It's no good, my lord,' the wildfowler said. 'We won't catch up and the water's getting too deep. We're near the mouth of the river and it's powerful dangerous out here now—'

He broke off as there was a grating rumble a way to their right, like the roll of distant thunder out to sea. Benbow's eyes darted nervously and he wiped the sweat from his upper lip. Lucas gripped the side of the boat, his knuckles turning white.

'What was that?' He could hear the tension in his own voice, an echo for the fear he saw in Benbow's eyes.

'Shingle, my lord.' The wildfowler would not meet his gaze. 'Shingle banks at the mouth of the river. Happen yon yacht must have run aground.'

The pictures flashed through Lucas's mind like a nightmare. Shingle was dangerous, far more dangerous than a sand bank, for it was unstable and could shift at any moment. The place where the river met the sea had always been treacherous. One winter the entire shingle bank had shifted from one side of the river to the other in a storm, lying submerged barely beneath the surface like an iceberg, waiting to trap the unwary sailor.

Lucas could hear splashing through the mist, unintelligible shouts and something that sounded ominously like a scream broken off. The wind stirred again and the mist twitched aside for a brief second, showing *Breath of Scandal* lying only some hundred yards distant, canted crazily on its port bow at the mouth of the estuary, the waves already breaking on its hull.

'Damn it, Benbow!' Lucas exploded. 'If we don't get the punt over there, I shall swim.' He was already ripping his jacket off as he spoke.

The mist swirled back and unsighted him, and immediately Lucas felt hopelessly disorientated. The anger and the frustration and the fear rushed through him in a tidal wave, but there was no time. Even as he stood poised to dive off the punt there was another growling roar, far louder than the first, that seemed to fill his ears and bounce deafeningly off the wall of mist that pressed around them. The sea swelled and boiled about them, rocking the punt so that Lucas was tipped off balance and fell over the side into the water. He went down, choking, and the cold, salty shock of the sea filled his lungs and wrapped him in its murderous embrace. It felt like hours before he surfaced and Benbow grabbed his arm and dragged him, coughing and spluttering, into the bottom of the punt.

The wind gathered strength, ripping aside the shreds of the mist once and for all, and the pale sun fell as the full horror of *Breath of Scandal*'s plight was revealed to them. Through streaming eyes Lucas saw the yacht's sails fill with the breeze and then the boat flipped over as easily as though it had been a toy.

There was the crash of falling timbers and it lay, stern upturned, capsized in a second, too quick for Lucas even to understand what he had seen. Benbow gave a gusty sigh.

'Seen it happen before to a lugger out of Harwich,' he said. 'Too quick.' He shook his head. 'What with the shingle shifting and the breeze filling the sails, they stood no chance.'

'Rebecca,' Lucas said. His lips felt stiff and his throat was sore with salt water, but it was nothing to the pain in his chest that seemed to expand and break until he felt his lungs would burst. He wanted to shout but could not get the air in. 'Rebecca…'

Benbow was still shaking his head, one brawny hand on Lucas's shoulder. 'I'm rightly sorry, my lord… There was nothing we could have done.' He gave another sigh. 'Tragic. Nasty as they come, these accidents—' His tone changed and Lucas felt his hand stiffen and fall away. 'Holy saints alive,' the wild-fowler whispered.

Lucas looked up, pushing the streaming hair out of his eyes.

'Great God and all his saints preserve us,' Benbow said, with true reverence. 'I never thought to see the day…'

The grey water was still breaking over the capsized hull of the yacht, but beyond it the mist was receding out to sea like a drawn curtain. It shimmered in the pale sun, floating like a cloud. It was going to be a beautiful day. For a moment Lucas stared, uncertain what it was that Benbow had seen, and then his own gaze caught the movement. Beyond the ruined yacht a small figure bobbed in the gentle swell of the waves. She was swimming strongly, but she was swimming away from the wreck towards…

Lucas's lips formed a soundless whistle. He looked up sharply at Benbow and saw the old sailor's eyes alight with an almost religious fervour. Out of the mist slipped the ghost ship, so slow, so gentle it seemed to move soundlessly over the water.

First the prow, the snarling dragon figurehead insolent in crimson and gold. Then the clean, clear-cut lines, the two raking masts, the white topsails catching the breeze and the sun striking on the black lettering of the name…*The Defiance.*

A rope snaked down from the side of the ship and Lucas saw Rebecca reach up, catch it, and swing like a monkey up into the arms of the man who stood on the deck, the water running from her streaming skirts. The privateer ship turned gently into the receding mist and the sun caught its edge in a gleam of gold, and then it was gone as stealthily as it had come.

'Well, I'll be damned,' Benbow said, leaning on the punt pole. He looked extremely shaken. 'My lord…'

Lucas was silenced. He was not sure whether he wanted to laugh or perhaps to cry for the first time in his entire life. For Rebecca was surely safe, but he had no notion whether he would ever see her again. Rebecca, with her determination and her tenacity. He might have known that she would not do anything as lame as give in to kidnap and drowning.

He wrung the water from his shirt and stared in the direction that the ship had gone. Rebecca had not wanted to come to Midwinter and he had obliged her to do it and now she had escaped him, and taken all his hopes with her. He wished that they had had more time to put matters to rights between them. He wished that he had told her he loved her.

His clothes were starting to dry as the sun strengthened and turned the salt sticky on his back. He could see a yacht coming out of harbour now and tacking towards them on the freshening breeze—the *Ariel,* with Cory Newlyn in the prow. He turned away from the open sea and set his face towards the shore. The punt rocked gently on the swell.

'Reckon we won't see the likes of that again,' Benbow said.

'Reckon we won't,' Lucas agreed, but he was not thinking of the ship.

'What do we do now, m'lord?' The wildfowler asked.

Lucas smiled ruefully. 'We go home, Benbow. What other choice do we have?'

Chapter Twelve

'Thank God I taught you to swim, Beck.'

Rebecca opened her eyes. The light was pale golden and was flooding in through a porthole in the stern, making water patterns on the pale panelled walls. For a moment she thought that she was asleep and dreaming, and then she remembered. She sat up with a groan. When Daniel had scooped her up onto the deck of *The Defiance* she had felt well and strong and exultant to be alive. She had hugged him tightly, asked a barrage of questions and laughed in delight as his grinning crew pressed around to shake her hand. It was mortifying that her strength had then withered swiftly and she had fainted—actually fainted—for the first time in her life.

Daniel sat down on the end of the bed and placed a tray in front of her. He looked just as she remembered him: the strong, tanned face, dark, curly hair and slashing white smile that warmed his eyes and lessened slightly but not entirely the dangerous image that he cut.

'You have slept for hours, Beck,' he said, appraising

her thoroughly. 'It is good to see there is colour in your face again. Would you like some soup?'

Rebecca's stomach gave a long rumble. Daniel laughed and pushed the wooden tray towards her. There were rolls and delicious-smelling vegetable broth. Rebecca took a few spoonfuls and gave an approving nod.

'You do not stint yourself, Daniel.'

'Did you think I lived in squalor, with cutlasses hanging from the ceiling?' her brother asked plaintively. 'I assure you we are far more civilised than that.'

'I suppose so.' Rebecca looked around the well-appointed cabin. There was a desk of cherrywood and two matching chairs and paintings of seascapes on the white walls. And on a low shelf the afternoon sun sparkled on a slender vase of engraved glass with the picture of an anchor and the motto *Celer et Audax*. It was a match for the one in her studio.

Suddenly his words penetrated Rebecca's wandering thoughts and she put the spoon down with a clatter.

'You say that I have slept for hours? Then they will think me dead—'

'I sent a message telling them that you were safe,' Daniel said calmly, holding on to the tilting tray. 'Besides, Lucas Kestrel saw you come aboard the ship. He knows you are here.'

'Lucas?' Rebecca's heart jumped. 'How could he know? Did he come after me?'

'He did,' Daniel said. 'In a fowling boat. Madness

under such dangerous conditions, but most impressive.'

Rebecca swallowed the lump in her throat. There was a fierce ache inside her. Lucas had come after her, no matter the odds, no matter the danger. Evidently he had cared enough to try to save her. And now, no doubt, he would think her guilt proven beyond doubt when she had clambered aboard *The Defiance*. She sighed sharply, turning her face away. 'Damn it, why do matters never turn out right?'

Daniel got up and strolled across to the porthole. 'They may yet do so,' he pointed out reasonably.

Rebecca applied herself to the rest of the soup with gusto.

'I must go back,' she said, her mouth full. 'I cannot leave them all wondering what has become of me.'

Her brother turned to look at her. 'I thought you would say that.' There was something odd in his tone. 'We need to talk first, Beck.'

Rebecca nodded and looked around. 'My clothes…?'

'Ruined.' Daniel went across to the chest beneath the window. 'There may be something here that will fit you.'

Rebecca gave him a look. 'I shall not ask where they have come from.'

'Best not.' Daniel flashed her a grin. 'I will see you on deck shortly.'

He left Rebecca to rummage through the chest and come out with a curious selection of clothes that made her feel like a refugee from a Drury Lane theatre. There was a full green skirt with voluminous petticoats, a tight black jacket and a huge lace shawl. Grimacing, Rebecca scrambled into the outfit, cast one quick glance at the mirror on the bulkhead, pulled a face and went out.

The fresh air hit her as she went up the companion-way and out on to the deck. *The Defiance* was not a small ship as schooners went, but it was exceptionally trim. The paintwork was fresh and the decks scrubbed like a warship. Daniel was in the bow, chatting to one of his crew. He turned when the man touched his arm and nodded towards Rebecca, and gave her another flashing grin, coming down the steps to meet her and draw her into the shelter of the wheelhouse. The sun was starting to set now, laying a trail of gold across the pale sea. From somewhere about the ship came the smell of roasting chicken.

'You look better than I had expected,' Daniel said, holding her at arm's length and nodding approvingly. 'It is good to know that Molly's clothes, if not Molly herself, have come in useful in the end.'

'What happened to Molly?' Rebecca asked lightly.

Her brother shrugged. 'She left me. She said that she had thought life on ship would be exciting but it was no more than one bout of seasickness after another. She asked to be put ashore in Ireland. I hear that she runs a waterside tavern there now.'

'I see,' Rebecca said, fascinated by this insight into her brother's personal life. 'Well, I am grateful for the loan of her wardrobe.'

'We are prevaricating,' Daniel said, with a slight smile.

'So, where do we start?' Rebecca asked.

Daniel laughed. 'At the beginning?'

They talked as the sun went down in a trail of red and gold and the coastline of Suffolk shifted in the haze on the horizon. They spoke of old times and home and family, of Rebecca's life in London, the engraving studio and her work. At some point the lantern in the wheelhouse was lit and someone came to bring them ale and fried chicken, but no one interrupted their conversation. Rebecca told Daniel, as she had told no one before, of her fears of not being able to work again, and the loneliness that had stalked her through the long months following the deaths of their aunt and uncle. Daniel nodded, his face grave and still in the falling twilight.

'So how comes it that you are here in Suffolk?' he asked, 'and guest of the Duke of Kestrel, no less?'

Rebecca hesitated, but she knew that there could be no further concealment. She told him of Lucas coming to Clerkenwell to look for the Midwinter engraver and how he had persuaded her to accompany him back to Midwinter so that she could help unmask the spy once and for all.

'Did you know that I was here?' she asked.

Daniel smiled. 'Oh, yes. I hear—and see—many things, Beck. Everyone was talking of the Duke of Kestrel's supposed cousin, Miss Rebecca Raleigh, and the fact that Lord Lucas Kestrel was mad in love with her.'

Rebecca blushed. 'That was merely part of the plan to hide my true reason for being here.'

'Was it?' Daniel's dark blue gaze was searching.

He tossed aside a chicken wing and reached for another. 'Perhaps we may return to that, Beck.'

Rebecca was not certain she wanted to talk about Lucas. She wrapped the voluminous shawl more closely about her for the evening breeze was strengthening. 'How did you know that I was on Norton's yacht?' she asked, trying to turn the subject.

Daniel laughed. 'I did not. I did not come to rescue you, Beck, much as I would like to take credit. I knew that Norton intended to take *Breath of Scandal* out today and I was waiting for him.'

Rebecca stared. 'You knew… Did you know he was the spy?'

'I knew that he and Lily Benedict between them had been involved in a conspiracy. I even heard rumours of a third who was their ally, but I never knew his name.'

'Sir Edgar Benedict,' Rebecca said. 'We were all misled by the tale of the housebound invalid.'

Daniel whistled. 'Cunning. A man who could come and go as he pleased behind the cover of his illness.'

'Then you were not…' Rebecca hesitated '…you were not their contact?'

'Certainly not.' Daniel sounded amused, to her relief. 'I may be a smuggler, Beck, but I am no traitor. Norton worked with a French privateer. I almost caught the Frenchman once,' Daniel added wistfully. 'That would have put an end to their games much sooner, but unfortunately his Majesty's Navy intervened and I had to run for my life. And then they merely took the privateer's cargo and allowed him to escape, the incompetent idiots.'

'It seems a shame,' Rebecca said softly, 'that you are outside the law when you do so much that is good…'

Daniel gave her a sharp look. 'What do you mean by that?'

Rebecca shifted a little. 'Why, merely that there are stories about you too, Daniel. Many and many a story, of how you harry the French and save those who wish to escape Bonaparte's tyranny.'

Daniel drained his tankard. 'Steady, Rebecca.' His tone was dry. 'Next you will be telling me that I take from the rich to give to the poor.'

'Don't you?'

'Not at all.' Daniel's smile was twisted. 'I discovered early on that I have an aptitude for this way of life and I make a good living from it. If in the course of my work I discover certain information that might be useful to the British government I might pass it on to them by my own means. If I can help anyone fleeing Bonaparte, then I shall try to do so. It is as simple as that.'

Rebecca let it go. She knew that her brother had his own code of honour and one of his principles was that he would never tell her more than she needed to know, in the same way that she would never contact him and draw him into danger. It was an unspoken agreement between them and she would not contravene it now.

'Which brings us rather neatly back to you, Beck,' Daniel added. 'Tell me about Lord Lucas Kestrel.'

'You mean the pretence of a love affair?' Rebecca said.

'No, I mean the genuine article.' Daniel got to his

feet and took a few paces away, leaning on the deck rail. 'When Tovey brought you the money that night in London he saw more than he expected,' he said, over his shoulder. His voice was moody. 'Lucas Kestrel stayed with you all night, Beck, yet you say there is nothing between you. I hope you are lying.'

Rebecca stared at him. So this was what Daniel had meant when he said that they had to talk. She felt a shot of anger. 'You choose a fine time to play the protective elder brother, Daniel! What is it to you?'

Daniel turned back for the rail, repressed violence in the lines of his body. 'What do you think it is to me? I am only too aware that I have failed utterly in my responsibility to protect you, Rebecca. Oh, whilst Uncle Provost was alive I could square my conscience and think that you were safe. A letter here, a little money there—' He broke off and turned away. 'It was never enough, I knew that, but it had to do. And then you were left all alone and I did not even hear of it for months, and then Tovey came and said there was some nobleman prowling around and that you had become his mistress! It was what I had always feared for you.'

Rebecca got up and came across the rail. She put a hand on his arm. The wind was cold, carrying spindrift in its wake. 'It was never like that with Lucas,' she said, knowing she had to tell the truth to sooth her brother's conscience. 'I love him.'

Daniel did not seem soothed. She could feel the tension in his body. His face was set. 'That is even worse, if he is only playing games with you.'

'He is not. He wished to marry me.'

There was a moment of silence and then Daniel gave a short laugh. 'Now I'll admit you have surprised me. So he wished to marry you before, but he no longer does? What happened?'

'He found out about you,' Rebecca said.

'I see.' Daniel was silent for a moment. 'You had not told him.'

'No.'

'Because you were protecting me.'

'Yes. It is a habit of mine.'

Daniel gave an angry sigh. 'And now he does not want to marry an outlaw's sister?'

'It is not that.' Rebecca hesitated. 'Lucas and I have both kept many secrets from the other. We did what we thought was best, but in the end we hurt each other too much. There is no going back.'

Daniel leant his chin on his hand. 'Could you not resolve these matters once and for all?'

'I do not know,' Rebecca said honestly. 'There are many reasons why I should not marry Lucas Kestrel.'

'You say you love him,' Daniel pointed out, 'so give me one good reason.'

Rebecca made a slight gesture. 'My whole life has been wrapped up in my engraving, Daniel. I do not wish to give it up and I certainly could not continue to work were I to become Lady Rebecca Kestrel.'

Daniel shifted slightly. 'You told me that your work would decline anyway, because of this damage to your wrist,' he pointed out. 'That is something you are going to have to come to terms with, Beck, sooner or later. You are fortunate in that you now have another alternative in life.'

'I do not wish to think of Lucas as an alternative to starvation!' Rebecca protested.

'Then think of him as a man who loves you.'

'That is precisely the point!' Rebecca leant on the rail and took a deep breath of sea-scented night air. 'Lucas does not love me. He wishes to marry because he wants me and because he and I…we—' Rebecca broke off.

'We'll take that as read,' Daniel said, a smile lightening the grimness of his tone. 'It sounds as though he has at least acted as a gentleman should.'

'Oh, do not be so stuffy!' Rebecca said spiritedly. 'I refuse to marry because of Lucas's misplaced chivalry and sense of honour.'

'Then you are a fool,' Daniel said bluntly. 'You are in love with the man. You said so yourself. He wishes to marry you. He may to all intents and purposes be desperately in love with you, Beck, and simply not very adept at showing it.' Daniel shrugged self-deprecatingly. 'Not all men are adroit with such feelings. Certainly—' a hint of dryness entered his tone '—Lucas Kestrel has been doing a good enough job of *playing* a man deeply in love, if all I hear is true.'

Rebecca was silent. With all her heart she wanted to believe Daniel's words. She wanted to think that it would not be a compromise match, born out of gallantry and need. That was a great deal, but it was not enough for her. She loved Lucas and she wanted him to love her too. Abandoning her engraving was a different matter and one that she would have to learn to accept. She realised that now. Her whole world was changing, but she should not hide behind her loss and use it as an excuse to refuse Lucas.

'I cannot imagine myself as a lady,' she said, a little forlornly.

'Why not?' Daniel was bracing. 'You were born one.'

'I am accustomed to working for my living.'

'So?' Daniel sounded severe. 'You need not become idle just because you marry a rich man, Rebecca. Your life is there for the taking. You can do what you wish with it. I never thought to see you refuse a challenge because you were afraid.'

Rebecca stared out across the darkened sea. Daniel's words were hard, but she knew they were true. She had been reluctant to give up the past, to trust Lucas and to go into a different future. But now her heart felt lighter and she went across and flung her arms about Daniel and held him close, wordlessly.

He rested his cheek against her hair and said, 'Does that mean I can stop worrying about you again?'

'I suppose so.' Rebecca freed herself from his grip and stood at arm's length. 'I must go back now.'

'Thank the lord for that,' her brother said. 'We have been hovering offshore these two hours past. It is damnably dangerous.'

Despite that, it was Daniel himself who came with her in the long boat to Kestrel Cove and escorted her up the sandy path through the woods, leaving her only when she was on the threshold of Kestrel Court. Rebecca gave him another brief, fierce hug but they did not speak, and, though she turned to watch as his tall figure was swallowed up by the trees, he did not look back. She turned away then. The lights of Kestrel Court glowed bright through the autumn night and she gathered up the green skirts in one hand and strode forward boldly, belying the nervousness in her stomach. It was time to meet her future and make of it what she could.

'A shocking accident.' Owen Chance, the Riding Officer, had been closeted with the Duke and Lord Lucas Kestrel for over an hour, and Lucas was heartily wishing him gone. He had nothing against Mr Chance personally, for the fellow was a good man for a government employee and close as the grave. He and Justin had agreed that they had to take Chance into their confidence in order to hush up the matter of the Midwinter spies and the further complication of Rebecca's disappearance. Chance was the only one outside the family who knew she had been taken by *The Defiance*. Benbow was more discreet than a clam and everyone else had been told that Rebecca had been rescued by a fishing boat and was currently resting after her ordeal. The Midwinter tabbies were in a flutter about it, of course, but it was nowhere near as bad as the huge scandal that would ensue if the tale got out that Miss Rebecca Raleigh, erstwhile cousin to the Duke of Kestrel, had been taken aboard a pirate ship and one, moreover, which was the property of her brother, Daniel De Lancey…

It was that that preoccupied Lucas now. He seemed to notice every tick of the clock, and the agonising slowness with which the hands moved around towards midnight. Despite the message that De Lancey had sent, Lucas had been desperately uncertain that Rebecca would come back at all, and with every hour his doubts had solidified into an uncomfortable weight in his stomach. He wanted her back. He needed her. Damn it, he loved her and he would tell her as soon as she stepped through the door. *If* she stepped through the door ever again…

'I agree,' Owen Chance was continuing, 'that it is best to present the matter in the light of a disaster. Sir John Norton and Lady Benedict, wishing to give the invalid Sir Edgar a healthful sea outing, arranged the trip on the yacht, only to fall foul of a most terrible accident.'

Justin nodded. 'Quite so. That is the story that we have put about in the town.' He shrugged. 'Perhaps Norton should have realised that the sea mist made it an unsuitable day for a sail, but…'

'But it is too late now,' Owen Chance concluded. He smiled a little grimly as he finished his brandy. 'A most satisfactory conclusion, your Grace, sparing us all the unavoidable scandal of a treason trial.'

He got to his feet. 'Well, if you will excuse me, I shall be on my way.' He shook Justin's hand, then Lucas's. 'They are searching for *The Defiance*,' he said, and Lucas swallowed his irritation because he understood Chance's sincerity. 'HMS *Plockton* is out of Harwich—'

'I feel certain that Miss Raleigh will be very well and will be returned to us soon,' Justin said, a shade too heartily. He drew Owen Chance towards the door. 'This way, old fellow. I cannot emphasise how much we appreciate your help in this matter…'

Their voices faded away down the hall and Lucas got up, unable to keep still any longer. He strode over to the window and peered out into the darkness, but could see nothing at all. He thought that he had heard a sound. It was his imagination, of course. Or wishful thinking. He dropped down into an armchair by the fire and ran a hand through his disordered tawny hair. He had never experienced such a mixture of hope and fear. If this was love then he was not certain that he had not been better off before. Except that it was far too late now.

There was the softest click as the latch of the long window lifted. Lucas looked up. Even though it was the one thing that he had wanted to happen all day, he found he could not actually move, or even speak. He simply stared.

Rebecca was standing just inside the long windows. It *was* Rebecca, although she was wearing a full green skirt that looked as though it had come from a dressing-up box. Her hair was loose down her back and shadowed her face with a nimbus of dark curls. He could see the doubt and hesitation in her eyes as she looked at him. It exactly mirrored everything that he felt inside. Then she smiled tentatively and held out a hand.

'Lucas?'

Lucas was across the room so quickly that he barely had time to think. His arms went about her and he held her close. 'I was afraid you would not come back.' He scarcely recognised his own voice.

He felt her tremble on the edge of laughter and

tears. 'I was afraid that you would think it proved my guilt. I am sorry I never told you...'

Lucas pressed a kiss on her hair and tightened his grip about her. Then he remembered that he had something to tell her. It was easy in the end. 'I love you with all my heart,' he said. 'Will you marry me?'

She tilted her chin up so that she could meet his eyes. Her own were brilliant with tears of happiness.

'I will,' she said, a second before he kissed her.

Neither of them was aware of how long it was before the door opened and the Duke of Kestrel entered. They broke apart, tousled and incandescent with happiness.

'Ah,' Justin said, sounding as unruffled as though he had stepped into the Prince of Wales's drawing room, 'I am glad to see you returned, Rebecca. We were becoming quite concerned for you. I kept Chance talking a while for I did not wish him to meet your brother on the way out.' He looked from one to the other and started to smile. 'I take it that the wedding will be going forward after all? I am very glad. But you will be wishing me gone, I dare say. I shall bid you good night.'

'Such discretion,' Lucas said, as the door closed behind his brother. He sat down in the armchair and pulled Rebecca onto his lap. She snuggled close, pressing her cheek to his.

'Would you like me to tell you what happened, Lucas?' she asked, muffled.

'Just for once,' Lucas said, 'I would not.' There was a huge warmth and happiness in his heart and it needed no words. He put a hand beneath her chin and turned her face up to his. 'For now,' he said, 'there are better ways to pass the time.'

'It was Edgar Benedict whom we overlooked all along,' Justin said heavily the following evening, as they all sat around the fire in the study. 'We were told that he was a bedridden invalid and we accepted it without challenge.' He shook his head bitterly. 'I could kick myself for falling for that trick. It might have been Lily Benedict who was the French spy reported first in Dorset last year, but it was Edgar who had the freedom to come and go as he pleased whilst we were all assuming him helpless and of no account.'

'So now it all falls into place,' Cory Newlyn said thoughtfully. 'Edgar Benedict killed Jeffrey Maskelyne right at the start, and then Lily took a pot shot at me later, when they realised that I was trying to discover any information Maskelyne might have left behind.'

'She was not the only one,' Rachel Newlyn said drily. 'I almost killed you myself, Cory, when I found you wandering around the stables in the middle of the night in that suspicious manner!'

Cory laughed. 'A good job you did not, my love! I feel sure you would have been deeply upset to have been the unwitting cause of my demise!'

'Desolated,' Rachel agreed, a small smile playing about her lips. 'And then Papa almost shot both of us with his blunderbuss! It is a miracle we are all here to tell the tale at all.'

'I imagine that it was Lily Benedict who accidentally picked up the wrong book at the reading group,'

Justin continued, 'leaving Deb with the book that contained the code—'

'And leaving her also to fall foul of Richard's suspicions,' Lucas said. He drew Rebecca closer to his side. 'I am not certain where we should all be had it not been for this business.'

'Wifeless,' Cory said drily. 'A situation not to be tolerated.'

Lucas smiled at Rebecca. 'I never thought to find myself saying this,' he said softly, 'but I completely agree, Cory.'

'If you could keep your mind on business a little longer,' Justin complained. 'There are a number of matters that still require clarification.'

'Such as?' Lucas was finding it difficult to drag his attention from Rebecca.

'Such as why one set of engraved glasses turned up at the Woodbridge auction house when they should have been in Norton's possession.'

'I think I can help you there,' Rebecca said, a little shyly, remembering what Daniel had told her. She caught Lucas's look of surprise and gave him a smile. 'I believe there were two sets of engraved glasses, one held by the Benedicts and John Norton, and the other by their French spymasters. When they needed to change the code, they both required a new set of engraved glass. My uncle's records bear this out.'

Lucas nodded. 'And they lost one set?'

'I understand,' Rebecca said, careful not to mention Daniel's name, 'that Sir John had passed one set to his French accomplice, but that the French ship was stopped by HMS *Plockton,* who took the contraband cargo, including the glasses. The cargo was sold off at the Customs House and Sir John was put to the trouble of buying back his own set of glasses.'

'Or trying to,' Lucas said. He laughed. 'Then Ross Marney accidentally outbid him and the spies were put to even greater trouble to try to steal the glasses back!'

'It is some consolation to know that we caused them some difficulties,' Cory said, 'for it seemed that they ran rings around us for months.'

'I suppose that it was Edgar Benedict who tied Richard and Deb to the easel at the unveiling of Lady Sally's watercolour calendar,' Lucas said, chuckling. He squeezed Rebecca's hand. 'You missed a rare sight there, my love. I doubt there has ever been such a sensation in Midwinter!'

Justin was looking speculatively at Rebecca. 'Your brother is an excellent gatherer of intelligence,' he remarked. 'Do you think he might be interested in working for the government?'

Rebecca laughed. 'I believe he already does, your Grace, but only on his own terms.'

Justin nodded thoughtfully. 'And so we come to the final mystery that puzzled me, which was why the spies chose George Provost to be their unwitting accomplice.'

Rebecca shivered and Lucas drew her protectively closer.

'In the end it was quite simple,' Justin continued. 'Edgar Benedict was a member of the Archangel Club and a friend of Alexander Fremantle. Fremantle had already commissioned some work from George Provost and when Edgar Benedict saw it...' he shrugged

'…he thought Provost ideal to provide the spies with their pictorial code.'

'So simple,' Rebecca agreed. She looked at Lucas. 'And so dangerous in making you suspect me.'

Lucas smiled and leaned closer, oblivious of their audience. 'Do you forgive me?' he asked softly.

'Well…' Rebecca said. She raised a hand to his cheek. 'I suppose so…'

Their lips touched and in the same moment the door to the study burst open.

'Good evening, everyone! We are back!' Lord Richard Kestrel steered his wife Deborah into the room with a proprietorial arm about her waist. 'Have we missed anything of note?'

His gaze fell upon Lucas, who was by now kissing Rebecca with considerable fervour. He stopped dead. 'Good God, Lucas,' he said, 'we were only away for six weeks!'

Chapter Thirteen

The engraving studio looked very much as Rebecca had left it. Whoever Lucas had set to keep an eye on the place had done the job well. The glass on the display shelves was a little dusty and the floor needed to be swept, but the place felt the same. It smelled the same, of cold mustiness and quiet. Rebecca shivered as it seeped into her bones.

She had told Lucas the truth about having to give up her engraving because she had not wanted there to be any more secrets between them. She had been afraid that he would think she had agreed to marry him as a second choice, and he had received the news without comment, which had made her a little nervous. It was going to take time to learn how to read Lucas, but then she had all the time in the world. For now, though, she had a personal farewell to take.

Discarding her cloak, Rebecca sat down at once at her engraving table, then hesitated. In the drawer were the tools of her trade—the drills, the scribes, the cutters... She was afraid to touch them, knowing that this was goodbye. Very slowly, she picked up the wine glass with the half-finished engraving of the kestrel, reached for her diamond scribe, and began.

When there was a knock on the workshop door, she was not sure how much time had passed, engrossed as she had been in her work. She imagined that Lucas had come to collect her, for he had said that he would give her some time and now that time was up. She was ready for him.

She flung open the door and was taken aback to see a complete stranger on the step. Rebecca blinked and looked again.

'Miss Raleigh?' The stranger was muscular and had piercing blue eyes and salt-and-pepper hair with matching Viking beard. 'How do you do? My name is Marcus Woolf.'

Rebecca closed her mouth, which she realised had been hanging open for at least ten seconds.

'My goodness! That is...Mr Woolf! It is such a privilege to meet so famous an engraver.'

Marcus Woolf smiled. He was immaculately dressed in beige buckskins and a dark green jacket and he did not seem at all surprised by her stupefaction.

'I am very pleased to meet you too, Miss Raleigh, and to see your studio.' He swung round towards the display stands. 'May I?'

'Please...I should be honoured...' Rebecca followed him over to the engraved panes that she had hung from the ceiling and watched in a daze as he examined them, nodding his head slowly.

'Great artistry, Miss Raleigh, and an excellent technique. I am impressed.' The piercing blue eyes came back to rest on Rebecca's face. 'As soon as I saw the vase with the ship on it, I felt I had to come to meet you. Lord Lucas Kestrel mentioned that you were an exceedingly talented engraver.'

Rebecca felt somewhat at sea. She had not even noticed that the vase had disappeared from the studio window, but now that she looked she could see the pale space where it had stood until recently, and the dusty shape of the base on the sill. Someone had removed the vase, and recently. But why? And why had Lucas spoken of her to Marcus Woolf? They had only been back in town a matter of days. He must have acted as soon as they had returned. She frowned slightly.

'Forgive me, Mr Woolf, but I do not perfectly comprehend how you came to see my work, nor why Lord Lucas should have mentioned me to you. Perhaps he also told you—' she felt a lump wedge itself in her throat '—that I am no longer intending to work as an engraver? I cannot.' Rebecca felt a hopeless urge to cry.

Marcus Woolf did not move. 'That is a great shame, Miss Raleigh.' His voice sounded clipped, impersonal. 'But you said that you *cannot* do any more engraving. Why is that?'

Rebecca knew now that she was definitely going to cry. Her throat was made of sandpaper. Even she could hear how her voice was shaking, and despised herself for the weakness. 'I have damaged my wrist, Mr Woolf, so I cannot use the drills any more. It is only a matter of time before I have to stop completely.'

She realised that she *was* crying. Great fat tears

were bouncing off her cheeks on to the stone floor where they shone like miniature puddles in the candles' glare. She felt a complete fool, but she could not stop. She did not really want to stop. It was just inconvenient that Marcus Woolf happened to be there. His presence made the end of her own career seem all the more poignant.

'Excuse me.' She groped for her handkerchief. Unfortunately it was not up her sleeve. She gave a huge, self-pitying sniff.

'Allow me.' Marcus Woolf's handkerchief was made of silk and smelled of expensive cologne. Rebecca rubbed her eyes vigorously and blew her nose for good measure, appalled when her eyes filled with tears again, as though to make up the loss.

'Oh!' It was a mixture of exasperation and self-pity. She saw Marcus Woolf smile. 'Pray continue, Miss Raleigh. Do not feel ashamed. If I lost my ability to engrave, I would cry for a week without stopping.'

His jacket smelled of the same cologne as the handkerchief and it was a crime to cry all over it. On the other hand, his shoulder was surprisingly broad and comforting and after a moment Rebecca could have sworn that he was patting her on the head. She was just remembering his somewhat dubious reputation with women, when he said, over her shoulder,

'Lord Lucas, I think we should get Miss Raleigh something restorative to drink. She is suffering from shock.'

Rebecca raised her head from Marcus Woolf's shoulder and met Lucas's gaze. He was standing in the doorway, watching the scene with considerable interest. She felt puzzled and ruffled. She smoothed down her dress and made hopeless attempts to tidy her hair.

'Come along, Miss Raleigh.' Marcus Woolf had an arm about her now and was drawing her towards the *chaise-longue*. Lucas had disappeared into the scullery and she could hear the clink of the kettle on the hob.

Rebecca sat down and closed her eyes briefly. None of this made the slightest sense and if someone did not enlighten her soon she was sure she might explode with frustration.

'Excuse me,' she said politely to Marcus Woolf, 'but I should appreciate an explanation, Mr Woolf.'

Marcus Woolf's blue eyes were very amused beneath the shaggy salt-and-pepper brows. He sat forward on the sofa. 'Certainly, Miss Raleigh. This work of yours—' his nod encompassed the workshop '—is exquisite. The execution and the ideas...' He shrugged. 'Believe me, I see many, many pieces of work from aspiring engravers, Miss Raleigh, and I would give anything for even one of them to be as good as yours.' He gave her a shadow of a smile. 'So I wished to tell you that should you desire it, I would be delighted for you to come and work with me.'

Rebecca gulped.

Woolf smiled again. 'I appreciate that you cannot engrave any longer, but you can still draw, and your designs are superb. So, how would you like to design for me? I know it is not orthodox for a lady to work, but to waste your talent would be a greater sin. What do you say?'

This time Rebecca almost choked. Through her

streaming eyes, she could see Marcus Woolf laughing at her. He got up. 'No doubt you will wish to discuss this with Lord Lucas. I will leave you my card. Come to see me if you wish to discuss the offer. For now I had better be getting back to my studio.' He turned to Lucas. 'Good day, my lord.' He touched his hat and went out.

Rebecca turned to Lucas. 'I do not understand,' she whispered. 'You showed Marcus Woolf my work. Why?'

Lucas came forward into the studio. He was looking very pale. 'I wanted you to have a choice, Rebecca,' he said. 'When you explained that you were obliged to give up your engraving I wanted—' He stopped, swallowed hard. 'I wanted you to choose to marry me of your own free will, not because one way of life was closed to you. So I thought to find you an alternative. I wanted to prove that I loved you enough to let you go. With all that had happened between us, I wanted you to be sure—'

Rebecca crossed the distance between them and put a hand up to his lips to stop the words. 'Oh, Lucas.' She smiled mistily at him. 'There was no need, but you have made me very happy.'

'You said that you always loved your engraving more than anything else in life,' Lucas said.

Rebecca laughed a little shakily. 'So I did. But that was before I realised how much I loved you, Lucas.'

There was a fierce light in Lucas's eyes now. 'Do you?'

'So very much.' Rebecca gestured around the workshop. 'I needed to take my farewell of all this because it was so much a part of my past life. But I am willing to step into the future with you.' She held out a hand to him. 'And I think you must love me very much too. You had asked me to marry you, but you were willing to give me an alternative—working for Marcus Woolf.'

Lucas came close to her and took both her hands in his. 'I did not wish for an unhappy bride,' he said, and Rebecca could hear the rough undertone of emotion in his voice. 'I love you more than I ever thought possible, Rebecca, but I wanted you to want me.'

The laughter bubbled up within Rebecca. 'So you persuaded Mr Woolf to offer me work.'

'Not so. All I did was show him your engraving. He recognised your talent for himself.'

'And now I shall have to disappoint him.'

'Why should you do that?' Lucas was drawing her closer, but now he paused and looked down into her eyes. 'He has offered you the chance to design for him. Surely you cannot turn him down?'

Rebecca was puzzled. 'But if I am to be Lady Rebecca Kestrel I cannot work!'

Lucas laughed. 'You are more conventional than I had thought, my love. Why not accept his offer?'

Rebecca frowned. 'Do you not wish to marry me, then?'

'Of course. But I have realised that the two need not be mutually exclusive. I should be very proud to have a wife who designed commissions for the best glass engraver in town.'

Rebecca stared at him in stupefaction. 'But, Lucas—ladies do not do such things! Ladies do not work!'

Lucas was shaking his head in mock disapproval. 'I am disappointed in you, my love! Since when did you conform to what is expected?'

Rebecca looked at him in dawning hope. 'You do not tease me?'

'No, indeed. I have no independent fortune,' Lucas continued, 'and need a wife to support me.'

Rebecca caught the flash of amusement in his eyes. 'Oh! You are so—'

He stopped her words with his lips and they clung together as though they would never part. The kiss turned swiftly from tenderness to passion. Rebecca felt the four walls of the studio contract to the space immediately about them as they held each other with desperate need. She could feel Lucas trembling as he held her and the knowledge of it brought a mixture of terror and elation.

He let her go for a moment and she knew what he would see in her eyes: the excitement and the wanting, the hours she had spent thinking about him as she now knew he had been thinking of her, the memory of how it had been between them. Sharp desire twisted deep inside her and she almost gasped aloud.

Lucas pulled the gown off her shoulder and bent to kiss her neck, the hollow of her collarbone, her throat. There was a look of intense concentration on his face. If Rebecca had not heard the quickness of his breathing, seen his fingers shake, she would have thought him unmoved. Her mind reeled. Surely this could not be happening to her in the studio, in the middle of the afternoon? Yet she had waited for him for what seemed like forever. She felt unbearably impatient. She reached for him.

Lucas's hands circled her waist, then moved up to push the bodice of her dress farther down, leaving her in her shift. He unlaced the ribbons and slid his hand inside. Rebecca gasped against his mouth as the warmth of his hand cupped her breast. He lifted her slightly so that she was sitting on the edge of the workbench. He pulled her skirts up her thighs. She felt the cold hard edge of the table against her bare skin. Lucas was fumbling with the fastening of his breeches. His mouth took hers again at the same time as his fingers parted her, stroking with a sly seduction. Rebecca climaxed at once, in shock and fierce delight, and a second time, helplessly yielding, when he entered her. Her fingers were digging into his back and the bench creaked in protest at each thrust. It was shocking and erotic and everything that she had dreamed of.

'Oh, Rebecca…' Lucas's face was turned into the hollow of her neck.

Her legs were trembling when she slid to the floor and she had to grip his arm to steady herself. Lucas scooped her up into his arms.

Rebecca squeaked. 'Lucas, no! You will hurt yourself.'

'I have done it before, if you remember,' Lucas said.

At the top of the stairs he put her down and she turned, wrapped her arms about him, and kissed him fiercely. They tumbled onto the bed. Lucas propped himself up on one elbow and allowed his gaze to travel all the way down her body, from the bow unravelling in her hair, to her breasts peaking with desperate arousal beneath the thin cotton shift, to her tumbled petticoats, down her legs to her toes. Rebecca's whole body ached for his touch.

He smiled slowly. 'I do believe that you are over-dressed,' he said.

Lucas stripped their clothes off with ruthless efficiency and turned Rebecca gently so that she was lying on her stomach next to him on the bed. Lucas allowed his hand to drift down the silken length of her back and over the curve of her buttocks. There was so much passion in her. He had suspected as much when he had seen the eloquence and the beauty and the raw longing that was locked into those engravings. He had wanted to unlock it in reality and make her his, no matter that he knew he should not. And now he had done it, this time forever.

'Rebecca…' He leaned over so that his chest brushed the soft skin of her back, and spoke gently in her ear. 'I am going to take you again. I cannot help myself…'

Rebecca made a faint sound of assent and gave a tiny, voluptuous wriggle. Smiling a little, Lucas reached for the bolster, slid his arm beneath her, lifted her hips and pushed it under her stomach. Finding that she was almost on her knees, Rebecca stirred abruptly.

'Lucas, what—'

'Hush.' He soothed her at the same time as holding her still with one hand spread on the small of her back. She looked so provocative and open to him without any pretence of modesty that he felt his body tighten almost unbearably. 'I won't hurt you,' he whispered.

He held her hips and slid inside her, feeling her shudder with pleasure. Her back arched, her hair fell about her shoulders in glorious chestnut waves and she gave a moan of sheer, unbelieving excitement as she felt the relentless possession take her. Lucas revelled in Rebecca's uninhibited response, which drew an equally unrestrained passion from him. Dimly he knew that he should treat her more gently, but he was powerless to resist, powerless to control his thoughts, his desires and his need for her. He had never felt like this before. Never felt this sense of exquisite completeness. He held her still and took her with a sure, hard control.

Yet this perfect pleasure, this flagrant possession, was not sufficient. He needed to see her face, to hold her, to kiss her.

He drew back and tumbled her over and into his arms. Her face was flushed pink with arousal and there was a dazed, abandoned darkness in her eyes. He swooped down on her.

'Not enough…' He had spoken the words aloud and now he saw her eyes open wider and a smile creep into the slumberous blue depths. Her hand came up to stroke his jaw.

'There's more?'

'That wasn't what I meant.' He looked at her. 'I need to look at you.'

Her eyes smiled. He bent to kiss her. His hands were on her thighs, spreading them wide. He surged into her softness and heard her gasp, and cut the sound off with his plundering mouth on hers once more. One of his hands trapped her wrists above her head, holding her still. The other came up to caress her breast and slide over her heated skin in triumphant possession.

He could not get enough of her. As he started to move inside her the conflagration took them. She gave a wild cry and Lucas felt the flames rise and consume him, destroying his self-control and his self-sufficiency and all the barriers that had kept him alone. Mindless urgency overtook him and drove him to its final, shattering climax and he gathered Rebecca closer still, as, body and soul, they were fused as one.

The sensations died slowly to leave them still and peaceful. Rebecca was boneless and soft in his arms and he drew her closer into their shelter, filled with wondrous contentment and a searing peace. He felt her body soften further and slide into sleep, and rested his chin in the cloud of her hair, inhaling her scent and relaxing as sated pleasure and deep satisfaction beckoned him irresistibly to join her asleep. And this time when she awoke, he was still there.

Chapter Fourteen

The third of the recent Midwinter weddings took place on a bright, cold day, two weeks before Christmas. A wedding breakfast was held at Kestrel Court and the entire Kestrel family assembled to drink to the health of the bride and groom. It was late by the time that the bride managed to escape from her guests and find a little solitude. She slipped open the terrace doors and went outside, making sure that she latched the door softly behind her and that no one had seen her leave.

The gardens were filled with shadows. Rebecca went slowly down the mossy steps that led from the terrace to the lawn. The air was crisp and cold and the grass was frosty beneath her feet. Behind her the light from the ballroom spilled across the darkness and the rise and fall of the music floated on the winter air.

'All secrets known…'

The full moon was as bright as it had been on the night she had seen *The Defiance* sail into Kestrel Cove.

'All villains caught save one…'

Daniel was safe, and that was what counted, and perhaps one day they would meet again.

The winter jasmine smelled sweet and wistful.

There was the crunch of frost; a footfall close by. Rebecca swung round. 'Who is there?'

There was no sound but the breeze in the pines and the distant slap of the waves on the shore, but the silence was heavy with waiting. Rebecca shivered, her breath clouding the night air. 'Come out, whoever you are!'

A shadow detached itself from the deeper shadows under the frozen branches of the firs and started to walk towards her in the bright moonlight. Rebecca stared and caught her breath on a gasp. 'Daniel? Daniel!'

He reached her at a run and his arms went about her, hard and strong, scooping her up off the ground and spinning her around in an exultant pirouette. Rebecca hugged him close. He smelled of woodsmoke and tobacco. He was warm and solid and real. He was here...

'You should not have come,' she said, torn between laughter and tears.

Daniel De Lancey laughed. 'Did you think that I would miss my sister's wedding day?' he said.

Rebecca stood back a little so that she could scan his face. 'Thank you,' she whispered. 'Thank you for being here.'

For a moment they looked at each other, then Daniel gave her another convulsive hug before loosening his grip a little. He scanned her face in the moonlight. 'Are you happy, Beck?'

Rebecca did not misunderstand him. 'With Lucas? Yes, I am. I am very happy.'

'You are sure you love him?'

The wind stirred in the treetops again. Rebecca shivered. 'Yes. I love him more than anything. I never thought…never imagined it could be so…'

She saw the flash of Daniel's teeth as he smiled. 'That is all I wanted to know. He is a good man, Beck.'

Rebecca laughed. 'I know.' Urgency stirred in her. 'You must go, Daniel. I thought that you were safely away. They have been looking for you.'

'I know they have,' Daniel said, 'but I needed to be sure, Beck.'

Rebecca reached up and kissed his cheek. 'And now you may be. Good luck and godspeed.'

'And to you, little sister. Be happy.' Daniel returned the clasp of her hand for a brief second and then he was drawing away with one final backward glance, one last promise: 'I will see you again before too long, I swear it…'

The tears misted Rebecca's eyes and chilled on her wet cheeks and she turned, unable to watch him walk away. Perhaps it would always be as difficult as this to say goodbye to Daniel. She would never know if they would meet again. But Daniel had come to her wedding day and now she had to go back to her husband. Lucas would be wondering what had happened to her.

She retraced her steps around the side of the shuttered summerhouse and started along the topiary avenue towards the terrace, but before she had taken more than three steps, Lucas came out from the shadow of the firs and fell into step beside her, and she knew without a word being spoken between them that he had seen exactly what had happened. She stopped and looked at him. The moonlight fell on his face but she could not read his expression.

'You saw him,' she whispered.

Lucas smiled then. 'I did,' he said.

Rebecca started to smile as well. She felt so full of love she was afraid she might burst. 'And you let him go.'

'I would let him go time and time again to make you happy, my love,' Lucas said, then laughed. 'Besides, I do not wish to be remembered as the man who shot his brother-in-law on his wedding day!'

They stood and looked at each other for a long moment and then Rebecca raised her hand to his cheek. 'I love you, Lucas Kestrel.'

'I love you too.'

'You have shown that many times,' Rebecca said. 'And I am not sure that I deserve you—'

Lucas stopped her words with his lips. It was cold; they felt fused together, sealed one to the other for all time.

'I have one more secret to tell you,' Rebecca said hesitantly.

Lucas gave a little heartfelt groan, but Rebecca smiled. 'No, I believe…I hope…you may like this one. I am expecting a child.'

Lucas stared at her for a long, long moment, then he bent forward and kissed her lips very softly. 'When? After the masque?' he whispered.

Rebecca shook her head. 'No. Last time—in the studio.' She paused a little nervously. 'You are pleased?'

Lucas drew her into his arms so that she was held gently but securely. 'Nothing could make me happier, Rebecca.'

They stood clasped together and then Lucas laughed. 'Justin had better hurry. Who would have thought that he would be shown up by his younger brothers?'

'I wondered if Deb—' Rebecca said thoughtfully.

'Yes, I do believe she may be *enceinte*. Certainly Richard is looking extremely pleased with himself!'

Rebecca laughed. 'Poor Justin. Will Lady Sally accept him?'

'Who knows?' Lucas said. 'She is a law unto herself.'

He let Rebecca go and she glanced towards the lighted windows of the house. 'It is ungrateful in me, but this wedding party seems interminable. Do you think we might respectably retire now?'

'Not respectably,' Lucas said. 'However, you must be chilled to the bone and it is my duty as your new husband to help you become warm again...'

Rebecca nestled close to him. 'Could you?'

'I can try. I know several methods.'

Rebecca laughed. 'Then let us go inside and, without further ado, try them.' And together, entwined, they made their way towards the light.

Epilogue

Lady Sally Saltire awoke suddenly in her bedroom at Saltires. The moonlight was very bright, flooding her bedchamber and bathing the room in a curious, cold white light. She lay still for a moment, staring at the canopy of the bed. She had woken alone on so many nights. For most of her widowhood she had enjoyed the freedom her solitary state had granted her. It was only recently that the loneliness had crept in, invading the corners of her mind, so that she woke sometimes hoping to find that she was not alone, always to be disappointed.

She sat up with a sigh. She was wide awake now and a little sad. That was the trouble with weddings, Lady Sally thought with a flash of annoyance. It was all very well for Rachel and Cory, and Deborah and Richard and Olivia and Ross and Rebecca and Lucas, of course. They had each other. Worse, they were all quite ridiculously, unfashionably in love. Even that encroaching chit Helena Lang was likely to finally catch a husband before long. Which just left her wearing the willow, since Justin had made his feelings for her quite plain. She still felt shocked as she remembered his words to her at the wedding breakfast, words spoken low, for her ears only.

'Your lease has expired, Sally. Time has run out. I want you out of that Dower House as soon as possible…'

She gave a little, irritable sigh. Damn him! Recently she had thought… But it was too late for thoughts and regrets now. She had had her chance to marry Justin Kestrel fifteen years before and one could not turn back the clock. She vowed that she would be out of his house before her officious landlord even woke in the morning. Her pride demanded it. He had even told her to make sure that she did not take a single thing that did not belong to her when she left.

'I shall take nothing from you unless you take something of mine,' he had said. Perhaps he was tight-fisted and she had never before realised.

She felt that she needed a drink. There was water in the ewer on the washstand, but that was no good. Port, brandy, even sherry would be acceptable, but they were all downstairs.

Lady Sally climbed out of the bed and reached for the saucy négligé that barely covered the equally sheer nightdress she had fallen for on a recent visit to London. The sight and the slippery, sensuous feel of it gave her an obscure feeling of anger. It was more suitable for a trousseau than for a middle-aged widow on her own in the depths of the country.

The house was as silent as the grave. Lady Sally tiptoed down the staircase, flitting between patches of moonlight and finding her way to the study without difficulty in the bright light. She did not bother to light a candle. She could see the sideboard illuminated clearly because the curtains were not drawn. They billowed in the breeze. Some careless maid had left a window open.

Lady Sally shivered in the draught. She reached for the port decanter, then hesitated, her hand hovering over the bottle of brandy that Justin Kestrel had left behind on his last visit. She felt a sharp pain inside as she remembered that she had teased him about the dubious morality of the Duke of Kestrel patronising the smuggling trade. They had laughed together. It seemed a very long time ago now.

She had been intending to return the bottle to him, but now it seemed a pleasing if small act of revenge to drink his best French brandy instead. She opened the seal and reached for one of the crystal glasses. The neck of the bottle had not even touched the edge of the glass when a hand closed about her wrist and gripped it hard. Lady Sally did not cry out. Some sixth sense had warned her that she was not alone; besides, she recognised his touch.

She could hear the smile in his voice as he spoke.

'At last. I thought that you would never give me my chance, Sally.'

He let go of her. There was a scrape as he struck a light. The candles flared. Lady Sally looked at Justin, Duke of Kestrel, in the mix of candlelight and moonlight.

'Your chance?' She was annoyed to hear that her voice was not quite steady.

'To win the third wager.'

'I was not aware that there was one.'

She saw the flash of his smile. 'Your mistake. I told you at the wedding breakfast.' He quoted drily: *'I shall take nothing from you unless you take something of mine.'*

Lady Sally's breath caught in her throat. She looked at the incriminating bottle of brandy. 'I assumed that you meant I should take nothing of yours when I left your house.'

'Assumptions are dangerous things.'

'Then—'

He took hold of her wrist again, this time in a featherlight touch. 'I want you out of this house,' he said, drawing her inexorably towards him. 'Out of this house and into mine—and into my bed.'

Lady Sally put out her free hand and caught his arm, pulling him against her hard. 'In mine first.'

'If you insist.'

Their kiss was explosive, unleashing the passion of years.

When they broke apart, Lady Sally said a little hesitantly, 'It is a very long time since I did this.'

'For me too. It will be fine. In fact, it will be very good…'

His arms were hard about her. His touch on her skin left no doubt of where this would end, and soon. There would be no escape. They kissed again, demanding, hungry, desperate for fulfillment.

'Justin,' Lady Sally said, taking his hand and drawing him towards the staircase, 'do you think we could elope?'

'Of course,' Justin said. His arm was about her

waist now and the anticipation ran scalding hot between them. 'If that is what you would like to do.'

'I do not think I could bear to confess to everyone that I had made a mistake and should have married you years ago, so...I would rather they knew *after* the event.'

Justin laughed. 'So you would like to marry me?'

'Please.'

'Excellent. We shall elope immediately.'

They kissed for a third time, sweet and longing.

'Almost immediately,' Lady Sally corrected. 'For now there is a more pressing matter on hand.'

Justin scooped her up in his arms and took the stairs two at a time, kicking the bedroom door closed behind them and dropping her into the middle of the big double bed, where he joined her a second later.

The lost fifteen years fled away then as she looked at him. He was the Justin Kestrel she had known when she had been a laughing débutante of eighteen, too fearful and flighty to accept the fate that was hers. And then he drew her to him very gently and there was nothing but warmth and light—and the promise of the future.

* * * * *

Harlequin® Historical
Historical Romantic Adventure!

THREE RUGGED WESTERN MEN
THREE COURAGEOUS LADIES
THREE FESTIVE TALES TO WARM
THE HEART THIS CHRISTMAS!

ON SALE OCTOBER 2005

ROCKY MOUNTAIN CHRISTMAS
by Jillian Hart

Summoned on a dangerously snowy night to deal with two stowaways, Sheriff Mac McKaslin discovers they are none other than a homeless young widow— Carrie Montgomery—and her baby. But will the sheriff send them out into the cold...or find a warm place for them in his heart?

THE CHRISTMAS GIFTS
by Kate Bridges

When Sergeant James Fielder arrives with a baby on his sled, he turns to Maggie Greerson for help. This special interlude allows Maggie to fulfill her secret dream of having a child— and explore the attraction that has always drawn her to James....

THE CHRISTMAS CHARM
by Mary Burton

Determined to prevent her younger sister from marrying the wrong man, widow Colleen Garland enlists the help of her onetime love Keith Garrett. Will their rescue mission finally lead them on the road to true love?

www.eHarlequin.com

HHWEST42

If you enjoyed what you just read,
then we've got an offer you can't resist!

Take 2 bestselling love stories FREE!
Plus get a FREE surprise gift!

A BRAND-NEW BOOK IN
THE DE WARENNE DYNASTY SERIES
BY *NEW YORK TIMES* BESTSELLING AUTHOR

BRENDA JOYCE

On the evening of her first masquerade, shy Elizabeth Anne Fitzgerald is stunned by Tyrell de Warenne's whispered suggestion of a midnight rendezvous in the gardens. Lizzie has secretly worshiped the unattainable lord for years. When fortune takes a maddening turn, she is prevented from meeting Tyrell. But Lizzie has not seen the last of him....

Tyrell de Warenne is shocked when, two years later, Lizzie arrives on his doorstep with a child she claims is his. He remembers her well—and knows that he could not possibly be the father. Is Elizabeth Anne Fitzgerald a woman of experience, or the gentle innocent she seems?

The
MASQUERADE

MBJ2209